MA

MW00487867

FOUR GARDENS

MARGERY Sharp was born Clara Margery Melita Sharp in
1905 in Wiltshire. She spent some of her childhood in Malta,
and on the family's return to England became a pupil at
Streatham Hill High School.

She later studied at Bedford College, London, where she
claimed her time was devoted 'almost entirely to journalism
and campus activities.'

Still living in London, she began her writing career at the age
of twenty-one, becoming a contributor of fiction and non-
fiction to many of the most notable periodicals of the time in
both Britain and America.

In 1938 she married Major Geoffrey Castle, an aeronautical
engineer. On the outbreak of World War II, she served as a
busy Army Education Lecturer, but continued her own writing
both during and long after the conflict. Many of her stories
for adults became the basis for Hollywood movie screenplays,
in addition to the 'Miss Bianca' children's series, animated by
Disney as *The Rescuers* in 1977.

Margery Sharp ultimately wrote 22 novels for adults (not 26,
as is sometimes reported), as well as numerous stories and
novellas (many of them published only in periodicals) and
various works for children. She died in Suffolk in 1991, one
year after her husband.

FICTION BY MARGERY SHARP

Novels

Rhododendron Pie (1930)*
Fanfare for Tin Trumpets (1932)*
The Flowering Thorn (1933)
Four Gardens (1935)*
The Nutmeg Tree (1937)
Harlequin House (1939)*
The Stone of Chastity (1940)*
Cluny Brown (1944)
Britannia Mews (1946)
The Foolish Gentlewoman (1948)*
Lise Lillywhite (1951)
The Gipsy in the Parlour (1954)
The Eye of Love (1957)
Something Light (1960)
Martha in Paris (1962)
Martha, Eric and George (1964)
The Sun in Scorpio (1965)
In Pious Memory (1967)
Rosa (1970)
The Innocents (1972)
The Faithful Servants (1975)
Summer Visits (1977)

* published by Furrowed Middlebrow and Dean Street Press

Selected Stories & Novellas

The Nymph and the Nobleman (1932)†
Sophy Cassmajor (1934)†
The Tigress on the Hearth (1955)†
The Lost Chapel Picnic and Other Stories (1973)

† these three shorter works were compiled in the 1941 anthology Three Companion Pieces

Children's Fiction

The Rescuers (1959)
Melisande (1960)
Miss Bianca (1962)
The Turret (1963)
Lost at the Fair (1965)
Miss Bianca in the Salt Mines (1966)
Miss Bianca in the Orient (1970)
Miss Bianca in the Antarctic (1971)
Miss Bianca and the Bridesmaid (1972)
The Children Next Door (1974)
The Magical Cockatoo (1974)
Bernard the Brave (1977)
Bernard Into Battle (1978)

MARGERY SHARP

FOUR GARDENS

With an introduction by
Elizabeth Crawford

DEAN STREET PRESS

A Furrowed Middlebrow Book

FM55

Published by Dean Street Press 2021

First published in 1935 by Collins

Cover by DSP

Shows detail from an illustration by Leslie Wood. The publisher
thanks the artist's estate and the archives of Manchester
Metropolitan University

ISBN 978 1 913527 65 5

www.deanstreetpress.co.uk

Let other pens dwell on guilt and misery.

JANE AUSTEN.

Introduction

Margery Sharp (1905-1991) was determined from an early age to become a successful, self-supporting author and over a period of about fifty years published twenty-two novels for adults, thirteen stories for children, four plays, two mysteries, and numerous short stories. Her early novels were witty and worldly, her sixth, *Four Gardens* (1935), was, as a reviewer observed, 'a quiet book', according the author 'something of the Jane Austen touch, springing from a detached, quiet power of observation, a delicious, satirical way of relishing affectation, and a respect for sensible, genuine people.' (*New York Times Saturday Book Review*, February 1936). Indeed, Jane Austen was clearly not far from Margery's mind for she gave to the novel the epigraph, 'Let other pens dwell on guilt and misery', a quotation from *Mansfield Park*, and one which another young novelist, Stella Gibbons, had just three years earlier bestowed on her debut novel, *Cold Comfort Farm*.

Clara Margery Melita Sharp was born with, as one interviewer testified, 'wit and a profound common sense', the youngest of the three daughters of John Henry Sharp (1865-1953) and his wife, Clara Ellen (1866-1946). Both parents came from families of Sheffield artisans and romance had flourished, although it was only in 1890 that they married, after John Sharp had moved to London and passed the Civil Service entrance examination as a 2nd division clerk. The education he had received at Sheffield's Brunswick Wesleyan School had enabled him to prevail against the competition, which, for such a desirable position, was fierce. At the age of 15 Margery's mother was already working as a book-keeper, probably in her father's silversmithing workshop. By 1901 John Sharp was clerking in the War Office, perhaps in a department dealing with Britain's garrison in Malta, as this might explain why Margery was given the rather exotic third name of 'Melita' (the personification of Malta).

Malta became a reality for the Sharps when from 1912 to 1913 John was seconded to the island. His family accompanied him and while there Margery attended Sliema's Chiswick House High

School, a recently founded 'establishment for Protestant young ladies'. Over 50 years later she set part of her novel *Sun in Scorpio* (1965) in sunlit Malta, contrasting it with the dull suburb where 'everything dripped', to which her characters returned. In due course the Sharps, too, arrived back in suburban London, to the house in Streatham in which her parents were to live for the rest of their lives.

From 1914 to 1923 Margery received a good academic education at Streatham Hill High School (now Streatham and Clapham High School) although family financial difficulties meant she was unable to proceed to university and instead worked for a year as a shorthand-typist in the City of London, 'with a firm that dealt with asphalt'. In a later interview (*Daily Independent*, 16 Sept 1937) she is quoted as saying, 'I never regretted that year in business as it gave me a contact with the world of affairs'. However, Margery had not given up hope of university and, with an improvement in the Sharps' financial position, her former headmistress wrote to the principal of Bedford College, a woman-only college of the University of London, to promote her case, noting 'She has very marked literary ability and when she left school two years ago I was most anxious she should get the benefit of university training'. Margery eventually graduated in 1928 with an Honours degree in French, the subject chosen 'just because she liked going to France'. Indeed, no reader of Margery Sharp can fail to notice her Francophile tendency.

During her time at university Margery began publishing verses and short stories and after graduation was selected to join two other young women on a debating tour of American universities. As a reporter commented, 'Miss Sharp is apparently going to provide the light relief in the debates', quoting her as saying, 'I would rather tell a funny story than talk about statistics'. Articles she wrote from the US for the *Evening Standard* doubtless helped defray the expenses of the coming year, her first as a full-time author.

For on her return, living in an elegant flat at 25 Craven Road, Paddington, she began earning her living, writing numerous short stories for magazines such as the *Windsor*, the *Royal*, *Nash's*, and the *Graphic*, and quickly succeeding as a novelist. *Four Gardens* demonstrates Margery's rich imagination, drawing less directly on her own experience than did her first two novels, although the social distinctions between the Common and the Town apparent in Morton, the London suburb that was home to her heroine, Caroline Smith, might owe something to observations of life in Clapham or Streatham. The conceit of the novel is, as the *Times* reviewer put it, that 'Caroline's four gardens mark four different periods in her life, and as she loved them they show her state of mind'.

Margery was barely thirty years old as she told the story of Caroline's life through youthful, ill-fated romance at the turn of the twentieth century in the setting of the garden of an empty mansion, and then through wife and motherhood while tending her vegetable patch as her husband grew rich making boots for soldiers during the First World War. Prosperous middle-age followed, living in the large house at Friar's Green, 'a small, charmingly rural pocket of Kingston, rather like Ham Common', that war work had achieved, but where the gardener, 'stubborn as a mule and twice as bad-tempered', thwarted her every attempt to fashion it to her liking. Finally, Caroline is a widow, the boot business lost, settling for a roof garden outside her bedroom in a flat 'on the dubious borderline between Holland Park and Shepherd's Bush'.

Margery continued living in the Paddington flat as her literary career developed, becoming a favourite on both sides of the Atlantic. Her life took a somewhat novelettish turn in April 1938 when she was cited as the co-respondent in the divorce of Geoffrey Lloyd Castle, an aeronautical engineer and, later, author of two works of science fiction. At that time publicity such as this could have been harmful, and she was out of the country when the news broke. Later in the year she spent some months in New York, where she and Geoffrey were married, with the actor Robert Morley and Blanche Gregory, Margery's US literary agent and lifelong friend, as witnesses.

During the Second World War, with Geoffrey was on active service, Margery worked in army education, while continuing to publish novels. The couple took a set (B6) in the Albany on Piccadilly, where they were tended by a live-in housekeeper, and from the early 1950s also had a Suffolk home, Observatory Cottage, on Crag Path, Aldeburgh. The writer Ronald Blythe later reminisced, 'I would glance up at its little balcony late of an evening, and there she would be, elegant with her husband Major Castle and a glass of wine beside her, playing chess to the roar of the North Sea, framed in lamplight, secure in her publishers.'

Late in life Margery Sharp, while still producing adult novels, achieved considerable success as a children's author, in 1977 receiving the accolade of the Disney treatment when several stories in her 'Miss Bianca' series formed the basis of the animated film, *The Rescuers*.

Margery Sharp ended her days in Aldeburgh, dying on 14 March 1991, just a year after Geoffrey.

Elizabeth Crawford

PROLOGUE

I

ON HER Fifty-First birthday Caroline Smith sat an hour or so after breakfast considering her children.

Their presents, freshly unpacked, lay convenient to her hand: a picture, and a book. Each had cost money, each (she felt) had been selected with the same loving eye to her education. The painting was of magnolias, cream and tawny in a vessel of cream china: it had a frame of white wood, neither carved nor varnished; so that Caroline's first impression of the whole thing was that there wasn't much work in it. But it did not displease her: it looked nice and clean, and it had been given her by Lal.

Caroline caught herself up. That was just what Lal didn't want. 'Don't think about *me*, mother: look at it impersonally.' In such a determination Caroline now looked again, at the creamy magnolias, each petal nicely painted, at the gloss on the jar, the shadow behind; and at once her thoughts flew to Lally's dress allowance, and how the child must have saved, and whether it might not somehow be possible to make it up to her. 'A leather jacket,' thought Caroline, 'she's always wanting leather jackets!' Her thoughts wandered further: they ranged lovingly and in detail over Lally's entire wardrobe. If Lally went to Cambridge for May week she would want one—two—new dance frocks, and something for the afternoon. With sweaters, heavy skirts and sports suits she was already amply provided. She always rushed to buy them, as soon as she got her money, just as the girls of a previous generation had rushed to buy blouses . . . as the girls before *them* had rushed to buy shawls. . . . And then side by side with her tweeds Lally bought pictures of flowers, of elegant white magnolias in a pale china pot. . . .

Caroline detached her eyes from them—she was losing her grip, she felt, on complete impersonality—and turned instead to the present from her son. It was a work on the Cinema, lavishly illustrated, and written from a very lofty point of view. Leon himself (and he was hard to please) had described it as the Last

Word. But it was also, he had told his mother encouragingly, very simply written: she was to read it a chapter at a time, not skipping along as through a library book, and she would find it all perfectly clear. Caroline accepted the work with pleasure— with a pleasure all the more genuine in that she suspected him of secretly desiring it for himself. The cinema was his passion, the book cost forty-two shillings; she would read it at once, as swiftly as was compatible with his instructions, and then offer to lend it to him to take back to Cambridge.

In such antiquated but agreeable grooves had run, for a moment, Caroline's thoughts. For no longer. At the end of that period Lally, glancing across the table, had observed to her brother that the illustrations seemed familiar.

"Of course they are!" retorted Leon, "I've had a copy about for the last three months. . . ."

Caroline sighed again at the recollection. How *could* she have suspected him—her exquisite, fastidious and disdainful son—of so mean a stratagem? ('But it isn't mean!' said another part of her brain indignantly. 'It's just what a boy would do, and very natural!') Of course if Leon wanted a book he would buy it. He might go without an overcoat, might live, like his sister, in tweeds and sweaters, but on anything connected with his passion he spent like a duke. He went to see the same film—the same hundred feet of film—not twice or thrice but half a dozen times. He took other people, to watch the effect on them. He journeyed from Cambridge to London to see one item in a news reel. He had a camera of his own and—and everything that went with it. And even in other, secondary matters, such as tokens of family affection, he was never mean. He either gave generously, or forgot all about them; his natural affections being strong but patchy, just as his manners, with their trick of being either exquisite or non-existent, were patchier still.

Caroline picked up the book and opened it at the beginning. For frontispiece there was a portrait of Charlie Chaplin, which slightly surprised her, for she had been used to consider him purely as something you took the children to. Undeniably funny, that is, regrettably vulgar, but never nasty. A child who had been to see Charlie—so ran the theory—might come home and throw food about: but it would not come home and ask awkward questions. Strong in this conviction Caroline had often taken her own children, the youthful Leonard (not yet Leon) and the toddling Lily (now known as Lal).

"Lily and Leonard," whispered Caroline aloud.

In spite of all the children could and did say, the names continued to please her. She had thought them pretty at the time, she thought them pretty still; and when Lal, at the age of fifteen, first mooted the change, Caroline's instinctive opposition had been chiefly a movement of surprise. Even after ten years she remembered the scene quite clearly: Lal, not without some importance, coming specially to her mother's room: the reasoned flow of eloquence, the culminating announcement, and Caroline's own rather foolish cry. "But, my darling! It's so sweet!"

"I know," Lal interposed wearily. "The point is, I'm not."

Caroline, hair-brush suspended, regarded her covertly through the mirror. It might be a mother's partiality; to her eye Lal was very sweet indeed. But she did not wish to hurt her daughter's feelings, and while she was still seeking for some less provocative argument, Lal spoke again.

"How would *you* like to be called Carrie?"

"But I always was!" replied Caroline mildly. "I was always called Carrie, when I was a girl . . ."

"Then I think it was a shame!" said Lal with fierceness. "If you have a beautiful name like yours, no one has a right to spoil it."

"Beautiful?" repeated Caroline, quite puzzled. "You mean—Caroline?"

Lal stamped impatiently.

"Of *course* it's beautiful! Listen, Mother—Car-o-line—can't you *hear* how good it is?" Her voice lingered, rounded, died away in a melting fall: her eyes, dark and shining, widened with enthusiasm. "Car-o-line, Mother! Just *listen* to it!"

And—

'Sweet?' thought Caroline. 'Of course she's sweet! What does it matter what the child's called, so long as it makes her happy?'

II

A coal dropped, the clock struck, and Caroline sat once more by the breakfast-table. The strewn wrappings, here and there touched with marmalade, offended her eye; she began folding them together, white paper in one pile, brown in another; and so came upon a third present, a present from her husband. It was an opal pendant in a morocco case; and presently she would go upstairs and add it to the two dozen other cases—one for each Christmas, one for each birthday—that testified to her husband's increasing prosperity during the last twelve years. Also, no doubt, to his continued affection. Caroline fingered the stones reflectively, half-tempted, in this hour of sentiment and leisure, to try and follow up the thought to some definite conclusion; but as always, before the perennial mystery of Henry's real feelings, her mind went shying away down the first by-path that offered.

'Aesopus tulips!' thought Caroline at once.

A little stiffly, she rose to her feet, slipped the pendant in her bag (so as not to tempt the maids) and went over to the french window. But she did not immediately open it. The old names still echoed in her ears, drawing her thoughts back and back, past Lily and Leonard, past Henry, to even shadowier figures yet. Cousin Maggie Platt, who had money in Consols; Ellen Taylor, so fortunately an orphan; and Vincent in the terraced garden, and her own widowed mother, with that striking resemblance (though from the back view only) to Alexandra Princess of Wales. . . .

PART I

CHAPTER I

I

On the brow of Morton Common, on a fine Sunday evening, two ladies walking up met a lady walking down.

The ladies ascending, on their way to Chapel, were Mrs. Chase and her daughter Caroline: the lady crossing them, on her way to Church, Miss Amelia Dupré. All three, as it chanced, were dressed very much alike, in light cloth skirts, light cloth jackets with leg-of-mutton sleeves, and hard straw hats. If anything, Miss Dupré's hat and jacket were rather the more worn. But there could have been no possible doubt, to the eye of any sensitive observer, that it was not Mrs. Chase who did not know Miss Dupré, but Miss Dupré who did not know Mrs. Chase.

The ladies walked on. A cadence of bells, not yet urgent, but rather cajoling, pleasantly enlivened the air. The houses—the mansions—on either side stood in Sunday quiet. Before each gate—the width of a carriage—Caroline slightly slackened her step, slightly turned her head, to catch a glimpse of flowerbeds. But she did so, this evening, automatically and without the usual enjoyment; until at the gate of Cam Brea she did not slacken at all.

"Mother?"

"Yes, Carrie?"

"Mother, *she* lives over a shop too!"

"But she belongs to the Common, dear," said Mrs. Chase patiently.

They walked on, Caroline still contemplative. She was no iconoclast; the social system, as exemplified in a high-class suburb of London, awoke in her breast no socialistic yearnings. It was the state of life to which it had pleased God to call her, and as such beyond criticism. But she was young enough to want everything clear-cut and logical, like the Creation of the World, from which admirable beginning there had been, she sometimes felt, a sad falling-off. If the Lord had created Morton fresh, thought Caroline (but quite reverently, and it was Sunday evening) He would have put the People in the Town *in* the Town, and the People on the Common *on* the Common. A nice thing it would be on Judgment Day, thought Caroline, if half the sheep and goats were left all mixed up together!

II

But Morton as a whole, despite occasional confusion, was not yet in danger. It had ceased growing: far enough out from London to make the daily trip objectionable, too close in for any compensating rural pleasures, it had built, during the last ten years, no more than one row of houses and a small boot factory. The houses replaced others, the factory population was quiet and well-behaved; and both Common and Town remained exactly as they were.

People on the Common inhabited large detached houses, employed whole-time gardeners, and drove carriage-and-pair. People in the Town lived in streets, rows, and crescents, had the gardener half-a-day a week, and transported themselves on foot, in 'buses, and occasionally on bicycles. Or such rather were the types: for as Caroline had observed, the frontiers were not strictly geographical. Her example, Miss Dupré, dwelt absolutely over a shop; but for all social purposes counted as a person on the Common. Her father had been an Admiral. The position of the Vicar fluctuated. If his wife had money, or if he had no wife at all, he belonged to the Common, but a wife and six children would bind him almost inevitably to the Town. Dissenters were Town *en bloc*. Doctors, like the Vicar, could move from one sphere to the other according to personal qualifications; so could the Principal of the Girls' High School. Other schoolmistresses were Town. Within so complicated a system the inhabitants of Morton had naturally to tread with care; but so practiced were their steps, so keen their social noses, that no gaffe of any magnitude had occurred since 1879. In that disorderly year, indeed, there had been two: the seduction of a Major's daughter by a chemist, and the engagement of a grocer's daughter to a gentleman's son.

The two escapades ended very differently—the first, in a marriage by special license and a small establishment in Wales, the second in a foreign tour for the young man and a plaster for the young lady. The young man's father, it was felt, had handled the match extremely well: for not only did his son rapidly recover his wits, but the plaster of two hundred pounds was persistently rejected, against all family advice, by the grocer's daughter. She had been done no injury, she said, which could be paid for in money; and if the expression had now and then rankled, the money was indubitably saved. Nor did Miss Pole (for such was the young lady's name) even go into a decline; always quiet and reserved, she merely became more quiet and more reserved still;

until a year or two later, in the properest manner possible, she quietly married an estate agent's clerk. The union produced one daughter, Caroline Maud; and the estate agent's clerk dying soon afterwards, Caroline and her mother, now Mrs. Chase, returned to the parental roof.

It was a kindly roof, if commercial. Under it dwelt Grandfather Pole (who could move his ears), Grandmother Pole, who was deaf, and a smart middle-aged lady who gave people change. Caroline liked all of them, and particularly her grandfather, who, though never directly affectionate, let her crawl behind the counter, play games with the shop cat, and eat the sugar out of candied peel. When at last he died, and the shop passed into other hands, Caroline wept bitterly; but whether mostly for her grandfather, or mostly for the sugar, even she herself could scarcely tell. The two were inextricably mixed, like the smell of her mother's jacket and the feel of her mother's kiss, and the effort to disentangle them proved too hard a task for her infantile brain. Already deeply conscientious, however, she determined, after long thought, to square all possible debts by crying twice as much as she felt naturally inclined; and night after night lay forcing the tears into a disappointingly dry pillow. This practice—though never its origin—Mrs. Chase rapidly discovered: and as rapidly put an end to by taking Caroline into the double bed. Within that vast yet cozy plain, curled snugly to the warmth of her mother's back, Caroline could weep no more. Her eyes denied her; even her militant conscience threw down its arms; and with a last sigh of relief she went gently backsliding into sleep.

She was then seven years old, and could now, at seventeen, remember no more of her grandfather than a cat, a warm bed, and a pair of mobile ears.

"Mother," said Caroline, faintly.

Mrs. Chase looked round; but without so much alarm as the sudden change of tone might have seemed to warrant. She was used, on fine Sunday evenings, to an occasional failure of her daughter's powers. "What is it, dear? Have you a headache?" Caroline nodded.

"It's just come on. Just behind my eyes."

Mrs. Chase nodded back. Both question and answer—like the preceding faintness—were purely conventional, designed partly to take in Caroline and her mother themselves, but chiefly to take in the Deity. The deception thus accomplished, Mrs. Chase took up her cue.

"If you think Chapel will be too much for you, dear, I should take a nice walk on the Common instead. It won't matter for once."

Caroline hesitated. She *had* deceived the Lord, of course, but it was simply out of politeness; she still did not wish seriously to hurt His feelings.

"Won't it really, Mother?"

"No," said Mrs. Chase firmly. "You've been looking peaky all day. But come and meet me afterwards, dear, and we'll walk back together."

Under the hard straw brim Caroline's eyes shone with gratitude: it was at moments such as these that her love for her mother, usually no more than a warm comfortable glow, seemed to leap and tremble into passionate flame. She longed to risk her life, work her fingers to the bone: she looked forward with eagerness to Mrs. Chase's declining years. In the twinkling of an eye she demolished her present narrow but secure income, and saw instead herself as a sempstress, working far into the night while her mother lay in bed. . . . Emotion overwhelmed her, she put up her hand and pressed Mrs. Chase's arm.

"I'll wait for you at the gate," said Caroline earnestly.

. . . But for all her tenderness, all her passionate and genuine affection, she would not, for anything on earth, have told her mother where she was going.

It was not for a walk on the Common.

CHAPTER II

I

THE house called Richmond Lodge stood not on Morton Common itself, but separated from it only by the fenced enclosures of Morton Dairy Farm. It was a villa-residence of the classic type, white-plastered, bow-windowed, with four acres of ground; and had been conspicuous in its heyday for certain scarlet-and-white sun blinds universally acknowledged—sun shining, plaster brilliant—to hit one in the eye. But no such fopperies now enlivened its façade: the house was empty, had been empty fifteen years, and in the opinion of Morton house-agents gave every promise of being empty forever. It was too big, and had only one bathroom. The basement was like an Egyptian tomb. All water had to be carried from the kitchen, all coal from a cellar by the stables. Even during the first six months, while paint and plaster were still moderately fresh, prospective tenants fled in dismay; as the years went by, and the walls began to peel, they could scarcely be got past the gate. A superficial decay belied the solidity of the shell, so that the tomb-like air of the basement became the tomb-like air of the whole house. In the books of the agents its name fairly stank; in Morton as a whole it was regarded as an eyesore. Only one person had a good word for it, and that was Caroline.

She considered it highly romantic; but since her words in general (and the word romantic in particular) carried very little weight, even she never spoke it aloud. Richmond Lodge was her guilty secret, the one point on which she ran deliberately counter to public opinion. Even paragraphs in print, such as now and then came out in the *Morton Chronicle*, could not shake her conviction. The house itself appeared to her grand, melancholy, and imposing; but the garden—the green and shaggy wilderness, half-glimpsed over a gate or wall—had the allurements of Eden. Like Eve after the Fall, she hovered longingly without; but where Eve had only memories, Caroline had imagination. There had been an old sale bill, now rotted away, which spoke of waterworks and pavilions; there had been a Scottish head gardener, who, before departing to an earl's, had dropped a word of orchid houses. Orchids and crystal falls—China pagodas ten stories high—with such and suchlike did Caroline, for five or six years, happily decorate her imaginary landscape; but as fairy tales lost their charm, so did the waterfalls. She began to hanker after the real, after the material Richmond Lodge rather than an imaginary pagoda: and thus found the criminal act of trespass come quite readily into her mind.

No sooner had she left her mother, therefore, on that particularly fine Sunday evening, than instead of turning back to the Common Caroline walked briskly on in the direction of the Dairy Farm. A public foot-path, little used by ladies on account of the cows, ran diagonally across its pastures: there was no one about save a courting couple and a boy with a dog. Caroline slipped through the gate and began to walk faster yet. The bells still rang, but faintly and behind her: before, just past the second gate, lay the shady turning to the wicket of Richmond Lodge.

And here Caroline paused. She was on familiar ground. Every solid but weather-beaten paling—every unclipped laurel and spreading may-tree—was as intimate to her eye as the pattern of her bedroom wallpaper. Hour after hour of childish loitering had etched them in her mind. The gate itself, loosely fastened with wire, she could see distinctly whenever she closed her eyes. It was five-barred, very heavy, and as much wider than the usual wicket as the Lodge was bigger than the ordinary house. . . .

'I'll have to climb over,' thought Caroline recklessly.

She looked down at her skirts. They were voluminous in cut and of a colour specially chosen to stand up to dirt. Gathering a breadth in either hand, and showing at least six inches of ankle, Caroline glanced once over her shoulder and advanced to the attack.

She had not to advance far. She took, to be accurate, exactly four steps; and even on the third her feet wavered. But it was no ignoble fear, no internal treachery, that held her so at gaze. It was nothing less than a miracle.

For the gate stood open.

Caroline's skirts dropped. She stared incredulously. The wire, in a rusty spiral, lay just beyond her foot: a broad curving scar showed how the gravel had been forced back. The marks of human agency also included two decapitated nettles and a broken switch.

It was not (Caroline decided rather arbitrarily) a miracle to prevent her having to climb, but a miracle to prevent her having to trespass. If gates were open, people could naturally go in. To examine the matter further, she felt, would be not only ungrateful, but also a waste of time.

In another moment, Caroline was through.

II

The garden, very much overgrown, dropped in a fall of three terraces connected by wide stone steps. The first was entirely lawn, now rank and flowery as a meadow; the second and third, cut up by old brick walls, seemed designed as a succession of smaller gardens of different characters. One had a sundial and roses, one a jungle of pampas-grass. There were no waterfalls; but at the bottom of all lay a long stone pool, moss-encrusted, in which the decaying baskets of lily roots could still be seen. Nor did any pagodas rise among the greenery, but instead three summer houses, one like a Greek temple, one like a Swiss chalet, one like a woodman's cottage. This last was also a tool-house: when Caroline pressed her face to the window she could see cobwebbed rakes, rusty trowels, and a scythe that might have belonged to Time. 'They ought all to have been oiled!' thought Caroline indignantly. 'There probably *is* oil somewhere, if one could only get at it.' Impulsively she tried the door: grinding, protesting, reluctant as a guilty caretaker, it gave way before her. Caroline stepped inside, sneezed, and made a hasty inventory. There was everything else, but no oil-can. A broom of twigs, still serviceable, caught her eye. She made a mental note of it and stepped outside again for a second tour of inspection.

Her attitude towards the garden, it will be observed, was by this time radically changed. So long as she stood outside everything within wore the colours of enchantment. She had expected (should she ever enter) to move breathless on tiptoe, chary of her shadow. For a single moment, on the very threshold, the spell had still bound her; but once fairly within, once with her feet on the actual paths, mastery changed hands. A garden was a fruit of the earth, and as such made for man; and in return man, by the sweat of his brow, must labour for his garden. Such, though all unconscious, was Caroline's conviction; and no one could so labour who walked dream-bound on tiptoe. Her step, as she now

redescended to the rose garden, was therefore a proper gardener's tread—slow, considerate, with long abstracted pauses for
survey and meditation. She also, without thinking, removed her
hat and gloves.

The path from the tool-house, skirting the first terrace, was
bordered with crab-apples. They needed pruning. The path itself
was flagged and level, but under a mat of grass that overlapped
the flower-beds. 'There ought to be two gardeners and a boy,'
thought Caroline regretfully. She descended the steps, noted
a fallen urn, and under the great central pergola picked up an
empty nest. It fell apart in her hands, a bundle of dry twigs; and
looking about for somewhere to put it her eye was caught by a
movement under the crab-trees. A branch swung back, an arm
was withdrawn: Caroline looked again, and saw that from the
garden above some one was watching her.

III

She at once dropped the nest and put on her hat. It was an
impulse not of vanity, or of Sabbatarianism, but of pure delicacy: She did not wish to seem presumptuously at home. For the
figure above which now revealed itself as that of a young man,
appeared very much at home indeed. He lounged easily against
the balustrade, hatless as she had been, and smoked a cigarette.
Had the house then been let, wondered Caroline, or was he the
son, perhaps, of the absentee owner? That he had a right to be
there was indubitable: and uneasily conscious of her own short-
comings, she stepped diffidently forward.

"I'm afraid," said Caroline bravely, "that I'm a trespasser."

"So am I," said the young man.

She was so surprised that for a moment she could not speak.
For to trespass with—with modesty was one thing: to trespass
thus brazenly quite another. All her diffidence gone, and quite
forgetting that there was no real need to speak to him again, she
said rebukingly,

"When *I* came in the gate was open."

"I know," said the young man. "I opened it."

He smiled quite candidly, as though their common lawlessness, their mutual avowal, at once placed them beyond all other conventional bounds. Caroline did not see it so.

"How prim you look!" observed the young man from above.

Caroline was now in somewhat of a dilemma. To remain where she was (besides being wrong in itself) would undoubtedly encourage him: to ascend the steps, and so make her way out, would place her, for a moment at least, positively at his side. While she was thus debating the young man strolled thoughtfully down.

"The whole place," he said disapprovingly, "has been let thoroughly run to seed. They should at least have left a gardener."

Caroline was surprised anew. His whole manner had suddenly changed. He had become grave, competent, a responsible man of the world. She felt as though she were being consulted on some important matter of business.

"Don't *you* think they should?" demanded the young man sternly.

"I—I don't know who they are," stammered Caroline. "I haven't any idea—"

They were now absolutely face to face: she saw that he was tall, very slender, with light corn-coloured hair. And she saw another thing, that although, from his height and slimness, he was evidently growing fast, his sleeves came well down over his wrists and his trousers over his boots. This in Caroline's experience was rare, and a sure mark of those who lived on the Common.

"I'm perfectly respectable," said the youth suddenly.

In spite of herself Caroline smiled. Respectable! As though he were an errand-boy asking for work! In those trousers! But she repressed the smile at once, and walked sedately towards the steps. He at once followed.

"Where are you going?"

"Home," said Caroline briefly.

"Because of me?"

She nodded.

"Then you needn't, because I will. If you insist on driving me out I'll go this minute."

Caroline was again in a quandary. If the garden was not his, neither was it hers: they were there on equal terms. She hesitated.

"If it's simply that we haven't been introduced," said the young man, reading her thoughts with extreme precision, "I'll go straight-away now and fetch my aunt. You're sure to know her, she knows every one in Morton. She's Mrs. Macbeth, and my name's Vincent."

Caroline looked at him with interest. She could not help it. For the name of Mrs. Macbeth, in the world of Morton, was as the name of Louis XIV in the world of Versailles. She was extremely rich. She had a husband who was a sheriff, and who in the course of time might even become Lord Mayor. Her mother's cousin was married to an earl. She lived, in fact, more on the Common than any one else in Morton.

"You *do* know her, you see!" said the young man triumphantly.

"But she doesn't know me," said Caroline.

"Why? Don't you live here?"

"Right in the Town," said Caroline sadly.

The distinction was lost on him. Instead of recoiling (as she had half expected), the young man merely continued to look at her; and now recollecting that he was not only the nephew of Mrs. Macbeth, but also, in some sort, the relation of an earl, Caroline could not refrain from looking-back. She felt it might be her only chance to study, at close quarters, a member of the aristocracy.

"Has she had a row with your people?" asked the young man suddenly.

Caroline laughed.

"She did once with my grandfather. She said the butter was too salt. And she took away her custom, which was nearly ten shillings a week, and went to the Dairy Farm instead."

In the young man's face a light of comprehension was begin-ning to kindle. He looked at Caroline again, and noticed something vaguely wrong in the cut of her jacket. It didn't fit. He had seen her first, he now remembered, without a hat; and to the broad oval of her face, with its candid and open brows, the hard black straw was hopelessly incongruous. But still, with all these disadvantages, he did not want her to go.

He hit on a good expedient.

"My mother," he said tragically, "has just practically died."

In a moment—before, indeed, she had quite comprehended his meaning—all Caroline's stiffness was gone. She saw him no longer as an impertinent, but as a wanderer in despair. Her eyes softened, instinctively she put out her hand. But she quickly withdrew it again.

"*What* did you say?"

"That my mother," repeated the young man rather hurriedly, "had just practically died. She was most dreadfully ill for months— no one thought she'd ever recover—"

Caroline looked at him sternly.

"But she did?"

"Yes," admitted the young man, "she did. But she's had to go away—to Switzerland—and they wouldn't let me go with her."

Caroline melted again.

"What a shame!"

"Wasn't it? Especially as I'd never been there. They made her go all alone."

"What, to Switzerland?" cried Caroline, quite shocked.

"Well, there was the nurse and my two sisters, of course, but it was me she wanted. So then the pater decided to shut up the house, and I was pushed off here. It—it's simply killing me!"

In spite of a lingering disapproval, Caroline was quite fascinated. He was like no one she had ever met before. He called his father pater. He had a mother who in illness was sent not to Bournemouth or Torquay, but right to Switzerland. In the company of Mrs. Macbeth—in the largest house on the Common— he was being killed. . . .

"How?" asked Caroline.

"There's no one to talk to," said Vincent.

For the next half-hour he talked to Caroline. In a rapid, even flow he told her all about himself, all about the Macbeths, and a good deal about Art. He was going up to Cambridge, and had to cram three hours a day. The pater wanted him to be a solicitor, but he, Vincent, did not. He, Vincent, wanted to be a critic. He had read all Ruskin, all Browning, and *Heroes and Hero-wor- ship*. He offered to lend Caroline these books and discuss them with her afterwards. He had a sister who played the violin and practiced three hours a day, but he, Vincent, while hardly practicing at all, played better than his sister. He told this not out of conceit, but to impress on Caroline's mind the fact that in Art no mere industry, however close, can compensate for one flicker of the Divine Spark. At Mrs. Macbeth's there were two daughters who played the piano; when their practice hour came round, Vincent had to leave the house. He had to go and wander about Morton, a place without an art gallery. Today, by his first stroke of luck, he had discovered the garden. He had also discovered Caroline; and if Caroline would only have pity on him, his reason might yet be saved.

"But—but what can I do?" asked Caroline in astonishment.

"Listen to me," said Vincent simply. "You go for walks by yourself, don't you?"

"Every afternoon. Mother can't, much, but she thinks it's good for me."

"Then walk up here sometimes. That's all."

Caroline hesitated. They were now, owing to her tactful manoeuveres, back by the wicket gate. In another moment they would have parted. She did not wish to part in the least; but propriety was strong. . . .

"It's not my fault," said Vincent suddenly. "I want you to meet my aunt, and you won't. Anyway, I shall see you home."

"No," said Caroline. Then the baldness of it troubled her, and she added, "I'm not going home. I'm going to meet my mother."

"I'll come and meet her too. Then everything will be all right."

"No," said Caroline again.

They both felt it to be a crisis. Vincent looked at her face, then folded his arms on the gate in the attitude of one prepared for a long argument.

"Why not?"

"Because I don't wish you to," said Caroline primly.

"Have I offended you in the last five minutes?"

"You know you haven't."

"Do you think I'm going to try and kiss you in the lane?"

Caroline looked at him squarely.

"It's because you live on the Common and I live in the Town."

There was a pause, a taking of breath on both sides; then Vincent began to laugh.

"If you think I care about that—"

"If you don't I do," said Caroline. "And if you can't understand why, you'd better ask Mrs. Macbeth." She looked at him again, but gently, without antagonism. "You see? Even now, you feel a little . . . shy, at the thought of mentioning me. If I'd been some one on the Common you wouldn't a bit." He smiled, as though the distinction still amused him, but Caroline went doggedly on. She had a horror of false pretences; she wanted to leave nothing in doubt, nothing for him to find out afterwards. "If you did meet my people you wouldn't like them. Mother's different—she's different from every one—but Cousin Maggie and Ellen you'd simply hate. And I"—a slow deep colour began to rise in her cheeks—"I should get teased about you."

He stared down at the nettles, at last serious as she could wish. 'He's really sorry,' thought Caroline, 'almost as sorry as I am. . . .'

"So we can't be friends after all."

"Only in the garden," agreed Caroline soberly. There was another silence, still mournful—almost like being in church. Then Vincent looked up; and to Caroline's final astonishment he had changed again.

"Well, I shall be there practically every day," said Vincent cheerfully. . . .

IV

Mrs. Chase appeared early, but no longer alone. On one side of her walked Cousin Maggie Platt, on the other Ellen Taylor; and though this was no more than Caroline might have expected, her heart nevertheless sank. On her present delicate mood—on any mood, indeed, save the exceptionally robust—they both jarred.

"And how's Carrie?" asked Mrs. Platt heartily.

For no reason at all, Ellen giggled. The giggle was her natural form of expression, like a duck's quack or a weasel's squeak. A weasel—something thin and sandy and malicious—that was Ellen all over, thought Caroline unkindly. She had reddish hair, pale eyebrows, and when not toadying Cousin Maggie would toady any one else who came to hand. Slipping an arm through Caroline's she giggled again.

"How's the headache, Carrie dear?"

Caroline did not reply. Mrs. Platt, forty-one and her mother's cousin, could command a certain complaisance; but Ellen was only nineteen.

"The air's done you good," said Mrs. Chase. "Would you like another stroll, dear, before we go in?"

"No, thank you," said Caroline. "I'd rather have supper." She spoke less from appetite than from a strong though obscure instinct to heighten the contrast, to make everything not pertaining to her adventure as prosaic and commonplace as possible. And Sunday cold supper—scones and milk, and perhaps an egg—what could be more prosaic than Sunday supper?

"If you're as hungry as all that," said Cousin Maggie bluntly, "you'd better come back to me. I've got half a cold ham."

Between mother and daughter flashed a swift glance. 'No!' said Caroline mutely. 'It's only her way!' pleaded Mrs. Chase. 'Not on any account!' said Caroline.

"All right, don't if you don't want to," said Mrs. Platt good-humouredly. "I've got Ellen to keep me company. *Her* pride isn't stronger than her stomach." She patted Ellen on the shoulder, and punctually Ellen giggled. "I thought you'd like to talk to her about the fête."

"They can talk going down the Common," said Mrs. Chase.

Two and two they passed through the gate, the two women in front, the girls behind. But no talk of the fête—joint Church and Chapel, in aid of the Destitute Children's Dinner Society—immediately arose. For if Caroline was preoccupied, so also was her companion; the only difference being that whereas Caroline's preoccupation demanded silence, Miss Taylor's demanded speech.

"Wait till they're a little ahead!" murmured Miss Taylor.

Only half-comprehending, Caroline looked at the figures in front of them; and received the customary thrill of pleasure from the sight of her mother's back. It was so slim and straight, so very ladylike! In profile Mrs. Chase was too thin; but from the back she was elegant. Beside Cousin Maggie's tremendous bulk—purple, braided, swollen across by enormous sleeves—she looked like the Princess of Wales.

"He was there again!" murmured Ellen Taylor.

She turned confidentially, and Caroline had a moment's fleeting wonder as to why, when Ellen was so thin, her bodices were always too tight. This one in particular—a light green alpaca—was rucked under the arms into a succession of discoloured creases. . . .

"Who was there?" said Caroline aloud.

Ellen stared reproachfully; and at last exerting herself, Caroline recollected a long unconvincing history, whispered unpleasantly close to her ear, of some agnostic young man whom Ellen was converting to Methodism.

"Frederick Watts?"

Ellen giggled coyly.

"In the next pew, dear. And he stayed behind to talk to Mr. James."

Her voice went on, but Caroline ceased to listen. She was sleep-walking with open eyes, stepping off and on the curb, smiling at her mother's acquaintances, nodding to her own. Half-way down the hill they met Miss Dupré walking up. But save as a dim ambulant shadow—such as might be cast by man, woman, or child—Caroline did not notice her.

CHAPTER III

I

"I DO so wish you could have been a peasant, dear," said Mrs. Chase wistfully.

Caroline bisected her doughnut—they always had doughnuts for lunch on Sunday—and reached for the jam.

"Not peasants, Mother. Gypsies."

"Well, a gypsy, then." Mrs. Chase looked at her daughter thoughtfully, trying to visualize Caroline's soft brown hair under a striped handkerchief. But it was not to be; in the fête's chief attraction—a Gypsy Encampment of Old Spain—neither Caroline nor

Ellen, nor indeed any other member of the Chapel, was invited to take part. It had been tacitly, almost subconsciously, reserved for the people on the Common; whose wives and daughters, decked in the spoils of foreign travel, were to have the whole of the wide Town Hall gallery to themselves. The use of this gallery was an innovation, from which much was hoped, for not only did many people habitually go up there to enjoy a view of the crowd, but many others, of the more economically-minded sort, went up to put themselves out of temptation. This year temptation was to be ready for them: lovely Carmencitas, a rose behind the ear, would pounce or languish every few yards, and even the one way of retreat (by an obscure back staircase) had been thought of and provided for. It was to house a fine stuffed alligator, with an admission fee of threepence.

"I do wish you could, Carrie!" said Mrs. Chase again.

Caroline shrugged her shoulders placidly. A coffee-stall, in conjunction with Ellen Taylor, seemed to her far too natural a fate to make any fuss about. It didn't matter.

"*I* don't mind, Mother. Besides, where should we get the clothes?"

It was characteristic of Mrs. Chase that she considered the question carefully. Though there was no possible chance of her daughter being so promoted, it pleased her to consider ways and means, to wrestle with unarisen difficulties, to turn out, in her mind's eye, a radiant gypsy princess clad chiefly in cast-off clothes. . . .

"There's Cousin Maggie still wears red flannel petticoats," she said at last. "She has them new every year and lovely material. I'm sure if I asked her—"

Caroline jumped up from table and began stacking crockery. The notion of an old-time Spanish gypsy relying for an illusion on a red flannel petticoat struck her as so deliciously funny that she wanted to laugh aloud. But she must not laugh yet, for that would provoke questions; and though with some little trouble she could probably have made her mother see the joke too, Caroline did not wish to share it.

There was only one person, just then, with whom she wished to share anything. Like everything else that pleased, touched, or amused her, Cousin Maggie's red petticoat must remain hidden in her breast—a delicious burden—a secret treasure-trove—until she could carry it to Vincent.

II

They had met, during that past week, already twice again; once as it were by accident—he lounging just within the gate, she casually passing by—once by definite appointment. For this, the third time, there was an appointment also: half-past two, in the rose-garden, unless it rained enough for umbrellas.

As soon as she reached the Dairy Farm Caroline began to run. The washing-up, the talk about the Bazaar, had put her five minutes behind, and she was neither old enough in experience, nor coquettish enough by nature, to realize the value of such a grace. She ran without a thought, as fast as her belt and heels permitted, and was no more than eight minutes behind altogether when she slipped in at the gate.

Vincent was not yet there.

Caroline stood breathless, partly from her speed (which through the upper garden had considerably increased), but chiefly from surprise. The idea of his being late too had never occurred to her. Still unbelieving, she circled the pergola, descended to the water-garden, and returned under the crab-apples. He was not there. But now her mind had begun to work again, to consider possibilities; with the result that, instead of going back to the gate (where her presence might be construed into a reproach), she walked instead to the nearest bench and there sat down.

She sat for ten minutes.

At the end of that time, without any real intention, she turned round, reached behind her, and pulled a long straggling dandelion from the overgrown flowerbed. It left a small brown patch, about the size of a playing-card. Caroline pulled again, but too recklessly; the soil was hard, she held a handful of crushed greenery, but the roots remained in the ground. This so annoyed her that she went straight to the woodman's cottage, thrust open the door, and selected the best of the trowels and a small fork. Both had loose handles, and were also extremely rusty: but then there is nothing so good for rust (reflected Caroline) as digging in the earth.

Laboriously she went to work. Her chief want was a kneeling-mat, in default of which she had to squat on her heels, a position at once inconvenient and tiring. But the work progressed. The two loose handles she wedged with twigs, and she also instituted a stone-heap and began stoning as she went. Inch by inch, a good clayey brown, the soil reappeared; Caroline laid aside the tools and crumbled it lovingly between her fingers. All her childhood she had dreamed of just that sensation: it had been a curious chance that in Morton, where gardens were common, she should have been put to live over a shop. . . .

The work progressed. Inches stretched to feet, the stone-pile toppled over; for half an hour, oblivious of love and time, Caroline dug and pulled and loosened the stubborn roots. Then a sound from the terrace made her raise her head. She stood up, brushed the earth from her fingers, and saw Vincent laughing at her.

III

It was that afternoon they found the window.

"Come round to the house," said Vincent at once. "I've something to show you."

Caroline followed obediently. She would have liked him to admire her flower-bed, but he appeared to have forgotten it already. They went up between the crab-apples, through the shrubbery, and so not to the house itself, but round to the yards and outbuildings that lay behind. Caroline liked them—they were so small and neat and practical—but Vincent did not, and she was all the more surprised when instead of going straight through he led her on past the wash-house to the inner block of sculleries.

"There!" he said triumphantly.

Caroline looked up, and saw a small square window, extremely dirty, on a level with her head. Between the upper sash and the frame was a gap of about three inches.

"It's open!"

Vincent nodded. Without a word—and so all the more impressively—he upturned an abandoned box, mounted, and began gently working the bottom sash. But no gentleness could avail him: the whole window being as it were soldered together by time, damp, and a good deal of rust. Vincent considered the position afresh, chose a spot where the sashes overlapped, and brought his shoulder heavily against the wood. There was a loud cracking sound: when he jerked at the sash again it moved creakingly upwards. Another cautious thrust gave him an opening two feet square: he flung over a leg, ducked and disappeared.

"Caroline!" called Vincent from within.

Without any intention of following, she nevertheless got up on the box and looked through the window. Within all was dark, a uniform twilight furnished with shelves, doors, and a heavy table. This last stood conveniently under the window, and was already printed with Vincent's boots.

"Come along, Caroline!"

Caroline held back.

"I don't think we ought."

For answer he reached up, caught her round the waist, and drew her gently through.

IV

Through room after room, down corridor after corridor, they roamed with a gradually increasing confidence. For the house was indulgent: no caretaker started up, no door creaked to alarm them. They found parlours and bedrooms, and a boudoir hung with satin: they found a strange-smelling conservatory, whose walls, covered with bark, left a dry powder on the finger-tips. Plants dead in their pots circled the dry fountain: a marble lady, too naked for Caroline's comfort, supported an empty flower-basket on her marble shoulder. Caroline moved away, tried a tall double-door, and found herself on the threshold of the drawing-room.

It was a room—ah, such a room!—vast, ghostly, glimmering with mirrors. It had a parquet floor, still slippery to the feet, that seemed to stretch on and on in an unending perspective. At the door where she had entered, and at the tall windows, curtains still hung. Above the curtains were birds like eagles, gilt under a powdering of dust, with loops of ribbon curling stiffly from their beaks. More loops and more birds decorated the mirrors. Overhead, like an enormous bunch of grapes, hung a vast chandelier in a holland bag.

"It's like the Crystal Palace," murmured Vincent behind her.

"When you get there too early," said Caroline softly.

They spoke in whispers: they moved on tiptoe. Even so, their feet made an odd sound.

"They've left the fittings," said Caroline.

She put out a hand, and touched a curtain. It felt stiff and dusty, as though it wanted a good shaking. But the stuff was silk, a heavy rib like Cousin Maggie's best gown.

"It must have been lovely when it was new," said Caroline. "It must have been rose-pink . . ."

She looked round, and saw that Vincent had left her to look out of the windows. He could not see much, for all save one had the heavy slatted shutters that made the room so dark. One of these had fallen away, rotting from its hinge; and against this sudden patch of light Vincent stood sharply outlined. For a long minute Caroline watched him: observed the light corn-coloured hair, the aristocratic narrowness of the head, the more regrettable narrowness of his shoulders: and felt rise in her heart an emotion so strange and overwhelming, that when at last she stirred to move again, her feet almost failed her.

As noiselessly as possible she crossed the room between the old mirrors. They reflected her one after the other, but so dimly, through such veils of greyness, that she slipped by like a shadow. And she had a curious fancy, too unaccountable to be examined, that perhaps the real room—the room with the real Caroline and Vincent—lay on the other side. . . .

She came up beside him, he did not move. He was still looking over the garden, as she herself still glanced back into the room. Then all at once he turned.

"This," said Vincent, "is our house."

"Yes," said Caroline. (But on which side of the mirrors?)

Without any warning he put his arm round her shoulder and drew her towards him. Caroline did not speak. She felt at once tranquil and breathless, bewitched yet unafraid. But her heart beat loudly.

"Caroline?"

She put up her face, and waited for him to kiss her.

CHAPTER IV

I

Now for Caroline there began a strange double-textured life in which the familiar and the dream-like had curiously changed places. The shop in the High Street, the Chapel Bazaar, Cousin Maggie Platt, even her own mother—were all become unsubstantial, a set of familiar ghosts among whom Caroline herself moved wraith-like as the rest. Wraith-like, but clumsily: for she developed at this time a completely new habit of knocking things over. Two large earthen pots, ready painted for the coming fête, fell untimely to her hand; also a terra-cotta group, the gift of Cousin Maggie, representing Anglo-Saxon warriors. To the rebukes that followed she listened patiently but without emotion, only once surprising her mother by the childishness of her defence.

"I'm not really clumsy," said Caroline.

In a sense it was true. In real life—in the house and garden— she was not clumsy at all. She moved surely, almost elegantly, about the large rooms. They gave her a sense of ease and freedom; as a liberal author may form the mind, so did their spaciousness and proportion form Caroline's looks. Without blossoming into beauty, she brought away with her a slow tranquillity in movement, a calmness in repose. She ceased, in fine, to slouch when walking and to fidget when she sat; nor did she now run headlong, skirts and hair flying, down the winding path from shrubbery to rose-garden. But it was not from any lack of eagerness: at the first sight of Vincent's figure her heart would pause, and then beat again, just as on that first afternoon in the shadowy drawing-room.

They talked about Ruskin.

In the rose-garden if it were fine, in the drawing-room if it were dull, Vincent discoursed at length on the Stones of Venice. He carried the book in his pocket and read passages aloud. If Caroline didn't understand anything, she was to stop him and ask; but her quickness and intelligence delighted them both. She followed not only Ruskin, but Vincent himself, through every highroad and byway of elevated thought: she discovered Baroque and Gothic beauties (which Vincent afterwards went and looked at) in the most unpromising parts of Morton. It was a little blossoming of the intellect, half adolescent emotion, half genuine mental excitement; and whether due chiefly to Ruskin, or chiefly to Vincent, Caroline never stopped to ask.

There was only one vexation: that whenever Vincent came to earth—just grazing the mountains, as it were, between two flights of oratory—he always seemed to be laughing at her.

"But *why*?" Caroline asked. "What do I *do*?"

"You look so good."

"That's nothing to laugh about."

"I suppose not," said Vincent; and then he would take her by the shoulders, and kiss her very gravely indeed, to show his extreme serious-mindedness.

But they kissed, on the whole, remarkably little. Vincent's chief urge was to instruct, and the more opportunities Caroline offered him the more indispensable did she become. Indeed, the relief of her society (as Vincent continued to repeat) was all that prevented him from going completely mad; since at Mrs. Macbeth's, amidst every material luxury, he suffered perfect agonies of mental isolation. His aunt read nothing but novels, his uncle nothing but *The Times*: the people who visited them read nothing at all. To Caroline this new view-point—from which, so to speak, she and Vincent together looked down on the whole Common—was naturally very agreeable; and all the more so in that she presently discovered, on the roll of these illiterate guests, the name of Miss Dupré.

"Her father *was* an admiral, you know," said Caroline, not quite able to believe her ears.

Vincent smiled wearily.

"The first time I tried to talk to her about Browning, she pretended not to hear; the second time she said she was in a draught. And before she went home, she told my aunt I ought to be getting more exercise."

"Exercise?" repeated Caroline. "But what had exercise to do with it?"

"Heaven alone knows. But the result of it was that next morning at breakfast my aunt ordered me to walk four miles a day. *I* don't mind." He smiled again, this time quite normally. "I'm walking four miles now, Caroline dear."

II

He could not, of course, always be punctual; and both the rose-garden and the water-garden, where Caroline principally waited, began in consequence, and at the end of a few weeks, to show considerable improvement. Without any theoretic knowledge, without the least experience, Caroline was a good gardener. She never hurried. Faced by weeds like a green carpet she began methodically to pull them up, not in handfuls—leaving the root intact—but one at a time; and thus, inch by inch, she recovered first the soil of the flower beds, then the flags of the pathway. The soil was caked hard and surfaced with loose stone: Caroline removed the stones by basketfuls and got a larger fork from the tool-house. Digging, with its resolute thrust and heave, appealed to her particularly, and in the size of the beds, and the paucity of rose-trees, she found ample scope. The rose-trees themselves presented more of a problem, for she felt pretty certain they needed pruning; but knowing nothing of the art to begin with, and gathering very little more from the article in the Encyclopaedia, Caroline was forced to content herself with removing all obviously dead wood and nipping all superfluous buds. The result was at any rate not injurious: the remaining buds bloomed: and by the middle of July she could count forty blossoms at once.

"When are you going to give me one?" asked Vincent idly.

Caroline looked at him in surprise.

"But it's not my garden!"

"No one would think so, to see you working in it," said Vincent.

Caroline looked round at the beds, down at the clean paths, and vainly tried to come to a conclusion. It *was* hers in a sense, she thought of it as hers, and yet—

"It's taking something away," she said at last. "You feel like that about the house. It's ours, because we enjoy it, but you wouldn't take anything out."

He came a step nearer, smiling into her eyes.

"Give me a rose, Caroline."

They were standing close together now, under the central pergola. Without a word, breathless as once before, she put up her hand and pulled a crimson spray. But perhaps because she was not looking, perhaps because of a sudden trembling, her hand came down scarred.

"Caroline! You've hurt yourself!"

She looked indifferently, still half bemused with that momentary sweetness, and saw a double red line start across her wrist. Vincent caught her fingers.

"I wish you wouldn't, Caroline. You've got lovely hands, and you let them get scratched to pieces."

Pleased but puzzled, she waited eagerly for him to go on. A lovely hand, according to all Morton standards, was either small and dimpled or long and slender; whereas her own—

"Aren't they—aren't they too big, Vincent?"

"Too *big*? Nonsense!" He shifted his hold to her wrist, displaying, as it were, the square capable palm and long straight fingers. "They're beautiful. If you have to go in rags, Caroline, you must never wear cheap gloves."

A scarlet bead formed and ran.

"And if you can't garden without getting scratched, you must give up gardening."

"That's silly," said Caroline.

But she spoke almost unconsciously; nor did he hear her.

CHAPTER V

I

"CAROLINE!"

"Yes, Mother?"

"Here's Ellen Taylor come to tea!"

Caroline ran back into the kitchen and counted the buns. There were only three, and halfpenny ones at that. She opened the cake-tin, found it bare as she had supposed: of Sunday's currant loaf there remained, in the bread-pan, no more than a heel. Caroline whipped round to the buns again and cut them all in half.

"And how's Carrie?" asked Ellen from the doorway.

Caroline noted with resentment that she was already removing her hat. It was of blue straw, trimmed with half a bird, and such was Caroline's unreasonableness that she even resented that. Every one wore birds: she herself had a pigeon's wing: but Ellen's birds were different. They did not suit with her ferrety countenance, and so losing the character of ornament, looked simply like dead creatures.

"I've just seen the alligator!" said Ellen importantly.

"What alligator?" asked Caroline.

"You know, Carrie! The one Mrs. Macbeth's lending the Bazaar, to block up the back staircase. Her carriage was going down to the station—empty, of course—and she told them to leave it at the Vicarage. I saw it carried all up the path!"

"Then you shouldn't have looked," said Caroline priggishly.

Ellen giggled.

"Tell that to Mrs. Macbeth's friends, my dear. *They've* all seen it. I looked as hard as I could, and saved myself threepence." She picked up the bun-plate, with one swift glance reconstructed the original three buns, and set it briskly down again. "Do hurry up with tea, dear; I've come to start the flowers."

"What flowers?" asked Caroline.

"For the Bazaar, of course! There's nothing else you *can* do with a coffee-stall. Shall we have garlands or an arch, do you think?"

"Unless you have a man, arches fall down," said Caroline practically. She took up the tray, carried it into the sitting-room, and found rolls of coloured paper over the whole table. Mrs. Chase would have pushed them aside, but Ellen stopped her.

"Don't for me, Mrs. Chase. I'm going to work as I eat. Mrs. Platt says she believes I'd work in my sleep, if only I could keep my eyes open!" She picked up her scissors, snipped a row of petals, and laid them beside her plate. The making of paper flowers was her specialty; she had quite a gift for it, and could twist blue roses, green poppies, and even yellow almond-blossom, by the hour together.

"Why don't you make them the right colours?" asked Caroline. Ellen looked superiorly.

"It's more artistic. Aren't you going to help?" Without much thinking what she did, Caroline took up a paper and cut out a small blue clown. It looked quite pretty. A whole row of clowns, along the front of the stall—

"I thought clowns," said Ellen, with an air of great brilliance, "were usually white?"

II

The departure of their guest left Mrs. Chase faintly apologetic.

"I had to ask her, Carrie. I know you don't like her much—"

"Much!" repeated Caroline, pausing in the act of clearing the table. "Much! I don't like her at all. It's a queer thing, Mother, and I don't understand it; but I don't like Ellen, and I'm sure she doesn't like me, and yet for years and years we've always been expected to do things together. We have to have a coffee-stall at the fête, and go for walks after Chapel, and be in the same parties carol-singing. I'm sure I don't know why."

"Cousin Maggie—" began Mrs. Chase.

"Of course Cousin Maggie likes her, because she's such a toady. She goes there to supper and eats and eats and agrees with everything Cousin Maggie says. It's the same with her music-teaching; she doesn't bother with the children one bit, she just goes from house to house flattering their mothers."

Caroline swung round for the tea-cloth, and caught in her mother's eye an expression of surprise and trouble.

"You must remember she's an orphan, Carrie."

"It seems to me," said Caroline impartially, "that she makes rather a good thing out of it. People have to be kind to her, because it's in the Bible—'widows and fatherless'; whereas if she had parents, they could hate her as much as they liked."

Mrs. Chase looked more distressed still.

"You shouldn't hate any one, Carrie."

"Except the wicked," said Caroline promptly.

"But we don't know any wicked, dear," said Mrs. Chase.

III

Caroline held up her hands—she had become rather vain of them—so as to frame a bough of cedar and the sunset behind.

"Look through there, Vincent."

"Chinese," pronounced Vincent at once.

It was the same evening and not quite seven o'clock; so far and fast can one travel in half an hour. At a quarter past six Caroline had replaced the last teacup, looked out of the window, and remarked that as the evening was so fine she would just slip up to the Hall and look at the decorations; at a quarter to seven she was discussing Chinese art with the nephew of Mrs. Macbeth.

"You ought to go to the Victoria and Albert, Caroline," said Vincent earnestly. "You ought to go once a week. That's the way to get your eye in."

Caroline dropped her hands.

"It would take a whole day—"

"Well, you've nothing else to do," pointed out Vincent absently.

She looked round at him, half-opened her mouth, and then shut it again. He would never realize, nor did she wish him to, that furniture had to be dusted, beds made, and china washed; and that if you did not keep a servant you had to do these things yourself. At Mrs. Macbeth's, no doubt, every one had early tea. . . .

"I'll think about it," promised Caroline. She stood up. "Let's go into the house, Vincent. We haven't been for ages."

They went up through the shrubbery, and—as other house-holders might use a front door—quietly in at the window. Just inside Caroline had placed a door-mat of newspapers, on which to wipe their feet. Usually Vincent led straight to the drawing-room, but today, after so long an absence, they wandered from room to room, on a leisurely tour of inspection. Only before the conservatory did Caroline hang back, for the marble lady inside still embarrassed her. She went instead through the other door into the drawing-room, and there, between the grey mirrors, waited for Vincent to follow.

The mirrors glimmered. As always, they gave her a feeling of insubstantiality; her own figure, so reflected, was too incongruous to be real. You saw the dusty eagles, folds of silk or gilded scrollwork, and then a queer, ungraceful silhouette with swollen shoulders and a tiny head. 'I can't look like that!' thought Caroline incredulously—

The door opened. Vincent came in. For one moment, looking only at his excessively high collar, at the shepherd's plaid of his suit, she saw him to be grotesque too. Then the treachery flickered out, and her heart melted anew.

"How beautifully still you stand, Caroline!"

She flushed with pleasure. He was now close beside her, his hand just touching her skirt.

"Sometimes you *are* beautiful, Caroline; particularly when you don't know I'm looking at you."

She could not speak. As always when he was about to kiss her, she felt lightly enchanted.

IV

In the lane outside, between the wicket and the Dairy gate, they found it hard to leave each other.

"Tomorrow, Caroline?"

She shook her head.

"Tomorrow's the fête—three till half-past ten. If I do get an hour off, I don't know when it will be."

"Come in the morning, then. I'll be here at eleven, not a moment later."

"If I can, but I won't promise."

"You won't promise," said Vincent, "but you'll come. How nice you are, Caroline!"

They had now reached the foot-path gate, and still lingered. Vincent leaned, looked over; there was not a soul about.

"I think I'll see you home," he said deliberately.

"Vincent!"

"Well, at any rate as far as the Common. Why not?"

"We might meet your aunt."

"You know she never comes there—none of them do. You told me so yourself. They're afraid of the cows."

Caroline hesitated. The broad sloping pasture, delicious in solitude, stretched invitingly before them. It would mean another ten minutes, another quarter of an hour, of Vincent's company. And it was quite true about the cows. . . .

Her hand dropped to the latch; Vincent held open the gate, and they passed recklessly through.

For the first hundred yards the path skirted trees, a small clump of elm planted to shade the cattle; and for a hundred yards, animated but decorous, Caroline and her friend walked pleasantly on. Their topic was one peculiarly suited to their surroundings: in which hour of the twenty-four, asked Vincent, would one choose to spend one's life? He himself plumped for the dawn, Caroline for half-past five; and he was still trying to win her over.

"But I've never seen it!" protested Caroline. "I've never been up before six in my life!"

"I haven't been up before seven," said Vincent. "*That* doesn't make any difference. If you just think of the birds, Caroline—and the mists going off the mountain-tops—"

Caroline opened her mouth to reply; but no words issued. They had at that moment rounded the trees, opening a clear view of the whole field, and there, not fifty yards down the path, advancing rapidly towards them, were Mrs. Chase, Cousin Maggie, and Ellen Taylor.

Quick as a flash, and as detachedly as though she had never seen any one of them before, Caroline's eye flickered over and took in every minutest detail of their garb and bearing. She saw a slim little woman in an old jacket—lady-like, but shabby, especially about the gloves. An awful woman in dark puce, feathered-boa'd like an old clo', hatted like a Harvest Festival, with sweat running down her forehead. A girl in blue alpaca—too smartly cut, too tight in the bust—with eyes like a ferret's and a ferret's sandy hair. . . .

Caroline's heart stopped beating. Out of the corner of her eye she could see the beginning of Vincent's smile. He was highly amused, he had thought of something funny; he wanted to catch her eye and share the joke. Caroline looked steadfastly away, staring over the fields.

"Caroline—" murmured Vincent at her ear.

She would not hear him. Her one thought was to get him away. But in that wide expanse of pasture, unpeopled save for their five selves, how was it possible? There was no time for anything, neither to drop back herself, nor to hurry him on. There was no time even for a warning. Before Caroline had fully got back her breath, the parties were engaged.

"Well, if it isn't Carrie!" called Mrs. Platt from afar.

Caroline stopped dead, felt rather than saw Vincent stop too, and in the same moment, with unnatural acuteness, observed a badly-split seam in Ellen's glove.

"We thought," continued Cousin Maggie, "you'd gone over to the Hall. That's what your Ma said." Her round black eyes, unwinking as boot-buttons, never moved from Vincent's face. Ellen Taylor was staring too, less openly, with knowing sidelong looks under her pale lashes. Only Mrs. Chase kept her eyes on her daughter.

"It's a lovely evening, dear. I'm glad you went for a walk."

Caroline looked at her gratefully; but it was no good. Against the combined forces of Cousin Maggie and Ellen there was no prevailing. She looked at them again, and drew her breath.

"This," said Caroline desperately, "is Mr. . . . Vincent." She dared not look at him; but from the answering motions of the three women knew he must have bowed. She hurried on. "My mother—Mrs. Platt—and Miss Ellen Taylor."

"Very pleased to meet you," said Cousin Maggie.

Ellen giggled.

There was a short silence.

"We were just going to turn back," said Mrs. Chase. "It must be nearly eight. Isn't that a cow over there, Carrie?"

Caroline saw her opening.

"Several cows, Mother. Mr. Vincent has just been seeing me past them." She turned, and for the first time since the encounter looked him in the face. "But in a party we shall be quite safe. Thank you very much indeed, Mr. Vincent."

He raised his hat, he was already turning; but Cousin Maggie detained him.

"You live round here, Mr. Vincent? If you do, you must come to the Bazaar."

He was understood to acquiesce.

"Three to half-past ten, in the Town Hall. We shall want some young lads," said Cousin Maggie heartily, "to throw their money about. That's what I keep telling Carrie 'n' Ellen here; if they don't bring some of their sweethearts, they won't make a sixpence."

Ellen giggled corroboratively. But she was no longer staring at Vincent, she was staring at Caroline: and against every effort of will Caroline felt her colour rise. Without looking round again she knew that he had somehow escaped; there was a general movement, a turning about, and Caroline found herself once more in motion. Too confused for thought, too miserable for speech, she followed automatically through the gate and out on to Morton Common. There, with some idea of getting home alone, she quickened her pace, but only to feel a hand thrust through her elbow and behind it the full weight of Ellen Taylor. Reluctantly she dropped back.

"Well, you *are* a one!" said Ellen archly.

Caroline did not answer. For the first time in her life she was experiencing the desire to hit out, to do a physical injury. She hated Ellen Taylor, hated every inch and part of her—the pale eyelashes, the silly voice, the tight blue bodice smelling faintly of sweat. . . .

"I wouldn't call him *handsome*, of course," continued Ellen, "but quite the gentleman. That's what I said as soon as I saw you. 'Well, whoever he is, he's quite the gentleman, Mrs. Chase!' I said; and your mother said so too. Have you known him long, dear?"

"No," said Caroline. "I met him ten minutes ago, just inside the other gate. I was frightened of the cows, and he offered to see me across."

"And he told you his name and everything!"

"He told me his name."

"Did you tell him yours?"

"No," said Caroline.

Ellen looked at her incredulously, greedy as a cat after cream. In another minute or two she tried again.

"Carrie!"

"Well?"

"You tell me about Mr. Vincent, and I'll tell you about Mr. Watts."

For answer Caroline shook free her arm and broke into a run. She could endure no more. If Cousin Maggie began at her she would run from Cousin Maggie—run from them all, run and run until Morton itself, and all that it contained, was left far behind. . . .

"Hoity-toity!" said Ellen Taylor.

CHAPTER VI

I

Mrs. Chase did not mention him. She was not silent, indeed talked rather more than usual: at supper about the Bazaar, at breakfast next morning about the news in the paper; and when Caroline wanted to go out before lunch, she made no objection.

"Only don't walk too far and tire yourself, dear. You'll be standing all afternoon."

Caroline turned away her head. She had lain awake, not indeed all night, but long enough to shadow her eyes; if she had looked into her mother's face, she would have seen shadows there too.

"Do you want anything from the shops, Mother?"

"Only the meat, dear."

Caroline nodded. She was trusted with everything else, but meat, as the most important article of diet, was still bought by Mrs. Chase.

"And don't forget it's dinner at half-past twelve, dear."

Again Caroline nodded; and before she was out of the house had forgotten everything in the world but Vincent and the garden.

II

She reached it at exactly eleven o'clock. He was not yet there.

Caroline walked through to the rose-garden, down to the dry lily-pool. Vincent had conceived quite an admiration for it—he could see Etruscan influences in the shape; but he was not there today.

She sat down. Here, there was still a good deal of weeding to be done, but she did not feel in the mood to begin serious work. With Vincent coming so soon it was not worth while. But the inactivity irked her, and after five minutes she got up and fetched a rake. The soil between the rose-bushes was in good order, but raking never did harm. It was also a pleasing and soothing motion. Caroline raked for a quarter of an hour, paused, raked again, and heard a church clock chime the half. If he came he was going to be late; there would be time only for a few words. What those words were to be she had not yet considered. Perhaps he would just take her hand, and laugh at her as he always did, and everything would be all right. If he just said 'Tomorrow, Caroline?' that would be enough. . . .

To her great surprise, she found that she was crying.

The tears gathered and fell. It was as though her body, wiser than her mind, had known all along that he would not come at all.

III

'There's still the Bazaar,' thought Caroline.

She looked at her watch: it was twelve o'clock, and she would wait no longer. There was still the Bazaar. She retraced her steps, picked up the rake, and was about to carry it back to the tool-house when a sound in the garden above made her pause to listen. First incredulously, then with a growing panic, Caroline strained her ears; and so distinguished, up by the house, but gradually drawing near, the unprecedented sound of human voices.

Unprecedented and threatening. With an instinctive motion of concealment she thrust the rake into the pergola and herself drew back. People—strangers—were in the garden: if they had not the power to turn her out, they had at least the power to spoil, to break in on an enchanted privacy. Caroline shut her eyes, and with more fervour than she had ever before used, prayed that they might go away.

'Send them away, O Lord God of Hosts!' prayed Caroline desperately. 'Send them out of our garden, O Lord we beseech Thee!'

The Lord did not hear. The people—the strangers—were coming down the path.

Caroline slipped by the pergola, out of the rose-garden, and into the close shrubbery. The figures advanced: there were three of them, a woman and two men. One of the men, Caroline thought, was a Morton house-agent. They halted at the steps.

"But this," trilled the woman's voice. "This is perfectly charming!"

"There's been work done here, at any rate," said the man.

The house-agent said nothing.

They went down the steps and began walking between the beds. Caroline could not move. She looked up the path, and saw her way clear; but her feet seemed rooted to the ground as the bushes she stood among.

"Charming!" cried the woman again. "Do you think I might have one, Mr. Brodie? After all, there's no one here to enjoy them . . ."

They were picking the roses.

Caroline put her hand over her mouth, and blindly, clumsily, began running towards the gate.

CHAPTER VII

I

THE fête began at three; but for the first hour or hour and a half no one did much business. Even the opening ceremony, performed by the lady of an M.P., aroused so little popular enthusiasm that she received her bouquet before an audience composed chiefly of stall-holders, clergy, and relatives of the child who presented it. In this slender gathering Ellen Taylor was well to the fore: she had a new blue alpaca, very showy about the sleeves, and when she returned to the coffee-stall she was no longer unattended.

"This is Mr. Watts, Carrie."

Caroline looked up from her urn and perceived a thin young man with prominent teeth. As the first Agnostic she had ever seen, he was a disappointment.

"I've brought him to have a coffee—so mind you put the three-pence in my tin," added Ellen *sotto voce*. Under her compelling eye the young man produced his coppers and stood sipping out of the spoon: he looked just the kind (thought Caroline dispassionately) that coffee didn't agree with.

"We shan't do much for an hour yet," said Ellen Taylor. "They'll all be having tea at home. Could you manage by yourself a bit, Carrie, while I take a turn round?"

Caroline nodded. The Agnostic hastily finished his cup and said that he too had thought of having a look. Caroline saw them go off, concealed the worst of Ellen's decorations behind an urn, and resumed her interrupted occupation of watching the clock.

He could not be here yet. Not for another hour at the earliest. Not till half-past four, or possibly five.

'He won't come at all,' thought Caroline.

But still, when she remembered the garden, and their long talks on Ruskin, and how she was the only thing that saved his reason—still, when she thought of all these, hope could not help but stir. If only he would come now, she thought, while Ellen was still away! So that she could just tell him in a calm and dignified manner, that she quite understood! No fuss, thought Caroline, and certainly no crying, but at least a proper good-by!

The arrival of a customer—a boy about Vincent's age, in a neat check suit—brought her back to earth. She sold him two small white coffees one after the other, and saw her mother approaching in company with Mrs. Platt.

"Well, here we are to start the ball!" said Mrs. Platt heartily. "A large white, if you please, Carrie, and plenty of sugar, and for mercy's sake mind my dress."

Caroline expressed her admiration. The garment was of light brick-coloured cloth, lavishly decorated with whorls and loopings of narrow black braid. Round the top of the collar—separating, as it were, the two reds—was a white quilling. Further touches of white enlivened the black and brick-red bonnet. The whole, with Mrs. Platt's holiday face thrown in, made a fine eye-filling sight.

"How are you doing, dear?" whispered Mrs. Chase anxiously.

Caroline rattled her box.

"One and ninepence."

"And Ellen?"

"Two and three."

"Give me another cup, dear," said Mrs. Chase.

II

The return of Ellen, still accompanied by Mr. Watts, brought more business. She had a way of sighting acquaintances in the throng, calling to them loudly, upbraiding their stinginess, till they were ashamed not to come and buy. Her box filled apace, but the whole procedure, though undoubtedly legitimate, and widely employed, in the cause of charity, filled Caroline with distaste. Other stall-holders cried their wares too, but none so loudly as Ellen. She had a peacock-like scream that at close quarters left an actual ringing in the ear-drums. Caroline, at the closest quarters of all, had a headache within the first hour.

"Filling up nicely, isn't it, dear?" said Ellen complacently. "In another half-hour there'll be a real crowd." She fidgeted among the cups, tinkling spoons, rustling the paper roses: she could not be still for one minute. Overhead, to a jingling of tambourines, the Gypsies of Old Spain settled about their fires. They were to do a series of tableaux, the first at five o'clock, when there would be enough people from the Common to make it worth while. . . .

"There's Mrs. Macbeth!" said Ellen suddenly.

Her heart thumping, Caroline looked around. At the other end of the hall, surrounded by a small group of the best people in Morton, Vincent's aunt had just made her entrance. She was moving slowly forward, bowing to left and right, and carrying a spray of orchids in her white-gloved hand. Unless the M.P.'s wife (with her bigger bouquet of roses) were actually in sight, no one could fail to think it Mrs. Macbeth's bazaar.

"Well, did you *ever*!" giggled Ellen Taylor.

"I think she looks very nice," said Caroline.

"Nice! She looks like the Queen of Sheba. If she comes for a coffee I shall charge her half-a-crown."

They continued to watch, Ellen frankly staring, Caroline from the cover of her urn. Mrs. Macbeth's immediate entourage, as distinct from her general train, had now resolved itself into two ladies and three gentlemen, all known to Caroline by sight. Of Vincent there was not a sign.

"She's coming!" whispered Ellen excitedly. "If Mrs. James doesn't stop her she'll be here in half a minute! Lend me some milk, Carrie, I'm running out. . . ."

Caroline heaved up her enamel jug—there were urns only for the coffee—and tilted it into Ellen's. The milk splashed and bubbled, frothing up to the brim; then the jug was snatched away and close at her elbow Ellen's giggle shrilled out.

"Half-a-crown to *you*, Mrs. Macbeth!"

'Toady!' thought Caroline.

The white glove reached out, the astounding bonnet dipped forward, and Mrs. Macbeth drank. Her entourage, however, hung back, apparently waiting for instructions.

"You'd better," said Mrs. Macbeth. "But if I were you I shouldn't drink it."

She set down her cup, saw the five more half-crowns paid in, and passed majestically on. The visitation was over.

"Well!" said Ellen. "That's practically fifteen shillings clear. Don't you wish you'd served her, Carrie?"

"No," said Caroline coldly. "I think it was the rudest thing I've ever seen."

"What? Because she said they needn't drink it? If it comes to that, I don't think it's specially good myself."

"It's awful," said Caroline wearily, "but that's not the point. If it tasted like ditch-water she oughtn't to have said it . . ." Her voice trained away: she was too unhappy to speak: and a silence, one the one side despairing, on the other huffed, settled blankly over the coffee-stall.

III

The fête proceeded. To Caroline, automatically handing out cups—a third to her mother, one to Mrs. James, one to the youth in the check suit—it was a pure misery. The noise, the heat, the press of people began to affect her like a nightmare: she longed desperately to awake and find herself—if not relieved, at least alone. For he was not going to come; she knew he would not come; and yet her eyes could not help searching for him. They also played her tricks, endowing every masculine figure—even the Vicar himself, even Mr. Watts—with something of Vincent's air. Twice, as the crowd thickened, she thought she saw him approach; twice, as Ellen screamed, found the coffee overflowing her cup. Ellen was doing well; she had taken another ten shillings and finally run out of milk.

"Shall I get some more?" asked Caroline wearily.

Ellen shook her head.

"I'll sell it black, and that's fourpence. You do look tired, Carrie!"

"It's the standing," said Caroline.

Ellen nodded again.

"I'm beginning to feel my feet too." She looked over the crowd, now thinning for supper-time, and suddenly began to giggle. Caroline gripped the edge of the stall and tried to close her ears.

"Why wherever's your Mr. Vincent?" asked Ellen archly. "Don't say he's let you down, dear!"

"He's been," mumbled Caroline. "He came while you were away."

Ellen did not believe her.

"How many cups did he have?"

"Three," lied Caroline; and to her horror felt the tears start. They pricked her lids, swelled, and overflowed: she could no more stop them than she could lose consciousness. She tried to lose consciousness, to absent her spirit from the tormenting present; but her mind refused her. She had to see Ellen's inquisitive face, feel the roughness of the cloth, smell the coffee-grounds in the urn; she had to hear a gypsy tambourine tinkling shrilly from the encampment.

"Whatever's the matter, dear?" asked Ellen curiously.

"I've got a headache," muttered Caroline. "I think I'm going to get a cold."

"Shall I fetch your mother?"

"No!" cried Caroline; and turning away her face almost ran out of the hall.

IV

At the back of the building was a little yard, rather weedy, where privileged persons could leave their bicycles. Caroline ran down the passage and let herself out into the cool air. Her cheeks burned, her head throbbed; but the pain in her heart was all that mattered. It made her want to cry out. She put her hand over her mouth and stumbled across the yard to where an old sugar-box lay waiting to be chopped up. Caroline turned it over, pushed it back against the shed, and so in the gathering dusk sat down to break her heart.

She wasn't angry with him. She had no reason to be. In all the months of their friendship he had never said a word that might be construed into. . . into a promise. A kiss wasn't a promise. It was a gift—a gift to a friend. And if, of two friends, one loved, how was the other to be blamed? 'He didn't know,' thought Caroline. 'If he had, he couldn't have laughed at me.'

She leaned back against the shed and let the tears run down. On her hand, lying in her lap, were three red indentations. She looked at them curiously, wondering how they had come there. The other marks she knew: a long scratch, now healed, from the pergola in the rose-garden, and a wider, shallower abrasion from the stones of the dry lily-pond. Vincent had been quite angry with her: he had thought her hands beautiful. *'If you have to go in rags, you must never wear cheap gloves'* . . . It was queer, he hated things to be cheap, even if they were quite good, whereas most people liked them all the better. . . .

'The Bazaar would just have suited him,' thought Caroline wryly.

It was her first stirring of humour, of critical and independent thought; but it did not last. The scratch on her hand seemed to redden as she watched; she had an odd fancy that there was perhaps a similar scratch on her heart. Not deep enough to be mortal—no piercing wound—but deep enough to hurt. Caroline put hand and heart together and sat brooding in the dusk.

Time passed, till in the back windows of the hall lights began to be lit. But how long she had sat there, or how long alone, Caroline could not tell. She knew only that when next she raised her head there was a dark and silent figure regarding her from the door.

"Who's that?" asked Caroline sharply.

The figure moved. It was the young man in the check suit.

"I'm sorry," he said, "I came to get my bicycle."

He did not move, however, but stood looking uncomfortably down at her. Nor did Caroline move either. The bicycles were there, six or seven of them stacked against the wall; all he had to do was take one and be gone. . . .

"It's in the shed," said the youth. "I always put mine in the shed. It's safer."

Resentfully, dragging her box with her, Caroline moved aside. He opened the shed door and from the black interior wheeled forth a bicycle so bright and speckless that it might just have come out of the shop. Caroline could not help looking at it, and as the machine moved by saw painted on the cross-bar a neat name and address. Henry Smith, of Cambridge Road, Morton, was evidently taking no chances: he had also a saddle cover, a safety chain, and two patent lamps. Caroline looked away again, and to her surprise found herself addressed.

"I do wish you wouldn't cry," said Henry Smith glumly.

"I'm not," said Caroline.

The statement did not seem to surprise him: as she found out afterwards, he expected women to be foolish. Instead of reasoning with her, therefore, he said soberly.

"There's a girl making an awful fuss in there."

"What girl?"

"The one at the stall with you. She says she thinks you've fainted in the street."

Caroline started up.

"Did she say that to Mother?"

"She's saying it to everybody. Your mother's just going home now. And there's another lady with her—a lady in light red."

He could have found no more effectual restorative. The image of her mother in distress, backed by that of Cousin Maggie in all the exuberance of alarm, would have roused Caroline from her death-bed. She jumped to her feet, ran a hand over her hair, and made at once for the door. Half over the threshold, however, another emotion made her pause and look back. The young man was still there, still leaning on his bicycle; and now regarding him for the first time Caroline saw that he was short and stocky, with a bullet head and rather small eyes. But the eyes were very direct: he had in a way rendered her a service; and without much thinking what she was about, Caroline turned.

"Thank you," she said, holding out her hand.

He took it carefully. She had a notion that he was trying to say something: but time so pressed that nothing more, at the moment, could pass between them.

PART II

CHAPTER I

I

ON JULY the third, 1904, Caroline Chase, with unusual perverseness, woke at six o'clock. As a rule she got up at seven: but today, because it was her wedding-day, she was to lie abed till eight.

In five and a half hours she would be Mrs. Henry Smith.

Outside it was misty but not raining. Later on there would probably be sun. 'Happy the bride,' thought Caroline conventionally; and plumping up her pillow prepared to sleep again.

She was not, it will be seen, unduly nervous. The idea of being nervous of Henry had never occurred to her. As for marriage itself—for the actual putting on of her womanhood—that too she could regard at least without panic. Ellen Taylor, now Ellen Watts, had already three children, and Caroline knew how children came. It was long, and painful, and at the end sometimes dangerous; but any woman could do it, and there was no other way. 'I shall call them Leonard and Lily,' thought Caroline suddenly; and then, remembering her mother in the next room, smiled into the pillow. How shocked Mrs. Chase would be, thought Caroline, if she knew what her daughter was thinking!

A ray of sunlight broke through the mist and splashed the looking-glass. It was no use trying to sleep. In one sense it would be even a waste—for was this not the last morning on which she would be able to lie by herself, secure in her privacy, thinking of Henry? She might also think of him when he was there, of course; but that would be different. Any man in the early morning (Caroline suspected) was simply a person for whom one got breakfast. . . .

She was not, it will be seen, unduly in love. But she had a great sense of the fitting: and for a bride on her wedding-day, should that bride happen to be awake at six, there was only one suitable occupation. She couldn't get up, for instance, and polish the silver. She couldn't go through the laundry-basket and set woollens soaking. She must lie where she was, and think about her groom.

But what was there—what had there ever been—to think about Henry? Turning him over, as it were, in her mind, Caroline decided that he was good, clever, eminently reliable, and genuinely attached to herself. They had been engaged eighteen months, after a preliminary acquaintanceship of nearly five years; during both of which periods Caroline had remained placid almost to the point of indifference. Sometimes it surprised even herself: for the advantages, in Morton, of having a declared and enviable young man to wait for one after Chapel, were very great. "Well, Carrie'll never be an old maid!" Mrs. Platt used to say heartily; and though Caroline winced at the crudeness, it was much better than having her say, "Well, hasn't Carrie a young man *yet*?"— which she would have said without any hesitation, and probably more often still. Mrs. Chase, too, was pleased. She liked Henry very much, and Henry seemed to like her; though of course no one on earth (reflected Henry's bride calmly) could ever really tell what Henry was really thinking.

He was very reserved. ('Or is it simply that there's nothing there?' wondered Caroline.) Day after day, year after year, they had walked and talked completely unchaperoned: from which conversations Caroline had gathered that he liked his work in Mathieson's Boot Factory, and that he was extremely desirous of marrying herself. It had been love at first sight, that day in the Town Hall: he had loved her at once, without doubt or hesitation, and had continued to love her ever since. That there were other young women in Morton he knew, presumably, as a statistical fact; but he never paid any attention to them. Whether they set their caps at him or cut him in the High Street, it was all one to Henry. He led, indeed, for a young man of twenty-seven, a singularly independent life. Both his parents were dead, and as assistant works-manager he earned very good wages. At his rooms, for which he paid a pound a week, he was pampered and respected as the very model of a lodger. Except for the Chases, he visited no one but his employer; and Old Man Mathieson had taken quite a fancy to him.

It was all, decided Caroline, most satisfactory.

But not exciting.

That was the strange part. For all these things in themselves—love at first sight, undying devotion, and general aloofness—were very exciting indeed; it was only in connection with Henry that they became so curiously prosaic. When he spoke of love—not, indeed, very often—Caroline always believed him. She believed every word, for no word ever over-passed the bounds of credibility. He never said, for example, that without her he would die: nor that her face was beautiful, nor that her eyes were like stars. He said he loved her very much indeed, and that she always looked nice and neat.

'Dear Henry!' thought Caroline, smiling.

If you had asked her why she was going to marry him, she would have said, For Love. But if the Recording Angel had asked her, she would have answered, Because I am twenty-four, because there seems no other future open to me, because I should like a house and children of my own, because he really seems to want me, and because I am really very fond of him.

There was a sound behind her, the door opened, and Mrs. Chase, in a wrapper, stood holding a cup of tea.

II

"Mother!" cried Caroline, genuinely roused, "you haven't any stockings on!"

With an air of mild recklessness Mrs. Chase advanced. Her flannel night-gown, a present from Cousin Maggie, and several sizes too large, had tucks round the bottom and tucks round the sleeves; in it, and with her hair done in two thin pig-tails she looked at once a little old woman and a very small girl.

"Here you are, dear," she said, "there's another lump in the spoon."

Caroline was not to be diverted.

"You haven't got your stockings on!"

"Well, dear, it's very warm," said Mrs. Chase, with an attempt at off-handedness. "It's going to be the most beautiful day you ever saw—" She sat down on the bed, draping the flannel well down, and looked at her daughter affectionately.

"Did you sleep well, Carrie?"

"Like a top," said Caroline.

There was a short silence. Caroline sipped her tea—the first she had ever had brought to her in bed—and wondered what time Henry would want his breakfast. Presently Mrs. Chase stirred.

"Carrie?"

"Yes, Mother?"

"Carrie, you—you do feel happy, don't you?" Caroline put down the cup and took her mother's hand.

"Perfectly happy, dear. And if you cry in Chapel, I shall turn round and give you my handkerchief."

"I've sometimes wondered whether you're . . . really in love with him, Carrie?"

"No, Mother, I don't think I am," said Caroline. Mrs. Chase looked at her in dismay. She had not herself really thought otherwise; but from a bride's own lips. . . .

"On the other hand," continued Caroline cheerfully, "I am fond of him—very fond indeed, and I'm not sure that isn't what he wants. I've never pretended, Mother, never one least bit. That time when he was in Birmingham for three months, I was glad to see him back, but I hadn't pined, and I told him so. He didn't seem to mind."

"He may have, all the same, Carrie." Mrs. Chase looked at her daughter again. How was it possible to explain, in the face of that impregnable tranquillity, that a man might hunger and thirst, and in the end perhaps fret himself to death, without ever having . . . seemed to mind . . . at all? "I'm sure he's in love with you, dear," said Mrs. Chase gently.

"Well, he must be," said Caroline. "I'm not much of a catch."

"Carrie, dear!"

"How can I be? I haven't any money, and I'm not even pretty. All you can say is that I'm well brought up." She squeezed her mother's hand, suddenly serious. "Don't worry, dear. I know I'm lucky. If I don't love him like—like Romeo and Juliet, I do trust him with all my heart. And I'll do my very best to make him a good wife."

Mrs. Chase bent forward and kissed her. They were neither of them demonstrative, it was a light brushing of the lips. Then she rose to her feet and padded across the room.

"There'll be breakfast in half an hour, dear, and if you like you can have it in your dressing-gown." The door shut: Caroline sank back on the pillows. She was feeling oddly solemn, almost as though she had already made her vows, not to Henry in Chapel, but there, and to her mother.

CHAPTER II

THE honeymoon was passed at Bournemouth, and Caroline spent three pounds of her own money.

She bought a plaid rug (for Mrs. Chase), a pink tea-set (for herself), and several pieces of Goss china. She would also have bought something for Henry, since it seemed mean to leave him out, but there was nothing he wanted.

"What should you do if you had ten thousand pounds?" asked Caroline idly.

"Buy Mathieson out," said Henry.

"Then soon you'd have twenty thousand," said Caroline. "You'd have to buy a factory a year." She turned her eyes from the sea—they were sitting on the West Cliff—and looked at him with genuine curiosity. "Would you, Henry?"

"Even with boots, there's a saturation point somewhere," said he practically. "If you make good boots they don't wear out, and if you make bad boots customers won't buy. At least not after the first pair."

"People shouldn't make bad boots anyway," said Caroline. "I hope Mathieson's don't."

Henry thrust out a foot.

"Fifteen-and-six, brown, black, or tan, round laces sixpence extra. But as soon as I get more of a free hand, I shall go in for heavy stuff."

"People don't wear them much heavier than that," objected Caroline, staring down at his feet.

"The Army does. That's what Mathieson's wants, only the old man won't see it. An Army contract, and then a small high-class trade on top. We can make as good shoes as the French any day, if only we'll set out to do it."

She looked at him almost in alarm. The magnitude of his designs, the calm assurance of his manner, filled her with awe. He was twenty-six, and he talked of the Army and the French as though they were. . . just something to do with the works!

"French shoes *are* nice," said Caroline at last. It was not, as she immediately realized, the most tactful remark that could have been made; but he was not offended.

"They are," agreed Henry promptly. "They're well sewn, and they've something about the shape that ours haven't. I don't know if they're so comfortable. When you go into a shop, Carrie, which do you look for first—comfort, or style?"

"Comfort," said Caroline. "But then I've got big feet."

He glanced down.

"Fives with a six fitting. Most women would wear fours."

"I've got big hands too," said Caroline. She held them out for his inspection—the square, capable palms, the long straight fingers with their mixture of strength and fineness. For the last five years or so she had been taking great care of them.

"You'd look silly with them small," said Henry consolingly. He took out his watch: it was twenty minutes to one. They got up from the bench and turning their back on the sea began to walk slowly home to the Polperryn Private Hotel. As usual, they had allowed a little too much time, and while Henry waited for her on the porch Caroline went upstairs to tidy her hair.

II

As always at their room door, she had a moment's hesitation. It was absurd, ridiculous; but she could not get over a feeling that it was the bedroom of some one else she was thus about to burst in on. Once she had actually knocked, and been answered, to their common embarrassment, by a chamber-maid doing the beds. 'It's perfectly silly!' thought Caroline; and stepped defiantly inside.

The room was large, light, and furnished, to Caroline's eyes, in the height of luxury. There was even an arm-chair, and in this, as though to assert her proprietorship, she now sat down. On the wide dressing-table lay a pair of man's hair-brushes, on the washstand a razor and strop; in spite of everything—in spite of Henry on the porch and the wedding-ring on her finger—the sight so surprised her that she looked hastily round for something of her own. A pink flannel dressing-gown, brand-new, restored her confidence. Caroline sighed, sat back, and took the pins out of her hair.

The whole trouble, of course, was that she did not yet feel like Mrs. Smith. With every circumstance of life completely altered, she herself (and to her own great surprise) felt almost exactly the same. Even the greatest change of all had been . . . not overwhelming. With Henry's head on her breast, in a darkness smelling of sea, her mind had still watched apart. "My dear, my dear!" she had said; and loved him because she was making him happy.

But she still did not feel like Mrs. Smith. She felt like Caroline Chase being allowed, after various promises and ceremonies, to go for a holiday alone with Henry. Reality, left behind in Morton, perhaps awaited her there; in the meantime she could only enjoy her holiday very much indeed, and keep one foot on earth whenever possible.

The last pin dropped in her lap, Caroline shook out her tail of hair, combed it through, and began to twist it up again. There was a woman opposite them—the guests at the Polperryn sat all at one long table, the proprietress at one end, her German husband at the other—a woman with straggling mouse-coloured wisps on which Henry's eyes always rested with disapproval; and Caroline had taken a lesson. She could never be pretty, but she could at least be neat; and her hair went up as trimly as a Dutch doll's.

"Carrie!" said a voice behind her.

She jumped guiltily; but it was only Henry with his watch.

"Didn't you hear the bell, dear? It went five minutes ago."

"I was thinking," said Caroline; and they went downstairs to one o'clock dinner.

III

There was Lancashire hot-pot, boiled potatoes, and a choice of rice-pudding or stewed figs. Henry took the pudding, Caroline the figs: but an old gentleman farther down hardily demanded both.

"It's a choice, Mr. Partridge," said the proprietress firmly.

"Then give me half a portion of each," countered the old gentleman.

The rest of the table looked on with interest. It was felt to be a test case. Mrs. Felsberg stood on strong ground, but the old gentleman—he was very old indeed, with tufts of white hair growing out of his ears—had his weapons too. He came for a month every summer, and took one of the best rooms: he paid in advance, and tipped all the servants. Mrs. Felsberg hesitated.

"I think," said Henry suddenly and slowly, "that that's a very excellent idea."

Mr. Partridge bowed.

"And failing a more reasonable solution," continued Henry, "I shall be very pleased to exchange half my pudding for half Mr. Partridge's figs."

All round the table ran a murmur of surprise and admiration. Henry's dignified manner, so far removed from levity, seemed to lift the whole proceedings on to a higher plane. As for Caroline, she sat a little straighter than usual and felt glad she had done her hair.

"Figs, please," said Mr. Partridge promptly.

Henry took up his spoon and began to draw a neat boundary down the middle of his plate. Others followed suit. Persons with an uneven number of figs began to cut one fig in two. The entire population of the Polperryn was in decorous but open revolt.

"Gertrude!" murmured Mr. Felsberg pleadingly.

Either to the whisper or to the mutiny, Mrs. Felsberg yielded. Her spoon descended first into the pudding-dish, then, without even a change of implement, into the dish of figs. A full portion of each was handed to Mr. Partridge. Two clergymen farther down asked for and received the same liberal dole. With a certain mournful dignity Mrs. Felsberg then rose from her seat, bowed stiffly to the table, and so sailed from the room.

"She's afraid of second helpings," said Henry grimly.

IV

Several times after this incident, Caroline and Henry, walking along the front, encountered Mr. Partridge in his bath-chair. He had the superior kind, with a donkey, so that walking beside him was not so tedious as it might have been; and Caroline in particular liked stroking the donkey's ears.

"He must be very rich!" she said to Henry one afternoon, as they sighted the equipage just ahead of them. "He has it three hours every day, and gives the man sixpence!"

Henry was less wonderstruck than she expected.

"If he'd no more than five hundred a year he could still do that. I wouldn't call a man rich unless he had . . . two thousand."

"I should call that *rolling*," said Caroline. "Has any one in Morton got it?"

"In Morton!" Henry laughed. "You'd make the Common turn in its grave, Carrie. Why, if old Macbeth had stuck it he might have been Lord Mayor."

It was Caroline's turn to be unimpressed. A Lord Mayor, for her, was so much a figure of Pantomime—a strapping principal boy with a cat as big as himself—that the idea of one living in Morton struck her as simply ludicrous. It was just the sort of joke they *did* make—they asked Idle Jack his address, and he said 101 The Common. It always got a good laugh—

"Mrs. Macbeth," said Henry thoughtfully, "would have made a Lady Mayoress all right. Remember her at that Bazaar, Carrie, the first time we met?"

"I should just think I do," said Caroline. "I remember her being frightfully rude about the coffee." She could remember other things as well; not clearly, but in flickering patches like a bad cinema. Ellen squealing, and Cousin Maggie in a red frock, and herself, more unhappy than she had ever been before or since, sitting out in the dusk with her back to a bicycle shed. . . .

"I drank seven cups," pursued Henry reminiscently. "And then you ran out of the hall, and Ellen started screaming. You *did* look ill in that bicycle yard, Carrie!"

"I thought my head would split," said Caroline. "Ellen didn't start screaming then, she'd been screaming all afternoon. Lately she's got better."

"She's passed it on to the three kids," said Henry grimly. "I know you were girls together and all that, Carrie, but if you could manage to have her round while I'm out, I'd be greatly obliged."

They both laughed, for Ellen was one of their jokes; and the sound was so pleasant that Mr. Partridge, now no more than a yard or two ahead, brought his donkey to a standstill and waited for them to come up.

Caroline was his favourite. He used to tell her long stories about South Africa, which he had once seen from a ship, and give her his views on the recent war, which were very gloomy.

"We've lost prestige," he said. "Whatever happens in the future, our prestige has been shaken. It's all the fault of that scoundrel Rhodes."

"But we did win, sir," said Henry consolingly.

"And Jamieson," continued Mr. Partridge. "A pair of filibustering rogues! If I had my way they'd both be court-martialled!"

"You don't mean you're a pro-Boer, sir?"

"I'm not pro-anything!" said Mr. Partridge testily; and he whipped up his donkey with such force, and so unexpectedly, that for a moment Caroline, Henry, and the donkey-man were all left behind. "What I say is," called Mr. Partridge over his shoulder, "why can't they leave the country alone?" Caroline stopped.

"Do pretend to agree with him, Henry!"

"But I don't," said Henry. "I think he's an old fool. Why should I pretend?"

"Because, if you don't, he'll be beating the donkey all afternoon."

Henry threw back his head in a rare peal of laughter.

"But he will!" said Caroline impatiently. "And I'm sure it's half-starved. . . ."

"Then I'll buy you a bunch of carrots, and you can feed it while I argue. Come down on the sands, Carrie, and let's have some time to ourselves."

With great willingness, and only too pleased to see him in a good humour again, she slipped her arm through his and they moved towards the lift. But it was not to be. The sound of Henry's laughter, cheerfully echoing, had reached Mr. Partridge; and once more so attracted him that he came hurrying back. Caroline and Henry walked as fast as they could, but the donkey positively galloped; and by the time the Smiths reached the lift, Mr. Partridge was there to meet them.

V

On the last night of their honeymoon, which fell on a Sunday, they went to a concert of sacred music and then on the front. There was a moon over the high tide, the sacred tunes echoed pleasantly in their ears; but Caroline, usually so amenable to any soothing influence, was for once insensitive. She had something she wanted to say, something which during the past few days had been gradually forming in, and taking possession of, her mind.

"Henry?"

"Yes, dear?"

"Henry, there's something I want to say to you, something rather important." She glanced sideways up at him, and to her surprise felt his arm, lying within her own, suddenly stiffen. "It's just this, dear—that if ever I . . . don't make you quite happy, I want you to tell me. Even if it's only a little thing, like not doing the bacon the way you like it. You're so good and—and unselfish with me, Henry, that sometimes I'm afraid you wouldn't. That I might just go complacently on and never know." She stopped again, fumbling for the right words. "I do so want to make you a good wife, Henry. . . ."

The arm relaxed.

"I don't think you need bother about that, Carrie."

"But I do bother! That's just what I mean!"

"I can't complain when I've nothing to complain of."

"But if you have, you will?"

"I can't imagine it," said Henry stubbornly.

They walked a little farther, closely arm-in-arm—a honeymoon couple for all the world to see. Caroline sighed.

"Be happy yourself, Carrie, and . . . stay fond of me, and that's all I want," said Henry out of the silence.

She leaned nearer, so close that her cheek brushed his coat. She felt for him a great affection.

"It sounds very easy. . . ."

From below, under the cliff, came a soft lapping of waters. The broad and lambent moon made everything distinct, even—Caroline thought foolishly—one's own emotions. How good Henry was to her, how confidently she could look forward! How good of God to let them be there, young and strong and fond of each other, in such a beautiful place as Bournemouth!

"I do love you, Henry," said Caroline sincerely.

His arm pressed tight against her own.

"I love you with all my heart, Carrie."

They had been walking quite slowly; now, at the turning of the path, Caroline stopped. The quick response, the unusual explicitness of his emotion, tempted her further.

"Why, Henry?"

There was a long pause. She waited eagerly, almost breathless. Except for her hands (which indeed he had never remarked on) she knew she was not beautiful. It must be something more important, something in *her*. . . .

"You're not always fidgeting about," said Henry at last.

Caroline looked again at the moon, and thought she would like to go on among the trees, and see it through branches.

CHAPTER III

I

IN THE train going home Caroline produced a large tin of shortbread tied with tartan ribbon. It was a present from Mr. Partridge, who had also given her his address, and two pieces of advice. The first was never to keep a man waiting for his food, the second never to have anything to do with Chartereds.

"What *are* Chartereds, Henry?" asked Caroline curiously.

"Shares," said Henry, "in one of Rhodes' companies. I'm sure he's a pro-Boer."

"Perhaps he's just old."

"Not too old to have sense."

"Anyway," said Caroline, brushing the crumbs from her lap, "I shall send him a Christmas card."

II

Just as she had expected, Morton was real. The first strangenesses—such as buying the meat, and seeing her mother, from the other side of the road, as a little middle-aged lady—soon passed off, and she fell into a regular, most undreamlike routine of housework and Henry.

Both suited her very well. The house, in Cleveland Road, was small, no more inconvenient than any other in Morton, with three rooms below and three above. It had a back garden, nothing much to look at, but convenient for the washing, and in front a narrow strip of grass which Henry cut with shears. He had once talked of cutting the back too, and perhaps planting a few flowers, but since Caroline never set foot there (except of course on Monday mornings) the project fell through. Inside all was neat, comfortable, and extremely solid. Mrs. Chase had given them her dining-table, Cousin Maggie a box-ottoman, and the rest of the furniture was good second-hand. Only in the matter of chintzes and wallpapers had Caroline thrown prudence to the winds, choosing them so light and flowery that even her mother felt a doubt.

"You'll never keep it clean, Carrie!" said Mrs. Chase, running a hand over the drawing-room wall.

"Yes, I shall," said Caroline. "With breadcrumbs."

"That means four spring-cleanings a year!"

"I've got nothing else to do."

"Not yet," said Mrs. Chase delicately.

Caroline looked at her trellis-work—pink and green on a silvery stripe—and smiled.

"Anyway, Henry likes it. . . ."

Mrs. Chase was at once silenced. Henry was the man. If he had liked white-wash and bare boards, Mrs. Chase would still have acquiesced. It would have seemed perfectly reasonable to her that Caroline, who was in the house all day, should have suited her surroundings to the taste of the man who was out of it.

"He likes the chintzes, too," added Caroline rather pugnaciously. "He likes everything I got. The ones Ellen said wouldn't wash are the ones he likes best of all."

"They *are* pretty, dear," said Mrs. Chase hastily.

Her opinions were evidently wavering. Ellen had been extremely dogmatic on the subject, and Ellen was married and had three children: but then Henry was a man. To Caroline, watching her mother's face, the whole chain of thought was amusingly obvious.

"I'll make you some tea, Mother," she said smiling; and went into the kitchen to laugh by herself.

But though Caroline laughed, there was less difference than she imagined between her own and her mother's attitude. To her too Henry, by the mere accident of his masculinity, was entitled to the casting vote in all their common affairs. Nor did Caroline grudge it him; she felt instinctively that a man knew best. In the world of affairs—the world of the Boer War and Mathieson's Boot Factory—this supremacy was only reasonable, since he went to the factory himself and took the newspaper with him; but even in the kitchen, if Henry said the sink was too low, Caroline at once felt he was right. In any rare difference of opinion, and on the rare occasions when she did not take his advice, she always felt slightly guilty. Even now, preparing the tea-tray for her mother, Caroline was cutting brown bread instead of white because Henry preferred it.

"You could always have had it if you wanted," said Mrs. Chase a little reproachfully.

"But I didn't," said Caroline. "I always liked white."

It was quite true. For twenty-five years she had liked white better; now, without the slightest effort, she preferred brown. It was simply another example of Henry's natural supremacy. And there were other foods as well—celery, for instance—which she had never in her life eaten before, and which she now ate two or three times a week. Even the female digestion, it seemed, could accommodate itself to the male.

"Mr. Watts likes it too," said Mrs. Chase thoughtfully.

Caroline looked up. She knew what *that* meant. Frederick Watts liked it brown, Ellen liked it white; so she nagged his head off every time she gave it him. She did give it him, of course, because he was the man; but she couldn't be pleasant about it.

"I was there yesterday," said Caroline. "She asked us for Sunday, but I told her we always went to you."

Mrs. Chase looked at her anxiously.

"You needn't if you don't want to, Carrie. If you've anywhere else you want to go, you go."

"Henry wouldn't go to the Watts' if you paid him to: and as for other places," said Caroline cheerfully, "there simply aren't any. We never go anywhere." She looked at the clock, saw it was later than she had thought, and without the slightest compunction hurried Mrs. Chase briskly through her tea so as to have it all washed up before Henry came home.

III

They never did go anywhere. For such old inhabitants—and a bridal pair at that—their social relations were extremely limited. Theoretically, they knew every one who went to Chapel, and Henry, at the factory, came into contact with non-members as well: but since Caroline was not particularly active in good works, and since Henry avowedly disliked making acquaintances, their callers were few. Mrs. Chase came, of course, and Cousin Maggie Platt, and Ellen Watts with her three little girls. Ellen, indeed, came practically every day, and it often struck Caroline as hard that the one woman in Morton whom she really disliked was also her most intimate acquaintance. But there seemed nothing she could do about it.

"If I were you, I should drop her altogether," said Henry, when she thus complained.

Caroline looked at him hopelessly. How *could* she drop Ellen? After having known her for years and years, ever since they were both girls? How *could* she?

"I've dropped Watts all right," continued Henry complacently.

"That's different. You wouldn't drop—" Caroline paused, baffled as usual by the extraordinary fact that there *was* no one in Henry's life whom he could not drop at a moment's notice. Except for herself, he had no sentimental tie whatever. . . .

"Old Mathieson?" hazarded Caroline at last.

"What about him?" asked Henry, who had been reading the paper.

"He's been good to you, hasn't he? You couldn't drop *him* just because you felt like it?"

"If Mathieson's been good to me," said Henry slowly, "it's because I'm damned useful to him. He can't run the works himself, and he doesn't want a partner because a partner means sharing profits. I'm the answer."

Instinctively, Caroline put out a hand to him.

"Henry! Aren't you—aren't you satisfied, then?"

"Satisfied!" said Henry ironically. "Who wouldn't be satisfied in Morton, with a steady job and Chapel on Sundays?"

IV

This matter of Henry's dissatisfaction was one of the few things Caroline ever really attempted to think about. For thinking—the deliberate exercise of the brain—did not come naturally to her. In normal everyday life she thought very little, governing most of her actions by a placid instinctive good sense, by the remnants of her girlhood upbringing, and by what Henry told her. But when it came to so urgent a matter as Henry's happiness, then she sat down, with her hands in her lap, and thought steadily and earnestly for half an hour at a time.

He seemed quite happy. That, in a way, was one of the difficulties. Like Caroline herself, he was very reserved. Even on their honeymoon, when she knew he was happy, there had been no outward signs of unusual joyfulness. He was always kind, quietly affectionate, and above all thoughtful—not opening doors for her, or anything like that, but quick to see when she was tired, or to carry a heavy parcel, or to wait until the 'bus had stopped. (Caroline hated men who jumped off moving vehicles while their wives were still on, and this hatred Henry had either diagnosed in her, or shared himself.) Nor did these attentions ever diminish: having started at a reasonable level, he was able to keep them up. But Caroline had an uneasy suspicion that they might become as it were independent of everything else, so that she would never be able to tell what Henry himself was really feeling. They might become almost a mask. Already, indeed, as he spoke that one ironic sentence, it had been . . . like a mask dropping.

'Or are they all discontented, underneath?' wondered Caroline. If Henry were merely conforming to a general rule, she would feel much easier: but her knowledge of men was very small. There had been Henry, and—long ago, before she was grown up—a boy in a garden: and there her experience ended. The boy she remembered as very discontented indeed—discontented even with living on the Common, so he was evidently that sort. Frederick Watts—at the thought of Frederick Watts, Caroline unconsciously shook her head. If *he* were discontented, it was no wonder. Always going to the dentist, always being nagged by Ellen, he was no longer even an Agnostic. But Henry was different. He had good health, a good position, and (Caroline hoped) a good wife. That he was ambitious she had long known: but to be already, at the age of twenty-seven, assistant works manager, was surely enough to satisfy any one. . . .

'Perhaps it's just his way of talking,' Caroline would tell herself weakly: at which conclusion, feeble though it was, the session usually ended. She had, however, a hope that with the birth of her child this impalpable veil—if indeed it existed—between herself and her husband would finally disappear: so what after all—thought Caroline, reaching for her needlework—was the use in thinking about it?

CHAPTER IV

I

For a while this hope seemed likely to be realized.

On Caroline's twenty-fifth birthday, and a month before her first child was born, Henry brought home a rose-wood work-box fitted with ivory spools.

"It's second-hand," he said honestly, "but I couldn't get a new one like it. If there's anything else you want as well, Carrie, just you say."

Caroline ran a finger over its surface. It would be no use in the world for darning, of course, but it was very pretty. And it was also so extraordinarily unlike Henry that she asked a question.

"It's the nicest I've ever seen. What—what made you choose it, Henry?"

To her extreme surprise, Henry flushed.

"My mother had one," he said shortly.

"Your mother? I didn't think you could remember her."

"I can't," said Henry. "Only the work-box."

He picked up one of the spools, clumsy under Caroline's eye: and she had a sudden intuition that when he was a very small child his mother must have given them him to play with. For cutting teeth, indeed (thought Caroline unhygienically) they would be the very thing. . . .

She shut down the lid, gently, and heard the lock snap into place. There was a key—the size of a watch key—hanging from a ribbon: and the ribbon was bright and new.

"You're feeling all right, Carrie?"

"Splendid," replied Caroline vaingloriously. She was feeling, in these days, a good deal pleased with herself, as though she were doing something clever. Theoretically she knew this was not so—that in point of sheer cleverness the bearing of children was very small beer indeed, and not to be compared, for instance, with matriculation, or playing sonatas, or even with the correct manipulation of a paper pattern. But cleverness was what Caroline had always hankered after, and now, in her new conceit with herself, cleverness was what she pitched on. And Mrs. Chase abetted her: Mrs. Chase thought it very clever indeed of Caroline never to have fainted once. . . .

Her good health continued, she still did most of the housework, and but for Henry's insistence would have rejected the monthly nurse. But on the nurse Henry was stubborn, and when the woman actually arrived Caroline took quite a liking to her. She was large, business-like, eminently placid—very much what Caroline herself might have been, had she never married and taken to midwifery. The doctor was new, still a little suspect, in Morton as a whole, on account of his comparative youth: and this was the one point on which Mrs. Chase showed any uneasiness.

"You do feel quite comfortable about him, Carrie?" she asked anxiously. "I know it's difficult to change, but there's no reason why you shouldn't have Dr. Reynolds as well. If you're the least doubtful, dear, I'll speak to Henry at once."

Caroline smiled at her mother affectionately. Speaking to Henry, in the minatory or mother-in-law sense, was one of the things Mrs. Chase as a rule most scrupulously avoided.

"But I'd rather have Dr. French, Mother. Henry says he's much more up to date."

It did not occur to either of them to wonder how Henry knew. The recommendation was enough, Dr. French was established as superior to Dr. Reynolds. But as things turned out his skill was not much tested. At three o'clock on a rainy August morning Henry, ringing at the night-bell, was directed halfway across Morton to a case of heart failure: and by the time he got Dr. French away, and back to Cleveland Road—Caroline and the nurse had done the job between them.

II

"Leonard Henry," said Caroline happily.

On either side of the bed Henry and her mother looked at her in surprise.

"Leonard?" repeated Mrs. Chase. "Why Leonard, dear?"

"I like it," said Caroline. "Don't you, Henry?"

Henry looked down at his son with an appearance of detached impartiality.

"It sounds all right to me."

"And you can call him Len for short," added Mrs. Chase. "It's a very nice name indeed, Carrie."

They all combined to praise her. Even the monthly nurse wore a face of calm approval. She felt Caroline had done her credit: she felt that she and Caroline between them had landed one in the eye to every doctor on the list.

III

Exactly fifteen months later Caroline bore her second child, a daughter whom she christened Lily. They were Lily and Leonard, just as she had planned: and in the years to come they often reproached her for it.

CHAPTER V

I

THE year Henry was made works manager, which was a bad one for the boot trade in general, he went up to Northampton and brought back to Mathieson's one foreman and a small nucleus of hands experienced in making Army boots. They were mostly unmarried men, without family ties, who would go where the work was, and when Old Man Mathieson saw their wages sheet he was for a time seriously perturbed.

"We can't do it," he told Henry. "There's not a firm near London has even thought of it. . . ."

Henry stuck out his jaw.

"It isn't a question of climate, sir."

"It's a question," said the old man testily, "of knowing a trade or not knowing it. Our people don't."

"We'll teach 'em. Will you give me four years, sir, to get a first Army contract, or throw up the job?"

"Four years!" Mathieson looked at the wages sheet again and almost groaned. "It's wasting the money I pay them and the money I pay you. It's waste all round."

"You've always your alternative, sir," said Henry shortly.

His employer shuffled the papers together and threw them down on the table. Before that veiled threat he knew his powerlessness. Henry was indispensable. With whatever bee in his bonnet—with whatever mania for Army boots—Henry would have to stay.

Henry stayed.

II

With paradoxical swiftness—each day long and placid, each month gone in a flash—the time slipped by. In herself, as in Henry, Caroline saw no change at all: but Leonard and Lily, almost while one watched them, turned from babies into small children and from small children into a small boy and girl. Caroline brought them up, however, without much difficulty: washing them, exercising them, correcting their pronunciation, and giving them either jam or cake (but never both at once) for Saturday and Sunday tea. On other days they had plain bread-and-butter, not out of meanness on her part, or from any shortage of housekeeping money, but from a deep Puritan instinct that what was pleasant and easily obtainable had perhaps better be gone without. In the same way, though it was both cheap and nourishing, they never had dripping-toast except as a special treat. Caroline also took them to Chapel, and forbade Lily to sew on Sundays: but their religious lives were not made burdensome, and on exceptionally cold nights they could say their prayers in bed. 'God won't mind this once,' Caroline would rule comfortably: and neither the children, nor Caroline herself, ever questioned her expert knowledge.

A complete freedom from doubt was indeed, in the upbringing of children, one of her most valuable qualities. It gave her both assurance and serenity. To every question she had a direct and simple answer. These answers were not, of course, always correct, but they provided a resting-place for the mind as the habit of obedience provided rest for both mind and body. In matters of biology she turned Leonard over to his father, helped Lily make a cat's nursery for the cat to kitten in, and for all public purposes retained the fable of the cabbage-patch. ("But we mustn't chase Tabitha," added Lily, after one of these elegant references, "because of the kittens inside.")

III

On an October morning, in the year of the Coronation, Henry came down to breakfast and found no toast made. This was so unusual that he went straight to the kitchen, where Caroline, one hand on the frying-pan, stood reading a letter while the bacon burnt.

"Carrie!" He reached out and turned off the gas. "What on earth are you thinking about?"

As though all five senses had returned to her at once Caroline sniffed, gasped, cooled her burnt fingers, and held out the letter.

"Read that, Henry."

"What is it?"

"*I* don't know," said Caroline impatiently. "It's just come. You read it while I bring in the bacon." He took the envelope, which was long and typewritten, and returned to the dining-room. Neither Lily nor Leonard was yet down, but in his curiosity he omitted to call them. He had also some vague notion that if it were bad news—though what he could not imagine—their absence might be preferable. He sat down to table and spread the papers flat before him.

He was still sitting there, almost as astonished as his wife, when Caroline came in with the dish of bacon.

"Well, Henry?"

"Well?" said Henry, looking up.

"Does it—does it mean what it says?" asked Caroline suspiciously.

"I don't see why it shouldn't. Old Partridge died last month, and left you two thousand pounds. I'm very glad indeed, Carrie."

"Well!" said Caroline. She sat down, half-poured out a cup of tea, and set the pot back on its stand. Henry picked it up and finished the pouring.

"He hadn't any relations, had he?"

"I don't think so—he never used to talk about them."

"Then he had to leave it to some one."

"But why *me*, Henry? Why not to you?" asked Caroline, taking her cup. "It was you who backed him over the pudding—don't you remember?"

"Figs or rice," corroborated Henry. "But it was you who used to agree with him about the war. Remember how he used to whip up that donkey?" For a moment they were both silent, smiling at the ridiculous picture. An angry old man, a galloping donkey, and behind two breathless young figures arguing about the Boers. . . .

"I must send a wreath," said Caroline suddenly. Henry looked at the letter.

"What's the use? The funeral's over."

"I don't care, they can put it on his grave. I—I was fond of him in a way, and it's a mark of respect. I shall send a really good one, with arum lilies." She paused, thinking it over, visualizing cushions, crosses, broken harps . . . a wreath would be best, something plain but handsome, with her name and Henry's on a black-edged card. "I shall pay two pounds," said Caroline aloud.

There was another silence, longer still. Henry rose from his seat and going into the hall called violently upstairs. A commotion in the bathroom sufficiently answered him, and he returned to find Caroline reading the letter through again.

"What am I to do with it, Henry?"

"Put it in the bank."

"But, Henry—"

"What is it, dear? You don't want to spend it on fal-lals?"

"Of course I don't!" She too got up, coming quite close to him, so that she could see into his face. "You—you wouldn't like it for Mathieson's, would you, Henry? You couldn't buy a partnership?"

"Not for two thousand pounds."

The words were ungracious, but she did not take them so. It was a matter of fact.

"But if you put it in—bought shares or whatever it is—wouldn't it give you more of a say?"

For a moment he hesitated. Caroline wished she knew more about it, that she could urge facts and figures, show all that two thousand pounds could do. For she could see that under his impassive demeanor, under his habitual brusqueness, Henry wanted it badly. . . .

The moment passed.

"Put it in the bank, Carrie."

"But, Henry—"

"I don't want it at Mathieson's, and I shall like to know you've got something safe. I'll go into the bank this morning and see about opening a deposit."

His tones were final. Caroline folded up the letter, and helping herself to some cold bacon, at last began breakfast. She felt flat and crestfallen, and not at all how she would have expected to feel after being left two thousand pounds.

"There's no toast," said Henry suddenly.

With an apologetic smile (in case he should think she was upset) Caroline picked up the rack, went out of the room, and there in the hall encountered Lily tumbling downstairs and Leonard sliding down the banisters. "*That's* no way to come down!" said Caroline severely. But her smile, from apologetic, had become suddenly genuine and radiant. 'A thousand apiece!' thought Caroline: and proceeded joyfully to the kitchen.

IV

By the end of the year (and as a direct result, Caroline could not help feeling, of Henry's remarkable unselfishness) the Director of Army Contracts looked favourably upon Mathieson's boots, and Henry was made joyful too. Or perhaps joyful was not the right word: he was calmly satisfied. On their first tender Mathieson's received a contract for five thousand pairs, to the perfection of which he was apparently devoting his life. Neither Inspectors nor Viewers had any terrors for him: he rather welcomed them, as a confident candidate welcomes the examiners. Of Northampton and Leicester he spoke respectfully but without awe. It was simply, he told Caroline, a question of capital: if only Mathieson's had the money to expand, if only the old man were less of an old woman, Morton might stand up to either. For Henry's goal lay still in the future: he wanted to make not five thousand but fifty thousand pairs of boots: and it thus seemed likely that his happiness would last.

V

Faced by the sudden danger of having nothing left to wish for, Caroline instinctively but sincerely began to worry about her mother.

For Mrs. Chase, though not yet elderly, was already old. Quieter, smaller, more ladylike than ever, she had become, with age, just such another as Miss Dupré: and as Miss Dupré had lived alone over the chemist's, so Mrs. Chase now lived over the grocer's. Caroline saw her daily, took Henry and the children to Sunday supper, yet never rang the door-bell, nor looked towards her mother's place in Chapel, without a sudden clutching fear lest the seat should be empty or the door remain unopened. It was foolish, but she could not help it, and once in the middle of the night she even disturbed Henry by waking suddenly and being unable to get to sleep again for just such unprofitable thoughts.

"*I* can't hear anything," said Henry, sitting up beside her.

"It's not that," said Caroline unhappily. "It's Mother."

"Your mother? She isn't ill, is she?"

"No," said Caroline. "She's not *ill*. . . ."

"What is it, then?"

"She's all alone, Henry, and I keep worrying about her. If she *were* ill in the night—"

He turned himself over.

"Well, you can't do anything about it now, can you?"

"No," agreed Caroline.

"Then go to sleep," said Henry practically.

Caroline lay down and stared at the ceiling. It was not particularly dark, for they slept with the blinds up and the curtains undrawn. She could see the pattern of the gas-bracket, and the top of the wardrobe, and also the top of a large coloured text, framed and glazed, which had been an additional present from Cousin Maggie. 'The King of Hosts,' said the text, 'My Shepherd Is,' and behind the great capital T was a village church with snow on the roof. Caroline tried to say a prayer, and turning instinctively on her face to do so woke Henry again.

"Why don't you have her to live here?" he asked suddenly.

The words, coming as they did in place of the expected (and deserved) rebuke, filled her with a perfect glow of gratitude.

"Really, Henry?"

"If you want to. I don't mind."

Caroline could hardly believe her ears. He was half asleep, of course, and for a moment she wondered whether he knew what he was saying: but she was too sensible to wake him more thoroughly to find out. With a sigh of contentment Caroline turned on her back again and went tactfully to sleep.

The next morning, after receiving a brief but explicit confirmation, she proceeded early to the flat over the grocer's and at once delivered her joyful tidings. Mrs. Chase was extremely touched, indeed almost overwhelmed by them: but she did not, as Caroline had anticipated, immediately begin packing.

"When will you come, Mother?" asked Caroline impatiently.

Mrs. Chase looked round the room almost as if she would be sorry to leave it.

"Carrie, dear—"

"Well, Mother?"

"Where would you put me?"

"In with Lily," said Caroline at once. She had worked it all out: Lily's bed under the window, Mrs. Chase's in the more sheltered position by the door. It would be quite simple. . . .

Mrs. Chase looked round the room again, and at the door to her bedroom, and at the other door to the passage and kitchen. She seemed at a loss for words, and Caroline, at first putting this down to a natural excess of pleasure, waited in sympathetic silence. But as the silence prolonged itself she grew uneasy: for the expression in Mrs. Chase's eye was hardly joyful at all.

It was positively reluctant.

"Cousin Maggie was round last night," said Mrs. Chase irrelevantly.

Caroline scarcely heard her. She was too much disconcerted by a new and incredible idea.

"Mother! Don't you—don't you *want* to come and live with us?"

"It's very, very kind of you, dear," said Mrs. Chase evasively.

"It's not kind at all. We want you. It was Henry's own suggestion."

Mrs. Chase straightened an antimacassar. She had dozens and dozens of them, crocheted throughout a long widowhood, and since they were all changed every week their laundering and mending provided quite an occupation.

"Cousin Maggie—" she began again.

"What on earth has Cousin Maggie to do with it?"

"She said," explained Mrs. Chase apologetically, "that she'd been lying awake at nights, wondering what would happen to me in case of fire."

Caroline felt unreasonably offended.

"I don't see what good it does, coming here just to frighten you," she observed tartly. "If she were going to *do* anything about it—"

"But she is," said Mrs. Chase. "She's perfectly willing to. As a matter of fact, Carrie—she wants me to go and live with her."

There was a short silence: then Mrs. Chase spoke again.

"I couldn't help it, Carrie."

"I know you couldn't. Only it makes me feel very . . . remiss."

"And I shan't, of course." Mrs. Chase paused. "You know, dear, I think I won't go and live with any one."

Caroline opened her mouth to argue, but the wind had been taken from her sails. It was just *like* Cousin Maggie: like her both in her genuine good nature and her lack of—of tact. . . .

"After all," Mrs. Chase continued, "I don't see why there *should* be a fire. I'm very careful."

"But suppose you were ill, Mother?"

"I should knock on the floor. The book-keeper sleeps underneath, and under the sitting-room there's the shop. You know, at my age, Carrie dear, there's a great comfort in having a place quite of one's own."

"But isn't it lonely?"

"I see you every morning, and Cousin Maggie nearly every afternoon. And I'm used to quiet, dear: if I lived in a bustle I should feel quite bewildered." Caroline urged her no more, but went rather quietly home. She felt much as the Good Samaritan might have done, had the Pharisee, instead of continuing on, turned sharply back and got to the traveller first. That the traveller in this case had no need of assistance was beside the point: and Caroline suddenly recollected, with the irrelevance of dislike, how rude Cousin Maggie had once been about the Chase's Sunday supper.

CHAPTER VI

I

SO THE days went, the months went, and Caroline Chase turned finally into Mrs. Smith. She did not even notice it: before she knew where she was she had been married five, then six, and then a full ten years. 'I'm middle-aged!' thought Caroline in astonishment; and after the tenth anniversary began to look, each morning, for the grey in her hair. But there was no grey to be seen: it was still a light chestnut brown, smooth and glossy over a brow scarcely lined, and this so surprised and charmed her that for a while she grew quite vain, brushing it elaborately every morning in the hope that Henry would notice. He never did, of course, and she soon tired of getting up ten minutes early; but the pleasure remained. Her figure, too, though matronly, was upright and agreeable: she looked just what she was, the good-humoured and sensible mother of two healthy and well-brought-up children.

Already they were big enough to receive twopence a week pocket money. Though Lily was a girl, and two years younger, she always had the same as Leonard; but their methods of spending it showed an interesting variation. Leonard was a squanderer: so long as his twopence lasted, he positively threw it about—he would walk straight out of the house, for instance, and buy a bar of chocolate and a *Comic Cuts*. Lily squandered too, but on a larger scale, often saving as much as sixpence or sevenpence before laying it out: she bought chiefly transfers, crayons, and coconut ice. It seemed highly probable (thought Caroline fondly) that she was going to turn out artistic.

They grew in spurts. At five and seven plump and docile, by seven and nine they had become leggy, freckled, and (according to Ellen Watts) far too full of themselves. Ellen's own three daughters, after a vociferous infancy, had settled down as they grew older to anemia and weak chests. Leonard and Lily called them the Whiners—a *jeu d'esprit* which Caroline, owing to Henry's ill-concealed amusement, had been powerless to repress. All four girls went to the same school, Lily and the youngest Whiner being in the same class; but any intimacy between them was solely the work of Mrs. Watts. She was always asking Lily to tea, with a special invitation for Leonard if he cared to come; and since Leonard never did care, and Lily refused to go without him, these invitations became something of a nuisance. There was also, continually recurring, the vexed question of music lessons.

"They can't begin too early, Carrie," explained Mrs. Watts, "I've seen it again and again. You ought to have started Lily a year ago."

"But I thought you'd given up teaching?" said Caroline tact-lessly.

Ellen bridled.

"It's not myself I'm thinking of, dear. Of course I *do* give lessons sometimes, just to oblige, and I'd be very glad to have the child: but it's Lily's future."

Caroline looked at her young daughter almost in surprise. The only future she had ever conceived for her was something very like her own—marriage with a nice steady husband, and two chil-dren, and not too much bother about housekeeping money. Of course it would be nice for her to play the piano as well, especially if the husband sang; but until that was ascertained (and as they hadn't a piano) why, thought Caroline, bother the child's head?

"She ought to be practising three hours a day," said Ellen firmly.

"We haven't a piano."

Mrs. Watts bridled again.

"Well, if *you* can't afford one, dear, I'm sure I don't know who can. We all know what Henry gets."

"Then it's more than I do," said Caroline angrily.

This was quite true. The exact figure of their income was some-thing Henry never told her. They had married on two hundred and fifty a year, and since then he had had two rises; but what those rises amounted to, and whether he might expect any more, Caroline had not been informed. Beyond once offering to pay the housekeeping money by the month (an offer which Caroline rejected, since she could keep a week more easily in her head) he never spoke of their finances at all. Nor did Caroline. She was never short, and in fact saved about five pounds a year; when there was anything special, such as linoleum or a new mangle, she just told him about it and gave him the bill. But she wasn't going to give him a bill for a piano. . . .

But after Ellen had gone Caroline's heart misgave her, and she interrupted Lily's homework to find out the child's views. Lily looked up from her addition, one finger still on a carry-five, and heard without excitement that she might, if she wished, learn to play on the piano.

"Like the Whiners?" asked Lily.

"I've told you again and again," said Caroline with asperity, "that you're not to call them that. Their names are Harriet, Gertrude, and Maud."

"But they do whine," said Lily.

"It's extremely rude, and I won't have it," retorted Caroline. "Would you like to have music lessons?"

"With Mrs. Watts, then?"

"Probably."

"Then I wouldn't," said Lily, "and nor would Leonard."

Caroline frowned.

"Do you mean that Mrs. Watts has said anything to you about it?"

"She's *always* saying it," replied Lily wearily. "She's always asking us whether we wouldn't like to play duets. Leonard"—she giggled appreciatively—"said he'd rather play draughts."

Caroline was so annoyed that she made a most revolutionary suggestion.

"If you like," she said deliberately, "you can learn at school. If you really want to, Lily, I'll speak to Father."

But Lily shook her head. In the company of Harriet, Gertrude, and Maud she had apparently lost all musical ambition. Nor was Caroline particularly sorry. She would have simply hated to pay out three guineas a year on the advice of Ellen Watts.

II

Every August they spent a fortnight at the seaside.

They went sometimes to Margate, and sometimes to Broadstairs, the arms of both which watering-places began to appear with quite monotonous frequency on Caroline's collection of Goss. Cousin Maggie brought her a piece from Felixstowe, and Ellen a piece from Southend—("It's a very small one," said Ellen, "but of course we're not well off like you.")—but the piece from Bournemouth remained unduplicated. Caroline remembered with affection the walks along the cliffs; but the train journey was too long, and in any case, with the children, they could hardly have stayed at the Polperryn. They took furnished rooms, not too far from the sea, for that was one of the things Henry was always so considerate about; Caroline continued to do the catering, but she had never to push a perambulator—like so many women of her acquaintance—through half a dozen back streets two or three times a day. At Broadstairs they were sometimes actually on the front, and as the children got older Caroline used to put them on a seat by themselves and go about her shopping in peace and quiet. Henry usually went for a walk, and then the whole family, assembling on the beach, would lunch off sandwiches and doughnuts and a bag of Victoria plums. These last, however shielded from the sand, were always a little gritty. If the children had bathed there would be Oxo as well, drunk standing at the Beach Cafe; and then Caroline took out her sewing, and Henry his paper, and the children dug or paddled all through the long, sandy, somnolent afternoon. Sometimes it rained, of course, and sometimes it was cold: but that was how Caroline, remembering and looking forward from one year to another, always visualized a summer holiday. Both she and Lily used to look forward from June, making a special two-month calendar to tick off the days; but Leonard, who took longer views, looked forward right from Christmas. Between these two pivotal dates their world revolved, and when Caroline, in her leisure moments, was not thinking about plum puddings, she was usually thinking about spades.

They both wanted iron ones, and Caroline considered iron dangerous.

"Lily gets her feet covered with sand," she told Henry, "and then digs on to them. She's hurt herself twice already, even with the wood."

"Then get Leonard an iron one and let Lily stick to what she's got," said Henry easily.

Caroline was silent. In Lily the instinct for female subordination, if it existed at all, was considerably weaker than in her mother and grandmother. When Leonard wanted her to be a bear, or a Red Indian captive, she always insisted on being the hunter or the cowboy for an equal length of time. If Leonard took her paintbox she recouped herself with Leonard's train. If Leonard had an iron spade, Lily would certainly want one too. . . .

"I'll think it over," said Caroline. For once she totally disagreed with her husband's opinion: but she would not for worlds have said so. However long she lived, and in spite of all Lal's subsequent efforts, she never managed to take a leaf out of her daughter's book.

CHAPTER VII

I

IN THE summer of 1914, when Leonard was nine and Lily seven, they decided to go to Bournemouth.

"To the Polperryn?" asked Caroline, feeling a trifle sentimental.

"If you like," said Henry.

"We'd have to take a double room, and two for the children. Lodgings would be a lot cheaper."

"Lodgings mean twice as much work for you."

"Oh, I'm used to it," said Caroline easily.

He gave her one of his rare looks of affection.

"I don't believe there's a woman in Morton works as hard as you do, Carrie: nor one that looks better on it."

He was gone, abruptly as usual, but the compliment left her in a pleasant and unaccustomed glow. All that day—working about the house, writing to the Polperryn—Caroline turned it in her mind: it was her first compliment for years, and a compliment from her husband, and she was sure Frederick Watts never said anything of the kind to Ellen. '*Well!*' thought Caroline; "Well!" she said aloud; and nearly went round to tell her mother. She did not, however, because she had planned to press Henry's flannels, and in her present mood would rather have done ironing for Henry than anything under the sun. 'How lucky I've been!' she thought, waiting for the iron to heat; and so fell musing (it was an unusual day altogether) on the extraordinary narrow compass in which a woman's luck lay. If a good man fell in love with her, she was lucky for life: if no man at all, or a man who made a bad husband, her luck was out. There was nothing to be done about it: on that one accident depended every female life. And indeed continued to depend, thought Caroline; for in spite of all the jokes about widows, she could never think of them without commiseration. There was Mrs. Platt, whose husband had left her money in Consols, and who certainly never pined; but she still wore his picture in a locket, and put flowers on his grave at Easter, and no doubt felt a little lonely whenever she climbed into bed. Even so, she was an exception: while with some widows their bereavement was so much a part of their characters that one simply never thought about them without thinking of their dead husbands as well. Ellen Watts, if the Lord took Frederick Watts first, would be just such a one; and at the thought of Ellen not only orphaned, but widowed as well, Caroline barely repressed a shudder.

'She'll wear weeds!' decided Caroline, testing the heat of the iron.

While the trousers were being pressed, however, her thoughts turned to the pleasanter subject of her own summer clothes. If they were going to the Polperryn she would need two new dresses: and she would have them with net yokes and low collars, the sort you could take out and wash. One such collar, bought in a summer sale, lay already in the dressing-table drawer, and with the flannels still warm over her arm she hastened upstairs to try it on. But in this, as in most of her attempts at personal vanity, she was foiled by the presence of her family. Lily and Leonard, who had no business there at all, were standing rapt before the table and breathing heavily on the glass.

"Mother!" squealed Lily, "look at Leonard waggle his ears!"

Caroline watched the performance; first together, then separately, her son's ears twitched briskly up and down.

"He's done it ten times running!" cried Lily with enthusiasm.

"So could his grandfather, dear," Caroline said calmly; and laying her husband's trousers on the bed, offered to take them both out for a walk.

II

All at once people began to talk about war.

Or that was how it seemed to Caroline. One day every one was talking about summer holidays, the next about mobilization. There was trouble in the Balkans—some one had been assassinated—but instead of leaving it alone Russia and Austria, and now Germany, were all joining in. When Caroline, in the middle of packing, stopped to ask Henry about it, he did not as usual give her a cut-and-dried answer: for once he seemed uncertain; and this at the time was what impressed Caroline most.

"Mrs. Macbeth and her daughter were going to Brussels," said Caroline, "and now they're not."

She looked at him inquiringly, waiting for a lead. Henry did not speak, but from his face she saw that he approved.

"I think they're very sensible," said Caroline sincerely.

She took up a red serge bathing-dress, shook out the moth-balls, and laid it at the bottom of the trunk. Henry's, which came next, was of dark blue wool, the regulation kind, and at the feel of anything so like a sock Caroline automatically ran a hand in and began looking for holes.

"You can leave that out," said Henry.

The garment still dangling, her wedding-ring shining bright through a thin patch, Caroline stood and stared.

"Do you—do you mean that *we* shouldn't go to Bournemouth, Henry?"

"You and the children can. I mayn't be able to get away."

"But you're not in the Army!"

"I make boots for it," said Henry stolidly.

It was the first time (she remembered afterwards) that he had ever spoken of Mathieson's in the first person singular. As though he *were* Mathieson's. . . . But at the moment she had only one thought.

"Henry, have you heard anything the papers haven't?"

"No."

"But you—you think it may happen?"

"I think it may."

Caroline dropped the bathing-dress into the trunk, a heap of summer clothes over it, and shut down the lid.

"Well, we're not going to Bournemouth without you," she said.

III

That afternoon Ellen Watts came to tea, bringing her three children with her. They were all going to Margate, and no rumour of war seemed to have reached Ellen's ears. She was perfectly normal and extremely irritating.

"Whatever's the matter with Lily, dear?" asked Ellen at once.

It was one of her most effective and characteristic ways of making herself disagreeable. She never asked if anything *were* the matter, but by at once assuming that it was could pass straight to the corollary of its being also Caroline's fault.

"With Lily?" Caroline looked out of the window and beheld her daughter and the Whiners standing in an unfriendly group on the edge of the grass. "Nothing that I know of. She was all right at dinner."

"She's too pale," stated Ellen, "and much too thin, and she finicks about her food."

Now this last charge was not unfounded. Lily, in the matter of food, had quite unsuitably well-defined tastes. She would eat any quantity of fruit, or bread-and-butter, or very lean meat: but she would not eat fat, or boiled puddings, or anything with custard on it. She simply would not touch them, and after one long-drawn battle in which the same slice of pudding appeared at six successive meals, Caroline had stopped trying to make her. It was the same with ground rice. "I shall just be sick, Mother," said Lily patiently; and she just was sick. . . .

Mrs. Watts too looked out of the window, following Caroline's glance.

"She'll never be pretty, dear," said Mrs. Watts frankly, "so you may as well make up your mind to it."

Caroline considered her pale lanky daughter and in her heart of hearts agreed. But she was not going to admit it to Ellen.

"Lily will be tall," she said complacently.

"Tall! My dear!" Ellen let out one of her shrill, infuriating cackles. "That's just what the men don't like. It makes them feel looked down on. And there's another thing, Carrie, though I don't like to say it: she's getting very sullen."

It was too much. Caroline put down her sewing and observed firmly that that was just where Ellen was wrong.

"She's quiet, and likes her own way, and she can be very obstinate; but she isn't sullen. It's one of the worst faults a child can have, and I should never," said Caroline confidently, "put up with it for a moment."

"Obstinacy *is* sullenness," said Mrs. Watts.

"Not in Lily." Caroline paused, trying to find words for the super-frankness, the candid egoism, which made her daughter's occasional stubbornness so peculiarly hard to deal with. Lily always had a definite point of view, and if her mother's happened to be different it was simply unfortunate. She never argued: she might even admit Caroline to be theoretically in the right; in which case it was simply that she, Lily, preferred to be in the wrong. "But you're just being stubborn!" Caroline once cried; and Lily, after thought, had amiably assented. . . .

"She isn't sullen in the least!" said Caroline with indignation.

Ellen leant across and patted her on the shoulder.

"My dear, you're quite right to stand up for the child, and as I say to Frederick, I think it's wonderful the way you *do* stand up for her and for Leonard too. But I can't help feeling you're not always as firm as you might be, and I've known you so long, dear, that I feel it's my duty to say so. Now we must be going."

She stood up, and tapping smartly on the window called her brood to her. They came, one behind the other, docile as sheep and with a certain sheep-like droop of the head and shoulders. Lily saw it too: she darted forward and held out a hoop-stick in the eldest Whiner's path. The Whiner stepped meekly over: so did her two sisters: and Lily's high squeal of laughter rang at their heels.

"Lily!" called Mrs. Watts tartly. "Aren't you going to come and say good-by to me?"

They came in; they did not seem in the least sorry to part with each other. Ellen and Caroline, less ingenuous, bade each other a cordial farewell.

"Kiss Mrs. Watts, dear," said Caroline automatically.

It was then the awful thing happened.

Lily hung back. She did look, for the moment, and as her mother was forced to admit, very sullen indeed. But in the face of Ellen's meaning glance Caroline felt bound to persist.

"Lily! Did you hear me?"

"Don't force her, dear," said Mrs. Watts acidly. "If she doesn't want to kiss me I'm sure I don't want to be kissed."

"Then I don't," said Lily, suddenly breaking silence.

Caroline stared at her in horror. Lily had kissed Mrs. Watts for years—never, indeed, with enthusiasm, but at any rate without protest: and now to choose this moment of all others to pile rudeness on disobedience and add stubbornness to both: For stubborn she was going to be, as Caroline at once perceived; and Ellen, from the complacent shrug of her shoulders, had evidently perceived it too.

"You're a very rude little girl," she said forbearingly. "And being rude to a visitor, as I expect your mother has told you, is the worst of all. But if you'll apologize, and say you're sorry, we'll forget all about it."

"But I wasn't rude," said Lily.

The two parties stood facing each other; on one side the children, Lily in front, behind her the three Whiners, on the other Caroline and Mrs. Watts. But neither alliance was staunch, and just at that moment one of the Whiners ratted.

"You shouldn't contradict," said Gertrude priggishly.

"Gertrude, go and get your hat on," retorted Caroline.

Lily opened her mouth. Having already been stubborn, she was about to be frank.

"I wasn't rude, because you said if I didn't want to kiss you, you didn't want to be kissed. You *asked* me. And I don't. I never have. I—"

"Lily!" cried Caroline sharply.

"Don't stop her," said Ellen with a smile. "I suppose now she's going to tell me *why* she doesn't want to kiss me. Go on, dear, why don't you tell me that too?"

"Because that really *would* be rude," said Lily mildly.

There was a moment's dreadful silence, then suddenly—in the nick of time—one of the Whiners burst into tears. Caroline could not believe it to be tact, but she felt grateful to the child all the same. She created a diversion, she at last got her outraged mother moving. Seizing a child by either hand, shepherding the third before her, Ellen shook the dust of the drawing-room from her feet. She went, scolding still, leaving Caroline to scold behind her; and it would be a very long time indeed—cried Ellen from the hall—before either she or the children darkened that door again.

The door slammed, Ellen was gone. She would be back next week, of course, and the Whiners with her; there was nothing to worry about there. Caroline half sighed, finding the thought less comfortable than it should have been. Then she turned to her daughter with looks of deep reproach.

"But I wasn't *rude,*" said Lily patiently.

CHAPTER VIII

I

THE few days passed in a confusion of rumours. The trouble in Ireland, now dropping into the background, occasionally recurred, and whenever it got into the headlines Caroline took heart. Trouble in Ireland was something homely, domestic almost—upsetting but familiar, like a spring cleaning. There was other news more reassuring still. On July the twenty-ninth the mid-weekly *Morton Chronicle* devoted its whole leading article to the reflooring of Morton Swimming-bath, and Caroline, reading that Mr. Macbeth favoured tiles, and the local M.P. cement, took heart again. But by August bank holiday the news was all of mobilizations, Germany mobilizing for fear of Russia, France for fear of Germany. Belgium, a small country where people on the Common sometimes went for a holiday, became of immense importance; it was all on account of Belgium, Caroline gathered, that England herself might be drawn in too.

But Henry was thirty-seven.

Through every phase of alarm and reassurance, that remained Caroline's one underlying thought. Henry was thirty-seven. Of Leonard she did not think at all. The recruit, as she saw him, was a young man of twenty-five—the sort of young man who never did well at home. Like the youngest Macbeth, who wouldn't settle down to anything except horse-racing. There must be thousands and thousands of them, thought Caroline, to whom a war would be a positive godsend. But men like Henry—men with wives and families and good positions—they surely would be allowed to stay at home. 'Perhaps it won't come after all,' thought Caroline hopefully. 'Surely some one will have some sense!'

Her views were strictly personal. She was sorry for the countries at war, but she had also a feeling—especially in the case of those Balkans—that it was their own fault. An unjust quarrel, the papers said, is being thrust upon us; and Caroline's only objection was that no one *could* have a quarrel thrust upon them if only they were determined to keep out. Henry, however, saw things differently: he talked about the importance of the littoral: and as usual—with a sinking of the heart Caroline re-acknowledged this fundamental truth—as usual Henry was right.

On August the fourth, as soon as he had gone to work, she went up to her bedroom and read all through the Litany.

II

All that day Caroline stayed indoors. The children went down the road and came home with Union Jacks. They said firmly and cheerfully that there was going to be a war. There was a meeting on the Common, and people in all the churches just as though it were Sunday. Caroline listened in silence and after dinner tried to damp their spirits by setting them to clean the boot-cupboard. They did it, however, to the tune of Rule Britannia, and she wished she had sent them out again. By supper-time, at seven o'clock, Henry had not returned. Caroline put his sausages back in the oven and played beggar-my-neighbour for two hours. Then the children went to bed, and the stillness of the house so got upon her nerves that she began turning out the drawing-room. The work, by gaslight, seemed queerly unfamiliar; she crumbled the bread recklessly, using half a loaf to one strip of wallpaper. As midnight approached she hid the clock under a cushion and by working harder still managed to lose all count of time. It might have been one or two, or three in the morning when at last a key sounded in the lock and she knew that Henry was home.

For a moment she could not move. Fatigue was swaying her, she had to hold by the bureau. Outside in the hall a match spurted as Henry lit the gas. 'He'll want his supper,' thought Caroline automatically; and with a great effort she walked steadily across the room, pulled open the door, and saw her husband's face startlingly near under the flaring gas.

He was white as paper.

"Henry!"

He looked at her and nodded.

"You're up late, Carrie. . . ."

"Henry—it isn't war, is it?"

Before answering he took off his coat and hung it carefully on a peg. There was something queer about him; he looked almost dazed. If she had not known him so well, Caroline might have thought he had been drinking.

"Henry!" she repeated urgently.

He turned back to her. She saw him moisten his lips.

"Yes."

"*War*, Henry?"

There was a long silence. Caroline put out a hand and felt her fingers close on something smooth. It was Henry's mackintosh, hanging from the stand. 'He hasn't worn it for weeks,' she thought foolishly, 'it's getting quite hard. . . .' Aloud she heard herself say,

"You won't have to go, will you, Henry?"

"No," said Henry. He moistened his lips again. "Mathieson's taken me into partnership. I shall have to stay here, and make boots."

He picked up a bundle of papers; and without another word—moving with a stiff clockwork stride, with eyes blindly fixed—walked past her into the clean drawing-room.

III

The next day, without asking any one's advice, Caroline went early to the grocer's and gave a five-pound order. The shop was already crowded; it seemed as though half the women in Morton were doing the same thing.

CHAPTER IX

I

ON AUGUST the fifth a booking-clerk at Morton Station, leaving his post to distribute cigarettes among a trainload of Territorials, was arrested as a spy and marched off to the police station. A troop of Boy Scouts, guarding the railway bridge, arrested an ex-colonel and one of the linesmen. An elderly stockbroker, flying a kite for his son on Morton Common, was arrested on the charge of signaling to the enemy. The German Charcuterie, owned by a Welshman named Evans, had its windows broken and its stock scattered in the street.

Also on August the fifth the local M.P. and his wife moved out of their house on the Common and handed it over for the use of the Red Cross. Dr. French threw up a now flourishing practice to join the R.A.M.C. Mr. Brodie, the estate-agent, who was forty-five if a day, enlisted in the London Scottish. The youngest Macbeth boy enlisted as a private. Every shop in the High Street was out of khaki wool. A first collection for Belgian refugees brought in seven thousand five hundred and eighty pounds.

In this manner—in these manners—Morton confronted the fact of war. As a community it was aggressively patriotic, not yet alarmed, and genuinely eager for service. It had no doubts. The Germans were brutal aggressors, the Austrians their tools, and Belgium was gallant little Belgium. England herself as usual championed the right, and like an amateur among professionals had somehow a higher status than the rest of the Allies. The response of the Colonies, subject of many a heart-stirring cartoon in *Punch*, aroused a deep and genuine emotion. 'From the ends of the earth!' thought Caroline; and the tears stood in her eyes as she read how the sheep-farmers of New Zealand were selling their land for a song, were almost giving away their flocks, so that they could more quickly come over and fight at the Mother-country's call.

As for Caroline herself, she did what she could. She refrained from going to Bournemouth, and bought ten pounds of khaki wool. And she gave up hoarding, either of food or sovereigns, and had a box For The Belgians on her hall table.

II

During the next few months Morton began and completed its first social revolution. The supremacy of the Common, so long unchallenged, crumbled away like a wall of sand; and as the old leaders fell so new ones arose. Chief among these was no other than Cousin Maggie Platt, who on Ladies' Committees sprang to sudden and lasting prominence. She could knit like a machine, she had a talent for slave-driving, and when first confronted by a pair of Mrs. Macbeth's socks, had told her to take them home, and unravel the wool, and so go on knitting and unraveling till she got them the same size.

After that Mrs. Platt ruled supreme. She had sole charge of the Wool Room, which she ran with martinet efficiency, making poor knitters knit the leg and toe only while the expert, headed by herself, did nothing but turn heels. The system produced a new kind of sock, known to Red Cross headquarters as Morton specials; but every pair went out wearable, and every pair had passed through Cousin Maggie's hands. . . .

In this splendid wake Caroline and Mrs. Chase followed as best they could, Mrs. Chase quietly knitting socks for five hours a day, Caroline, whose time was more broken up, sticking chiefly to mufflers. Ellen Watts of course knitted too, but she did not stop there; she put a notice in the *Chronicle*, addressed to the Mothers of Morton, to the effect that no pupil entrusted to her tuition would be taught any German music, and she also gave white feathers to civilians in the streets.

Caroline hated her.

She knew it was wrong. It was wrong to hate any one (except of course the Germans); all through her girlhood, moreover, it had been specially impressed on her that it was wrong to hate Ellen

Watts. But she could not stop. In Ellen's patriotism there was something half-hysterical, half-sanctimonious, that made Caroline sick. And there was also, though Caroline could not define it, another quality still which in Ellen's company made her not only sick, but somehow afraid. It was a kind of secret pleasure, a secret lustfulness. She was always going about whispering stories of atrocities, so that Caroline was afraid, for the children, to have her in the house.

III

During the first week of September, it was said, a hundred thousand Russians passed through England on their way to France. They travelled by night, in carriages with the blinds down, leaving no trace behind save an empty vodka bottle here and there along the line. In spite of the reinforcements, however, the war still went on, and there was even less and less talk, as winter approached, of spending Christmas in Berlin.

It was generally agreed that the war would last a year.

In Morton itself the chief local interest was the arrival and domestication of a family of genuine Belgian refugees, housed, through the liberality of the Macbeths, in Miss Dupré's old flat over the chemist's. There was a father (with weak lungs), a rather flamboyant mother, and two daughters, aged fifteen and sixteen, who went to the Morton High School free. For refugees they used an unfortunate amount of lipstick, and mothers who had hastened to invite them to tea began to make embarrassed motions towards a withdrawal of intimacy. It was interesting to see with what force and promptitude a fundamental Morton standard could still assert itself, and how soon the two Doré girls, from being guests of honor on the Common, found their proper level as flappers in the town. The Doré father, who had been a compositor, was gratefully received by the *Morton Chronicle*, Madame came to working parties like every one else, and Caroline soon found it hard to remember—or remembering, to realize—that they had been driven from their homes at the point of the bayonet.

"They weren't," said Henry, to whom she once mentioned this difficulty. "They were evacuated by the French."

Caroline looked at him in surprise.

"But at the Vicar's tea-party, Henry, when Mr. Doré gave that talk about his experiences—"

"Not his alone," said Henry sardonically. "The experiences of refugees in general. You needn't worry about this lot, Carrie; Doré gets better wages than he did at home, the two girls are learning English, and the Macbeths pay the rent."

Caroline was slightly shocked. She had herself, at working parties, several times paid for Madame Doré's tea; now she wished she had put the money in her box.

"But the others, Henry—!" she said. "The others need the money, don't they?"

"I believe they do," said Henry soberly.

Caroline sighed. Belgium was something she tried not to think about: the Raemakers cartoons, of a gaunt woman and starving child, made her feel sick at heart. Nothing the soldiers suffered, she felt, could be as bad as that—to see your children dying of hunger, and have nothing to give them, and never be able to rest even because of the Huns coming after. When the cartoons were very bad she used to cut them out before Lily or Leonard could see, but the precaution, as she knew, was probably futile. There were newspapers everywhere, Henry bought three or four a day, and the children were after them like magpies. Paper being at a premium, they collected them in bundles to sell to the butcher. They made sometimes as much as sixpence a week; but Caroline, in spite of the Doré disillusionment, compelled them to put half of it into her box For The Belgians.

IV

Henry looked ill.

He was working, in these days, with a contained and resolute fury, seeing no one outside the factory but Caroline and the children, coming home late and weary, eating his supper, and going to bed almost immediately after. For Mathieson's was at last expanding; there was talk of Government subsidies; and Old Man Mathieson, at this juncture, had practically thrown in his hand. He was seventy-two, he suffered from asthma, above all he was frightened, not only by the war, but by the immensity of the business that was springing up in his name. Henry carried everything. All Army contracts were in his hands completely. Mathieson, in theory responsible for the *de luxe* trade, was away first a week, then a fortnight, then wrote suggesting that the *de luxe* trade should be given up. Henry refused. Women, after a brief period of economy, were spending more money than ever. He promoted the assistant works-manager and kept an eye on things himself. With his stocky build and steady eye he still retained an appearance of robustness; but Caroline, who saw him at night and in the mornings, began to worry.

"When are you going to take a holiday?" she once asked daringly.

"After the war."

"But it may be another year!"

"In another year, then. Don't get upset, Carrie; I might be in the trenches."

To her horror, Caroline felt herself flushing. She was so bad a dissembler, moreover, that instead of holding her peace, instead of pretending not to understand, she at once blurted out what was in her mind. "I didn't think you knew!"

"That people in Morton say I ought to be at the front?" Henry pushed back his supper plate and regarded her calmly. "Of course I knew, Carrie. What they don't seem to know is that I couldn't go if I wanted to. An army's got to have boots."

"That's just what *I* say!" cried Caroline.

He looked at her again.

"It's these working parties, I suppose. Well, you needn't bother about me, Carrie; and if you can, don't bother yourself. Now I'm going to bed."

He got up, so wearily that her heart went out to him. He looked completely exhausted. But she never again urged him, however great either his need or her own anxiety, to leave Morton on holiday.

CHAPTER X

FROM the beginning of 1915 Caroline's imagination, usually so insensitive to the visual, began to be haunted night and day by a precise and unvarying image. Once or twice she tried to set it down on paper: a white hill, topped by a small white house, and up to the house a black path. Along this path travelled two shapes, the first a small boy, figured in white like the hill, the second a moving cloud of darkness. The darkness was the war, the boy her ten-year-old son; they were racing—but racing like snails, racing with nerve-racking deliberation—for the little house. Both paces were uniform, but the cloud moved faster: Leonard had nothing to save him but his eight years' lead. It was simply a question of whether the house were two years away, or five, or nine: for if only he could get inside the war would be over.

'I must be going queer,' thought Caroline.

She had not at first worried about her son at all. There was the difficulty of getting butter, her mistrust of margarine (only Leonard seemed to like it), a vague general anxiety whether he were properly fed; but the idea of his having to fight was new and terrifying. Yet if the war went on—and look at the war with Napoleon!—it was quite possible. It was even—thought Caroline in the early mornings—extremely probable; and she would lie awake, staring at the top of the text, praying urgent confused prayers to a God who was not only a gentle Shepherd but also a Lord of Hosts. 'He can't *want* war!' argued Caroline desperately; and before the problem of good and evil felt her spirit sink exhausted. She sometimes, in these days, envied the Roman Catholics, who could pray to a Holy Mother and be sure of understanding. Caroline thought about Her a great deal, seeing Her as the one sensible woman in a family of belligerent menfolk; and but for a Chapel-bred fear of encouraging the Pope would have liked to slip into the Catholic Church and burn Her a candle. 'Poor Woman!' thought Caroline sympathetically; and closing her eyes exchanged the top of the text for the white and ominous hill. . . .

II

It was in just such a half-waking, half-sleeping state that Caroline, at about three o'clock in the morning, became conscious first of a loud noise, and secondly that Henry was not in bed beside her. She sat up, and saw him standing by the window in his dressing-gown and shoes.

"What is it, Henry?"

"An air-raid. Don't be frightened, Carrie, and don't put the light on."

His tone, so calm and matter of fact, at once reassured her. In the little light she felt for her dressing-gown and slippers, and a pair of stockings.

"What about the children?"

"Get them up if you like, but they're probably just as safe where they are. They may sleep through it."

"I'm not going to take them in the cellar," said Caroline at once, "they'd catch their deaths of cold. Has there been a bang already, Henry? What woke me?"

"One up by the Common. I think they've gone over."

As if in ironic comment the windows suddenly rattled. Caroline ran on to the landing and met Leonard and Lily emerging from their rooms. They looked very wide awake, and Lily had put on her dressing-gown.

"What is it, Mother?"

"A car back-firing," said Caroline promptly.

They exchanged superior glances.

"It's an air-raid, Mother," said Leonard kindly. "We ought all to go down to the cellar and lie flat on our faces."

"You'll do nothing of the kind!" retorted Caroline. "Catching your deaths of cold! Lily, go and get your slippers, and Leonard, bring some blankets."

The brief domestic altercation did them all good, and by the time they had assembled in the dining-room the atmosphere was normal. Caroline took out her knitting, Henry a bundle of factory accounts, and the children a jig-saw. No third explosion disturbed their tranquillity: before half an hour passed Lily was asleep again and Leonard dozing. The click of knitting-needles,

the ticking of the clock, made a soothing and monotonous sound:
Caroline was almost nodding herself when suddenly, without
lifting his head, Henry spoke.

"Watts has gone."

Caroline stared blankly.

"Frederick? But he isn't fit! His teeth are simply awful, Henry!"

"He's going with the Red Cross. I saw him this evening, in the
High Street." Henry reached out to the ink-pot. "He was looking
ten years younger."

"Poor Ellen!" said Caroline.

"If she'd led him a quieter life," said Henry without emotion,
"he'd have been a conscientious objector."

Silence returned. Caroline finished decreasing her toe, cast off,
and immediately cast on again. She had lost all sense of time: she
would have gone on knitting till morning. Leonard, now sleeping
like his sister, lay with his head on a footstool and his mouth open.
It ought to have been shut, and Caroline, with some vague fear of
adenoids (as though they were something he might thus catch)
was on the point of waking him up when in the street outside
some one played two notes on a bugle. For a moment she did not
understand, music in the streets, and especially at night, being
associated in her mind solely with carols; but Henry knew better.

"The All Clear."

Stiffly, wearily, Caroline rose to her feet and put the sock back
in its basket. The children, suddenly awake, blinked sleepily from
the hearth-rug. So huddled in their blankets they looked absurdly
infantile: she wanted to take them in her arms and carry them
both upstairs. She yawned violently.

"Bed," said Henry, without looking up.

He was in the middle of a column: his pen still moved methodically up and down. Caroline took Lily by the hand, Leonard by
the shoulder, and marched them tenderly from the room. They
were so drowsy that their feet kept missing the stairs; by the
time she got them to bed they were already fast asleep. Caroline
tucked them in carefully, thinking that another time she would
have water-bottles, then closed the doors and went towards her
own room. On the landing, however, at a sound from below, she

paused to look down the stairs; and to her extreme surprise saw Henry putting on his overcoat.

"Henry!" she called. "Henry! Where on earth are you going?"

He turned and looked up at her with an air of annoyance.

"One of them sounded somewhere near Mathieson's. I'm going to have a look."

Before Caroline could stop him, he had opened the door and was out into the street. She stumbled downstairs, clumsy in her loose slippers, and from the cold door-sill, in the dead silence, heard the thud of his footsteps running down Cleveland Road.

III

Like every other war-time phenomenon, air-raids soon took their regular place in the domestic routine. Caroline had a gas fire put in the dining-room, and kept cocoa, biscuits, and her knitting all together in a sideboard drawer. She also bought a new dressing-gown, easy to get into, but shorter than usual and fastening like a coat-frock. The children put on sweaters over their night things, and rugs round their legs. Only Henry made a complete toilet, arriving downstairs a few minutes after the others. There Caroline got out her knitting, the children, in spite of every resolve to the contrary, rapidly fell asleep, and Henry sat down to his figures. Except for the bangs, it was extraordinarily peaceful. If the raid lasted more than an hour, Caroline made cocoa: if only sixty minutes, they went to bed without.

"The Whiners have it anyway," Lily once argued. "*And* they go down in the cellar."

"I never heard such nonsense!" said Caroline sharply.

It sometimes amazed her, when she came to think about it, that she was not more afraid. There were Henry, and herself, and the children, all in momentary danger of death or injury; and so long as they were all together she did not seem to mind. But if Henry were absent—as on one night when he had been caught late at the works—then Caroline began to panic, going constantly to the front door, and even out into the road, till she found the children following her. The children, she saw with relief, were not afraid at all, but rather enjoyed the excitement. The idea of being killed themselves, or of any one they knew being killed, apparently never struck them. And the suburb was lucky; apart from being kept awake it suffered little damage and no loss of life. Shrapnel broke a good many windows, and there was a hole up on the Dairy Farm, but Morton lay too far out from London, and, in spite of Mathieson's Boot Factory, was too insignificant to receive special attention. As often as not there would be no sound at all save for the clatter of anti-aircraft, between the first warning maroon and the final All Clear. The children went back to bed almost without protest, Henry did not bother to go out, and the next morning Leonard would be up early to look for pieces of shrapnel.

School, after an air-raid, began an hour later, so that the children could sleep on; and all the small boys in Morton found the time particularly useful for adding to their collections.

IV

For Caroline, one of the major events of the war took place towards the end of breakfast-time on an October morning in 1915.

There had just been an appeal for more Special Constables, and she could not help feeling that a Special's armlet would be a nice thing for Henry to have. That was as far as her thoughts went, and without weighing the question further she said cheerfully,

"Are you going to enroll, Henry?"

He looked up from his paper.

"Do you want me to?"

Caroline hesitated. Personally, she felt no desire at all to have him standing about cold streets when he ought to be in bed; but when every one *was* enrolling. . . .

Henry spoke again.

"I shouldn't do the least good, I need all the sleep I can get; but if it'll stop Ellen Watts nagging at you, I'll join today."

His perspicuity, as always, filled her with astonishment. And also with remorse, for she now saw quite clearly that it was only to make herself, Henry's wife, feel better that she had wanted Henry to stand about outside Morton water-works. It—it was disgraceful! She put down the tea-pot and humbly met his eye.

"You're quite right, Henry, and I don't want you to in the least. I simply hadn't thought about it."

"Don't worry," said Henry grimly, "it was bound to come up sooner or later."

But though his words were so final, and it was half-past eight, he did not immediately go. He sat staring before him, pushing a knife back and forth along a stripe in the cloth. Outside in the hall Caroline could hear Lily and Leonard in argument over their bicycles. They would be wheeling them about, making marks on the linoleum. . . .

The knife stopped moving.

"Carrie."

"Yes, dear?"

He was looking more serious, more troubled, than she had ever seen him. The trouble communicated itself.

"What is it, Henry? Is there—is there anything wrong at Mathieson's?"

At last he shifted his gaze.

"Carrie, would you like me to chuck Mathieson's and join up?"

She was too much surprised, too suddenly afraid, for any words.

"Would you, Carrie?"

"But, Henry—you can't! They wouldn't let you!"

"They couldn't stop me if I made up my mind."

"And you're over age. You're forty-two!"

"Brodie was forty-five." He pushed back his chair, as though suddenly conscious of the time, his duties, the need to be off. "You'd better think it over, Carrie. You'd be all right, you'd get allowances and so on, and there's enough in the bank to finish the kids' schooling. If you wanted advice—"

"Henry!" She jumped up, unable to hear any more. "Henry, I don't want to think it over! I don't understand! Surely you're more use where you are than out there as—as—"

"As an inefficient soldier?" finished Henry.

It was not true, but she let it pass. Whatever Henry undertook he would perform thoroughly, conscientiously, to the best of a first-rate ability. Just as he did at Mathieson's, only at Mathieson's he could make more difference. . . .

"Aren't you, Henry? Aren't you more use?"

"Yes," said Henry deliberately. "As I'm telling you, Carrie, there's only one reason for going, and that's if you want me to."

"I don't." She was now standing too, the tears, for some reason, running down her face. "You're doing your duty just as much as any one, in a way it's harder, and if you think I *want* you to go—I don't, Henry!"

"Right," said Henry. He looked at the clock, and with his usual nod—calm, unemotional, almost absent-minded—left her by the table and went off to work.

V

It was not until some months later, however, that Caroline fully realized how much he had been prepared to sacrifice. For if he did not know at the time, he must have had it in his mind. . . .

He told her at supper. He looked, as usual, tired and over-driven: if there was triumph in his heart, his voice did not betray it.

"I've bought Mathieson out," said Henry calmly.

Caroline stared at him.

"You've *bought*—"

"Mathieson's Boot Factory. It's now Mathieson-Smith's."

"But, Henry"—she put down the tea-pot to avoid dropping it—"where did you get the money?"

"Borrowed it. Mathieson's an old man. He was glad to get out."

Mechanically Caroline filled his cup, cut him a slice of bread. Borrowed it! Borrowed enough to buy half a boot factory! For a moment she looked at him almost with terror; but he seemed quite himself, quite calm and sensible; he was eating his sausages just as though nothing had happened. . . .

"*Borrowed* it!" said Caroline aloud.

"Partly from the bank, and partly from Mr. Macbeth. There's a mortgage, of course, but it'll be paid off. Don't worry yourself, Carrie: I know what I'm doing."

The word bank, the name of Mr. Macbeth, slightly reassured her. She immediately seized on them.

"I didn't know you even knew Mr. Macbeth!"

"I don't—socially. But as a business acquaintance he thinks quite a lot of me." For the first time Henry smiled. "And you can know *her*, Carrie, if you want to. She'll bring out the silver tea-pot any day you like to go along."

"But I don't!" cried Caroline, now thoroughly alarmed. "I should simply hate it! Ought I to?"

"You can please yourself. But I tell you one thing, Carrie— before we're finished we'll be as big as any one in Morton."

She got up, and went over to him, and put her hand on his shoulder. She was conscious that she had not so far shown either the pride or the pleasure which were so manifestly his due. She said gently,

"It—it's wonderful, Henry!"

"The war helped," said Henry absently.

Caroline's hand tightened on his shoulder till she was almost clinging to him. 'But he would have gone!' she told herself quickly. 'If I'd said the word he'd have gone months ago!' She looked down at his head, and saw with a pang of tenderness how thin and grey the hair was. 'He would have gone!' she thought again; and slowly her hand relaxed. But still the pleasure, the exultation, would not come to her: the idea of position and riches, even of a splendid future for Lily and Leonard, seemed to make no impression on her mind. She stood quiet and motionless, staring with troubled eyes at the astonishing vista so abruptly opening. 'Call on Mrs. Macbeth!' thought Caroline. 'I shan't do anything of the kind!'

Henry was now getting on with his supper, but she could not join him. The news had quite taken away her appetite.

CHAPTER XI

I

The beginning of 1916 Mrs. Chase died. Caroline grieved, but quietly and unobtrusively, feeling even a little diffident in her black garments. Black had come to mean the war, a man killed in the fighting; amongst other women so attired she had the sense of being an impostor.

She decided to wear her mourning for six months only, and then give it away. There were always, at that time, plenty of women who could do with it.

II

For the war went on. Verdun held out, Bukarest had fallen, at home people talked about Mr. Lloyd George and the shortage of eggs. Mathieson-Smith's was working at full pressure, but no sudden access of wealth—to Caroline's relief—had yet come to disturb the Smith home. Her own private thoughts, like those of every other woman with a family, ran almost exclusively on food. In some curious way she had put the war out of her head: it had become like some dreadful continuous noise to which, through force of habit, her ears were now dulled. She knitted, had made Henry put her two thousand pounds into War marks or offered saccharine for their tea. Caroline had not to wear that face either: if she did not know the rapture, neither did she know the despair: but things were not too easy for her.

She felt herself to be a woman apart, cut off both from the common joy and the common mourning. She was by no means shunned, and did not fancy herself so; but often a woman, in talking to her, would suddenly break off and fall silent, as though Caroline were incapable of understanding. Or perhaps she would change the subject, for there were several topics which Morton, in conversation with Mrs. Smith, had tacitly agreed to leave alone: such were profiteers, *embusqués*, and fraudulent Army contractors.

There was also one afternoon—and this was the worst of all— when Ellen Watts, with a telegram in her hand, came running down Cleveland Road calling Caroline's name aloud. A neighbour went out to her, but was thrust aside; Ellen ran clumsily on, found Caroline in the hall, and there began to abuse her with every foul name a woman can lay tongue to. Caroline forced the paper from her hand, and saw that Frederick Watts had been killed in France two days earlier.

The abuse continued. All afternoon, from three until five o'clock, the two women moved between kitchen and sitting-room— one white, silent, going steadily about her household tasks, the other loud, vociferous, pursuing step by step with a harsh incessant railing. A lifelong jealousy had at last found voice: words screamed and screeched, battering about Caroline's ears like the wings of evil birds. Once she put up her hands as though to fend them off: Ellen seized her wrists and wrenched them away. The names of Henry and Frederick, of Mrs. Chase and Cousin Maggie, of Lily and Leonard—all were mingled together in the bitter stream. For Caroline had a husband, and Ellen had not, and Caroline's children had a father, and Ellen's were orphaned; and Henry was a coward, every one in Morton knew it, he was making money out of the men who were being killed for him, he was cheating his country, he was taking the money and not even doing the work, his boots were made of paper so that the men couldn't march in them, and above all—above all!—he was alive and safe, and Frederick Watts was dead out in France. He was a coward and a shirker, Caroline ought to be ashamed of living with him—

"Now go," said Caroline whitely; and she took Ellen by the shoulders and thrust her out of the door.

It was not long after that Henry came in. He looked once at his wife's face and paused beside her.

"That woman's been here."

Caroline nodded.

"How long?"

"All afternoon . . ."

Without another word he left her and went to the kitchen. She could hear him filling the kettle. Very slowly, as after a long day's labour, she dragged herself up and as far as the door.

"How did you know, Henry?"

"I met her in the High Street." He turned, reaching for the tea-caddy; and Caroline saw printed on his cheek a red and angry mark.

III

It was at about this time, and after the lapse of so many years, that Caroline's thoughts turned once more to a garden.

CHAPTER XII

I

LIKE every other suburb, Morton had its patch of allotments. They occupied some acres of waste ground on either side of the railway line, and hither, on Sunday mornings, and in the light evenings of summer time, the elders of the district might be seen making their implement-cumbered way. They dug, they hoed, they planted marrows and lettuces, and in due time these vegetables came up and helped to defeat the U-boats. The allotments were uniform in size, but very various in degree of cultivation: some— perfect pictures, in the running for the M.P.'s prize—were fenced with brushwood (already sprouting) and adorned with rustic but lock-up arbors for the reception of spades. Others, unfortunately, were a disgrace, neglected, stony, or cynically bright with nasturtiums; but the vast majority lay somewhere in between, neither dust-heaps nor hot-houses, but growing beans and potatoes for one household, and perhaps a handful of Michaelmas daisies. In a mild way the allotments were popular, and it was a favourite family walk, after Church on Sunday, to go up to the railway lines and watch father dig.

Caroline's first idea was to join this community, to be seen herself digging and planting, if not on Sundays, at least on weekday afternoons; but the objections were many. She had, just then, a great desire for seclusion. She wanted to be alone, to labour silently and steadily at some manual toil; and the allotments, on a fine evening, were almost as bad as the working-party. They were also distant; they were a quarter-of-an-hour's walk away, so that she would have to leave the house for considerable periods at a time. It was at this juncture that Caroline remembered—what for years she had forgotten—that she had herself a garden of her own.

She went out and looked at it.

It was small, flowerless, with an unkempt grass-plot and no paths but the three tracks, one to each washing-pole, trodden by Caroline herself through an infinity of Monday mornings. Henry, she remembered, had once offered to plant tulip bulbs; and she had put the offer aside because—because just then, at the time of her marriage, a garden had no attraction for her. She had put gardens out of her thoughts; she did not wish to be reminded of them; and all because, years before that, there had been a garden on the Common where she met a boy called Vincent. . . . 'What foolishness!' thought Caroline severely; and stepping back into the house she went to the cupboard under the stairs and took out a large, newly-arrived parcel. It contained a spade, a fork, two hoes, a pair of gloves, and a book on gardening. Slipping the latter into her pocket Caroline next put the children's dinner ready, eating, as she did so, a large slice of bread and jam. Then she went into the garden, and began to dig.

II

She planted, as soon as the first strip was ready, runner beans and a row of lettuce; and she did so not in impatience, or from a desire to hurry on the food-supply, but because it was the digging she most enjoyed, and she wanted to spread it out. Other things were good too—hoeing, and pressing down the earth with one's fingers, and seeing a runnel of water glimmer and subside; but digging pulled at the muscles. Caroline dug with passion, just as the book told her, in three strips, carrying the soil from the first to the end of the third, mixing in vegetable parings from the scullery and a bag of fertilizer from the Morton seed merchant's. She was much too late, of course, for it was already March, but the beans, when she had planted them, sprouted with a will. 'The Runner Bean,' said her book, 'is not over-particular'; and Caroline gratefully acknowledged the truth of the statement.

She could not give them very much time. Her life, what with the house, the children, and the working-parties, was already tolerably filled. Domestic servants were both rare and costly, so that Caroline thought herself in high luck to have secured an elderly charwoman for three days a week. But there was usually a quiet space, between twelve and half-past, when the first work of the house was finished and before the children's dinner became a pressing consideration; and these thirty minutes Caroline began to guard and cherish as a precious treasure. She resented having to waste them on shopping, or on coffee with some other woman at the Morton Lyons; she hurried home as to an assignation. There were also, as the days lightened, evening half-hours when the children were at their home-work and she could slip out unmissed, and still hear, through the house, if any tradesman or visitor should come to the door. Neither Lily nor Leonard ever followed her; the garden did not interest them, and indeed they both seemed to regard their mother's new activity in the light of a mild but successful joke. So did Henry, of course, whenever he was not too tired: he called it her land-work, and found jokes in *Punch* about women being frightened by cows. But Caroline did not care. The garden, the quiet and solitude, were restoring her old serenity; and she was just as pleased that her family should keep away.

In April, when she was already buying bean poles, America came into the war. Caroline rejoiced exceedingly, expecting everything to be over in a week or two, but Henry still looked grave. It made the end certain, he said; but there was no occasion to get the flags out.

"But the end has always been certain!" cried Caroline indignantly.

She spoke in genuine surprise: it had literally never occurred to her that England might be beaten. England never *was* beaten— not in the long run. It was a historical fact, like—like the battle of Waterloo, and she told Henry so quite warmly.

"I suppose it all depends on the length of the run," said Henry. "There was Joan of Arc before Napoleon. But in this case, Carrie, you're probably right."

"Of course I'm right!" cried Caroline. "Of course we couldn't lose! Besides—"

She broke off, suddenly self-conscious. Besides—she had been going to say—besides, in this case, the Lord would never allow it!

III

The beans were sprouting, but Caroline still dug. She was now turning up the hard beaten patch outside the drawing-room window, and her excavations produced some odd treasure-trove. Once it was a Queen Victoria sixpence (which she put into the Belgian Box): once a portion of bubble-pipe, reclaimed by Leonard; and once, crumbling a handful of earth, she came upon a tiny brownish cocoon, caked with soil, but having a core hard as ivory. Caroline turned it between her fingers, rubbing it clean: and it *was* ivory, a tiny smooth bobbin that had once been wound with silk.

'The work-box!' thought Caroline.

It belonged to the work-box, to the rose-wood work-box given her by Henry just before Leonard was born. The children had played with the spools for years; then they grew too big, and the box was left standing on Caroline's work-table, holding a few odds and ends of wool, a broken magnifying-glass, and the prescription for Lily's cough-mixture. After that—years after—Lily had begged it to keep hair-ribbons in: she put black (for school) in one division, and coloured in the other, and Caroline had been very much pleased at her neatness. But it did not last, and as a rebuke Caroline took the box back again and let Leonard have it for some unexplained purpose of his own. That was Leonard all over, thought Caroline in parenthesis; he was just like his father. He never told her anything. But for his terminal reports, but for the annual prize-giving, she would never have known, for instance, that he was top in arithmetic; he never came home, like another boy, and boasted for her admiration. . . .

The bobbin lay in her palm, Caroline stood motionless while these thoughts, and many others, passed slowly through her mind. It was long since she had enjoyed so comfortable a pause for reflection. The garden was quiet. On the other side of the fences not a soul stirred. You could hear—it was so still—the rumble of trams in Morton High Street. You could hear St. Peter's bell chime the quarter past noon.

Caroline slipped the bobbin into her pocket and stooped again over the stubborn earth.

CHAPTER XIII

I

On the first Saturday in September Henry, coming home earlier than usual, found Caroline in the garden looking at her beans. They were now many of them four and five inches long, only wanting a little plumpness before they could be picked: and Caroline was tasting in advance the pleasures of doing so. She moved gravely between the rows, pausing every now and then for a long, childlike stare: she was looking at those beans (thought Henry) as though there were something extraordinary about them. He even had a look himself, half expecting to see an unusual-coloured flower, or some freak of growth: but no, they were simply common runner beans, with bright scarlet flowers and dark green leaves. . . . Then he too advanced between the beanpoles, and at once, from his step, from his whole bearing, Caroline knew he had something to tell her.

"You're nice and early," she said approvingly; and then waited.

Henry looked round.

"Where are the kids?"

"Up on the Common. I gave them tea early."

He nodded, but she felt doubtful whether he had heard. He was examining a bean-stick. 'It's something good,' thought Caroline, 'but he doesn't know how I'll take it.' To give him time she reached up and began twining a spray of loose tendrils round its appropriate twig. Then Henry spoke.

"How would you like to leave Morton, Carrie?"

For an instant, under the shock, she stood perfectly motionless, her hands still above her head, her face hidden in the greenery. Then she dropped her hands and turned to stare at him. It was not, she knew, in Henry's nature to make idle remarks: but then neither was it in his nature to be so completely unexpected. Leave Morton!

"Well?"

"I've never thought about it," said Caroline blankly.

"Now that your mother's gone I suppose there's nothing to keep you here?"

"No," admitted Caroline. "I don't suppose there is—"

There was a long silence. She tried to think intelligently, to consider the advantages; but the notion was too completely astounding. It also struck her, looking at Henry again, that there was perhaps no need for her to consider anything.

"Henry!"

"Well?"

"Are we *going* to leave Morton?"

"Unless you've any very strong objection."

"Of course I haven't, if you—if you think it would be a good thing."

"I do. I think it would be a very good thing. You don't seem to realize, Carrie, that I'm a rich man."

It was quite true. She didn't realize it in the least. There was always plenty of housekeeping money, bills were paid on the nail: but the idea of their being rich—like people on the Common—had simply never occurred to her.

"If we moved anywhere in Morton," said Henry, as though answering her thought, "it would have to be on to the Common. If you'd rather do that, Carrie—"

"No, I wouldn't," said Caroline quickly.

"Nor would I. But we've got to move some time. We want a bigger house, and a car, and Leonard ought to go to a good school. I'd like him to go to Harrow."

"Harrow!" Caroline gasped. "But, Henry—would they have him?"

"Quite probably. You can get a boy in just now where you couldn't before the war—and where you won't be able to after. But he's thirteen, and it ought to be seen to. Then if he goes to Oxford or Cambridge—"

Caroline looked at her husband with something like awe. To her, as to most other inhabitants of Morton, Oxford and Cambridge meant simply the Boat Race; the idea of sending Leonard to one or other of them was like the idea of sending him to the Never-Never Land. But Henry was different: where others gaped and wondered, he *knew*. He'd probably written to the masters there already. . . .

An awful thought crossed Caroline's mind.

He'd probably—it would be just like him—he'd probably got the *house* already!

More tragically than she knew, Caroline looked up at her own back windows, so dingy and familiar, then round at the garden with its flourishing bean-rows. It was all very small, of course, and obviously unsuited to people with a son at Cambridge: but she *had* liked it, and she had lately liked the garden so—

"There's one thing you *will* like," said Henry complacently, "and that's the garden."

Caroline turned quickly back.

"Henry, have you *bought* the house?"

"Not yet. I want you to go and see it. If you don't like it, Carrie, of course that settles it. There's a garden going down to the river—"

"Where is it?"

In considerable detail, with a plan drawn on the back of an envelope, Henry told her. It was at Friar's Green, a small, charmingly rural pocket of Kingston, rather like Ham Common, but on the other side of the river. The house itself was called Friar's End; and that alone was sufficient to indicate its standing. It had been, in fact, the old manor house, and had eight bedrooms besides the servants'. The gardens were beautifully Lald out, with a boat-house and stabling. Besides an eighteenth-century exterior there was also modern plumbing and electric light.

The fortunate—or rather unfortunate—owner was an Honourable Mrs. Cornwallis—

"Shall I have to go and see *her*?" asked Caroline.

"Of course. You'd better *go* in a car. I'll get one from the Daimler Hire."

"*When*, Henry?"

"As a matter of fact," said Henry casually, "I said you'd probably go tomorrow."

II

There was no time even to get a new hat. Caroline had been meaning to buy one for weeks, had put it off from day to day, and now, when she really needed one to give her confidence, had only a Sunday toque that had never really suited her. But there was nothing to be done; the following morning, what with housework, getting lunch, and leaving the children's tea, was gone in a flash; and even after she had climbed into the car (with her gloves already on) she had to climb out again to fasten the back door.

"Can't you get out frontwards, Mother?" asked Leonard critically.

He was waiting, with Lily, to see her depart; and Caroline observed with annoyance that they both looked extremely amused. She straightened her toque, walked composedly through to the back door, and as soon as they were out of earshot of the chauffeur told them that they were very rude.

"But it *did* look funny," corroborated Lily. "It looked like a bear getting out. . . ."

She would have liked to box their ears. For once in her life she was thoroughly, irrationally put out. Yet perhaps her annoyance was prophetic, for in the years to come Caroline's habit of descending from a car backwards—she could never learn any other way—was to be the subject of constant, hopeless reprimands from the grown-up Leon and Lal.

III

Through Morton and its outskirts Caroline made herself small in a corner. She had no wish to be recognized in her new grandeur. At the turning into the High Street, Cousin Maggie Platt stood waiting to cross the road; Caroline shrank farther back still and ducked her head. She felt, without knowing why, that she was somehow making a fool of herself. On the other side of the glass panel the Daimler chauffeur sat moveless as a statue; but if he had suddenly turned round and winked at her she would not have been surprised. Already she was exercised over the question of tipping him: would Henry do it when he paid for the car, or should she do it herself at the end of the trip? Would it be a shilling, or half-a-crown, or nothing at all? He looked practically a gentleman: he had a dreadful limp and a whole row of ribbons. It was odd to think that perhaps out there in France he had been wearing a pair of the very boots that Henry made . . . and now the chauffeur had a limp and Henry was going to have a house!

Caroline shifted against the cushions. It must be all right, because Henry said so. No one could be more patriotic than Henry. He was working himself almost to death: if the war went on much longer his health would be permanently damaged. It *was* damaged already: morally speaking he had as much right to a wound stripe as any one. Caroline looked at the chauffeur again and felt a great desire to ask whether his boots had been good. . . .

They were now approaching Kingston, and a glimpse of Ham Common recalled Caroline's wandering thoughts. It struck her as extremely pretty, but a great change after Morton. The minutes sped by. Kingston—which was very like Morton indeed—held them a moment with its traffic, then they were over the bridge and hastening towards Friar's Green. A bend in the road brought them plump upon it: the green itself, a white-railed duck pond, a small grey spire rising unobtrusively among trees. On three sides of the green square were cottages in rows, small houses, and a few shops; the fourth side, the one backing on to the river, showed only a stretch of old brick wall with trees behind. Behind the trees rose a group of white chimneys; and these were the chimneys of Friar's End.

IV

At the wide porch a butler came out to meet them. His manner was perfectly deferential, but Caroline, as she got out backwards, felt sure he guessed that the car was hired.

She announced herself, rather self-consciously, as Mrs. Henry Smith, and he replied that Mrs. Cornwallis was expecting her. To Caroline, following him through a wide shabby hall, the whole episode was beginning to feel like a nightmare. She was intensely conscious of herself—of her dress, her voice, the way she placed her feet. She felt like a cook-general going to be interviewed.

"Mrs. Henry Smith," said the butler contemptuously.

Caroline advanced from behind him, and found herself in a long drawing-room, shabby as the hall, but beautifully lit by three tall windows. Beside one of these stood a tall thin gentlewoman in a black dress. She bowed stiffly: she was the Honorable Mrs. Cornwallis; and Caroline, who had been preparing to shake hands, had to cover the movement by taking out a handkerchief. In her agitation she produced also two tram tickets and a bottle of eucalyptus. The whole episode was mortifying in the extreme.

"You've come to see the house," stated Mrs. Cornwallis.

"If it isn't too much trouble," said Caroline nervously. And she meant it: if it *were* too much trouble she was quite prepared, at the slightest hint, to get into her car and drive away, and never come back again. If only she could!

"Would you like some tea first?"

Caroline hastily refused, adding, in her confusion, that she had had it already. It was a foolish thing to say, since the time was only half-past three; but this remark, like practically every other Caroline made, Mrs. Cornwallis ignored. Slightly indicating that this was the drawing-room, she led the way out into the hall, displayed the dining-room on one side, the morning-room on the other, and so through to the kitchen and pantries. Here Caroline felt a stirring at once of pleasure and apprehension; they were beautiful and beautifully kept, but very large. They seemed designed to house at least four or five servants, though only one—an elderly cook—was at present visible. Like the butler, she looked faintly contemptuous. . . .

"This is the housekeeper's room."

Caroline glanced in and saw a small square apartment about the size of the dining-room in Cleveland Road. To her relief the housekeeper was not there, and she was able to look round. On the mantelpiece, conspicuous among a variety of groups and snapshots, were two large photographs in khaki frames. One showed a man of about fifty, the other a boy of nineteen; both were in uniform and across the corner of each frame was a broad crepe band. Mrs. Cornwallis was looking at them too: she did not speak: and at once Caroline knew that they were her husband and son.

They left the servants' quarters and went upstairs. They inspected the eight bedrooms, the two bathrooms, and turned into a short corridor whose windows looked north. Its rooms accordingly faced south, and would have a pleasant view over the garden and river.

"The nursery and night nursery," said Mrs. Cornwallis.

She did not offer to go in, and Caroline, understanding, nodded and passed on. It was getting worse and worse. She began to feel as though she were taking this woman's home by force, thrusting her out with a handful of money, yet no doubt (looking at the thing reasonably), Mrs. Cornwallis was glad to go: very glad indeed to be getting rid of a house ten times too large for her, and where she could have nothing but sorrowful memories. It was not, thought Caroline, trying to comfort herself, as though that boy had been married; he looked far too young, scarcely out of school; there were no grandchildren to be robbed of their garden. But the thought was less comforting than she hoped, and she was glad to go downstairs again. Mrs. Cornwallis led the way back to the drawing-room, and, inviting Caroline to sit down, took out a small sheet of notes.

"About the staff, Mrs. Smith. Should you bring your own servants with you?"

"No," said Caroline without thinking; and then she did think of the horribly superior cook, of the openly contemptuous butler, and realized with dismay that this woman wanted her to keep them on. It was dreadful; but there was a look—almost an appeal—in Mrs. Cornwallis's eye that she could not rebuff. She took the plunge.

"Would—do you think any of yours would mind staying on?"

"Except the housekeeper, who comes with me, I think they would certainly stay," said Mrs. Cornwallis decisively. "I can also recommend them. At present I have Hilton, Mrs. Dowing—the cook—and two girls, both very young but quite capable. A properly trained parlourmaid seems to be a thing of the past."

Caroline nodded. Servants *were* difficult to get; in a way she was fortunate. She said quite calmly,

"If we do come, I should be glad to keep them all."

For the first time Mrs. Cornwallis smiled.

"Both Hilton and Mrs. Dowing are elderly, of course, but by no means decrepit. You'll find them thoroughly good servants. They wished to stay here, and I'm glad it's possible." She looked at her notes again. "Mr. Smith, I believe, considered buying the house with its furniture, but said he would leave the final decision to you. Perhaps you would like to let me know about it."

Caroline gazed round the room in alarm. It was full of what looked to her like extremely valuable pieces. There was an ormolu cabinet, a lacquer chest, a large oil-painting of stags by a pool. Where on earth was all the money coming from? Surely, surely it would be better to discuss things again with Henry first?

Mrs. Cornwallis followed and misinterpreted her look.

"There are a few things, of course, that I should want to take with me; but I can let you have a list. No doubt I shall be hearing from your husband in a day or two?"

The question, so politely dismissive, brought Caroline thankfully to her feet. She was only too glad to go. Promising that Henry should communicate immediately, that Hilton and Mrs. Dowing should receive every consideration, she followed her hostess out into the hall. For all pretense had now been dropped; both women knew that Friar's End was already as good as sold, that Caroline, not Mrs. Cornwallis, was already its rightful mistress. She had only to say, 'Go today, for I wish to move in tomorrow' and Mrs. Cornwallis would go. As this knowledge, with all its bewildering implications, suddenly rushed through her mind, Caroline unwittingly halted in the middle of the hall.

"I am so sorry!" said Caroline impulsively.

The next moment she could have sunk through the floor. For there was an awful silence, a terrible ear-burning pause, before Mrs. Cornwallis, by a brief farewell, showed that this solecism too would be politely ignored.

V

In the car Caroline shut her eyes and tried to doze. She was too tired to think, too tired to look out of the window; she was as tired as if she had done a three weeks' wash. The thought of Friar's End was like a heavy burden; presently no doubt she would get used to it, might even, with time, cease to feel it at all. And for Henry at least, without waiting on time or anything else, there must be every sign of delighted anticipation—

Half-collapsed in the corner of the car, Caroline rehearsed her pleasure. She would praise the drawing-room, and the furniture, and the wing that faced south, and the convenience of keeping Mrs. Dowing. She would praise Friar's End itself, and the reasonable distance from both Morton and Town. There was something else to be praised, but she could not think what it was. For a moment she puzzled, then gave it up; being too tired even to remember that she had never looked at the garden.

PART III

CHAPTER I

I

A MONTH passed, and Caroline was no longer Mrs. Smith of 60 Cleveland Road, but Mrs. Henry Smith of Friar's Green; or rather that was now the name on her visiting cards; but she was not yet really convinced by it. It was like (reflected Caroline) being married to Henry all over again; only instead of being Carrie Chase allowed to go on a holiday with Henry Smith, she was now Mrs. Smith being allowed to inhabit the house of Mrs. Cornwallis. There was the same feeling of unreality, the same sense of being an inexpert but surprisingly successful impostor. She wouldn't have been in the least surprised if one day Mrs. Cornwallis had come back and turned them all out. . . .

As far as possible she kept to what she believed to have been her predecessor's ways, accepting without comment a routine which included baths every day (instead of once a week) and dinner at eight o'clock instead of supper at seven-thirty. To her inherited staff she made only one addition—a garden boy of fifteen, strong, good-humoured, too phlegmatic to hanker after munition-making. He was badly needed; the grounds at Friar's End were large, elaborate, and had for the last three years been in the sole charge of one sexagenarian gardener. He had concentrated on the lawns and knot-garden and let the rest go; but with the help of a good strong lad, he told Caroline, everything would soon be in order again. And that was all he did tell her, having obviously no intention of asking or taking anyone else's advice. When Caroline spoke to him he feigned deafness; when she gave him a written list of roses he simply turned the paper over and made a list of his own on the other side. He was as stubborn as a mule and twice as bad-tempered, and after the third abortive interview Caroline gave him up in despair.

On the whole, however, things were less bad than she expected. She soon got over her fear of the cook, and the fear of the butler lasted only a little longer. For Hilton—perhaps because like Caroline herself he had expected something worse—not only tolerated but approved of her. Caroline felt it and was grateful, and also surprised. She had never seen herself objectively, she knew that she was slow and dowdy, but not that she was dignified. As a girl she had wanted to be clever, but that dream was past, and it was now with a feeling of secret vanity that she considered herself not stupid. As for wisdom, that was something in the Bible—an attribute of the Almighty—and if she had been asked to name the wise upon earth her list would probably have stopped short at Queen Victoria and the Archbishop of Canterbury. Still—'I'm doing very well,' thought Caroline every now and again; and having set her new house in order turned diffidently but courageously to her new neighbours.

II

The society of Friar's Green was not large. It comprised a doctor, a parson, a middle-aged landscape-painter R.A., and two maiden ladies who bred Golden Labradors, all of whom Caroline saw in church the first Sunday morning. Their aspect was reassuring; they looked just like people in Morton. Also as in Morton, there was a working party at the Vicarage, where Caroline was soon spending three afternoons a week and paying the usual fourpence for her tea. Here indeed the air blew at first a little coldly; she was aware—not of antagonism—but of a critical, still charitably suspended judgment which was nevertheless predisposed to come down heavily on the wrong side. She was the New Rich. She was the wealthy Mrs. Smith—how extraordinary it seemed to her!—who had stepped into Mrs. Cornwallis's shoes. That she wore them at all was a misdemeanor; if she trod in them too proudly— or if with an affected humility—on would go the black cap. All this Caroline felt as the Vicar's wife first came forward to greet her: she saw the Labrador spinsters politely aloof, the Doctor's wife faintly smiling, at the other end of the table women from the cottages looking curiously over their work. Caroline smiled, sat, and accepted wool for a pair of bedsocks. When the talk turned on the inefficiency of the old sewing-machine she resisted the impulse to offer a new one; as she had previously resisted impulses to buy a Golden Labrador from the Misses Brodrick and a land-scape from the R.A. But she promised flowers for the church, and offered the use of her garden and boat-house to such Boy Scouts as wished to practice life-saving. By the end of the afternoon the Vicar's wife at least had lost her constraint. She promised to call the next day; and though this in a sense was unnecessary, Caroline did not dissuade her. There was a good deal she wanted to say and the Vicar's wife seemed the right person to say it to.

"First of all," began Caroline—she had been rehearsing the speech all day—"I want you to let me know all that Mrs. Cornwallis did for the village and in the church, and how much of it I can do instead. It's not"—in spite of herself she flushed a little—"it's not that I want to—to take her place; but I don't want Friar's Green to lose by our coming. I could see at the working party—"

"Oh, no!" cried the Vicar's wife rashly.

"Not you," said Caroline, "but it's only natural. So I want you to tell me things."

The Vicar's wife looked slightly embarrassed.

"As far as Mrs. Cornwallis is concerned—she had a pew of course—"

("I'm Chapel, really," put in Caroline frankly.)

"—but, apart from that I don't think she did anything at all."

The statement seemed to take them both by surprise—Caroline because she had expected something so different, the Vicar's wife because she had never before put it into words.

"Well!" said Caroline.

"She once lent the gardens for a treat, but the children broke a rose-bush. She wasn't by any means a Lady Bountiful. In fact she wasn't an agreeable woman at all." The Vicar's wife checked herself: but it was such a luxury to her to speak ill of any one, and especially of a parishioner, that she could not resist going just one step farther. "In fact, Mrs. Smith, the first time my husband called here, he was kept waiting in the gun-room for over twenty minutes!"

"Well!" said Caroline again. "When was that?"

"In 1910. She's had her troubles, poor woman, so one mustn't think hardly of her; but I hope that wherever she's going they won't expect too much . . . amiability." Mrs. Moore sniffed—one genuine, enjoyable, scandal-mongering sniff; then guilt overwhelmed her, her holiday was done, she was back in the mantle of the Vicar's wife. "The rest of the people here," said Mrs. Moore firmly, "are all very nice indeed."

III

Such was Friar's Green. The nearest big house, about a couple of miles away, was Tregarthan Court, where an elderly Lady Tregarthan, widowed of her baronet, still kept up a certain shabby state. To Caroline this seemed a piece of sheerest ill-luck, and she lived hoping against hope that a baronet's widow might be too proud to call; but Henry, when she mentioned the matter, took an opposite view.

"Of course she'll call," he said curtly. "Why on earth shouldn't she?"

"Well, we're not—we're not exactly her class, are we, Henry?"

"We're anybody's class in England—except perhaps dukes. You don't realize, Carrie—" He broke off, queerly baffled by her calm and attentive gaze. *"What money can do"* he had been going to say; but something restrained him. "Anyway, if *we're* not," he said abruptly, "the children will be."

The children! They were taking to the new life like ducks to water. They had shown no bewilderment, scarcely any surprise. They played in the garden, raced down the nursery corridor, as though—as though the place belonged to them. Leonard was to go to school in the spring; in the meantime he was being coached by the Vicar, two hours every morning, and picking up social acquirements right and left. It was he who negotiated the purchase of a Labrador, and he who initiated the riding lessons. Lily followed in his wake, shyer, quieter, but in the end with equal facility. She too was to go to boarding-school, a decision which had cost Caroline some heart-searching; but Henry was anxious for it, he said the child would make nice friends, and Lily herself showed so much eagerness that Caroline was quite upset. It seemed, to her ideas, positively unnatural; would *she*, at that age, have wished to go away from her mother for eight months of the year? And faced by this question, trying to think back to herself as eleven-year-old Carrie Chase, Caroline had the first inkling of how tremendous an abyss, how bridgeless a gulf can separate two generations. 'But I wasn't so different from *my* mother!' she thought. 'She wouldn't have let me go, and I wouldn't have wanted to leave her.' And now in letting Lily and Henry have their way, was she being wiser than her mother, or more foolish? It would be a bad lookout if the latter, thought Caroline apprehensively; for as she looked ahead, trying to plot out—as she had so often and so easily done before—her children's careers, it seemed as though all her old guides and landmarks were suddenly become useless. She could not see at all clearly. She had lost confidence. Their futures would undoubtedly be brilliant, but she could not help wishing—just now and again, particularly at night—that they were all safely back at the house in Cleveland Road.

IV

After a silence of nearly a year, Ellen Watts began to write. She wrote about once a month, in very pale ink, and the burden of her letters was ever the same. One or other of the Whiners was in need of country air; or she herself needed country air; or she herself and the whole three of them were all in need of country air together. Caroline read these letters with a troubled heart. As far as she hated any one, she hated Ellen Watts; yet Ellen was poor, she was a widow, the three children were genuinely delicate. In the face of her own fortunate circumstances, Caroline felt it her obvious duty to invite them all for at least a week; and though her spirits sank at the thought, she fixed the date for the first of June. Before posting the letter, however, she naturally told Henry; and Henry put his foot down.

Caroline was so much relieved, and so much ashamed of herself for being so relieved, that she at once began to plead for them.

"You'd never even see them, Henry. You wouldn't know they were here. And I'm sure I don't know how Ellen manages."

"She manages very nicely. She gets a pension and allowances for the kids, and last year Mrs. Platt took them to Margate. Unless it makes you really miserable, Carrie, I won't have them."

"I shouldn't be *miserable*," said Caroline, with something less than complete honesty.

"Then that settles it," said Henry; and Caroline wrote a very nice letter, enclosing postal orders for the children, but making no mention of the summer holidays. There was another subject she did not mention, a subject quite foolishly near her heart; she wanted to ask whether any one—either a new tenant, or the people next door—had finished off the runner beans; but on second thoughts dignity prevailed, and the folly died without written evidence.

CHAPTER II

I

THE day Lady Tregarthan called Caroline had been cleaning silver.

Cleaning silver, of course, was now none of her business; the maids did it, and very well too; but it was an occupation Caroline enjoyed, and with a certain stubbornness she set aside a random collection of ornaments, dubbed them valuable, and announced that she would do them herself. That she had been doing them at half-past four, just before tea, was another relic of her Morton past, when silver, like fine mending, was a pleasant afternoon relaxation; and thus it happened that Lady Tregarthan, being ushered towards the drawing-room door, met her hostess similarly bound but carrying a large tray of glittering bric-a-brac.

"Lady Tregarthan, madam," said Hilton sternly.

"Oh!" said Caroline. "Do come in and sit down." She still held on to the tray, in spite of Hilton's tentative gesture to relieve her, and as Lady Tregarthan passed, a faint smear of plate powder brushed off on her jacket. Caroline determined not to mention it—at any rate not just yet.

"I see you've been cleaning silver," said Lady Tregarthan loudly. "If I'd known I'd have come earlier and lent you a hand."

"Well!" said Caroline, quite struck. "Do you like it too?"

"Love it," said Lady Tregarthan. "When I was a small child I used to be allowed, as a Saturday treat, to clean the tops of my mother's scent bottles. That was how *we* were brought up. Now my married daughter lives in an American service flat."

Caroline listened with amazement; for Lady Tregarthan, she knew, came of one of the best (though most impoverished) families. And behind her surprise stirred something more agreeable still: a faint heavenly reassurance, as though in a strange and hazardous country she had suddenly caught the sound of her own tongue. . . .

The entrance of Hilton with tea put her once more in motion. She hastily replaced the ornaments, took off her gloves and apron, and gave them to Hilton to take away. It seemed too late, however, for shaking hands, so Caroline at once sat down by the table.

"China or Indian?" she asked, prompted by the sight of two tea-pots. (Hilton was a martinet in the house, but he had his qualities.)

"Indian," said Lady Tregarthan promptly, thus administering another shock.

"So do I," said Caroline. She swished the tea round in the pot and poured it out good and strong. "China's got no taste."

"Disgusting wish-wash," agreed Lady Tregarthan heartily.

They were getting on well; they got on better and better. They talked about servants, and rations, and the war and their children.

Caroline told her all about Lily and Leonard, and Lady Tregarthan listened with genuine interest. Then it was Lady Tregarthan's turn: she had no sons, for which she confessed she was now sometimes thankful, but she had a married daughter (also it seemed, a Lady like her mother), who lived mostly in London, but was at present staying at the Court owing to a slight indisposition. At those last words Caroline looked up inquiringly, but the visitor shook her head.

"No," said Lady Tregarthan grimly. "I only wish it were."

"How long have they been married?"

"Six years, my dear. I don't know what they think they're doing. James is with his regiment, of course, but what," asked Lady Tregarthan practically, "do they get all these forty-eight-hour leaves for?"

"It does seem a pity," agreed Caroline sincerely.

"Pity! It's sheer selfishness! There won't be another Tregarthan—I suppose that's *my* fault—and if they don't look out there won't be another Westcott. Marion doesn't care; she's what they call artistic; which as far as I can see means running around with Dago picture-framers, when she ought to be doing her duty." Lady Tregarthan slapped down her cup so that the china rattled. "How old did you say your girl was? Eleven. Then have her presented the moment she's eighteen, my dear, and get her married the next year. Then they don't have time to get ideas into their heads."

Caroline listened in a positive flutter. Lily presented! Lily in a white frock, and Prince of Wales's feathers! Whoever heard of such an idea! And yet here was Lady Tregarthan just throwing it into the conversation as though it were the most natural thing in the world. 'I suppose it *is* for her,' reflected Caroline. 'I daresay she'd manage it, if we asked her. But whatever will Henry say?'

The astounding visitor was taking her leave. Caroline got up and forgetting to ring for Hilton went out with her into the hall. They were already almost intimate; under a hundred superficial differences each had recognized and acknowledged in the other one of her own sort.

"You must bring your daughter to see me," invited Lady Tregarthan. "She'll find it remarkably dull, but that won't hurt her. If Marion's still down they can play tennis."

"We'd love to," said Caroline. "What day?"

For no reason at all Lady Tregarthan laughed. It was a queer, throaty, clucking noise, as though you had suddenly disturbed a very old hen.

"Thursday. Thursday at half-past four. I won't ask your boy, they're always a nuisance. You're sending him to school, I suppose?"

Caroline nodded. She wanted badly to say 'Harrow,' but as always the name made her slightly self-conscious.

"Best place for him," said Lady Tregarthan, and on foot as she had come, stumped purposefully down the drive.

Caroline did not immediately go in. It was a fine day, the sun beat pleasantly on her face, and she was also savoring, for almost the first time in her life, the sweets of a social success. For the visit had gone off admirably: it had been even enjoyable, so that she actually looked forward with pleasure to her return call. . . .

'I *am* doing well,' thought Caroline.

She liked Lady Tregarthan very much indeed. She liked her looks, her manners, her sound and practical good sense. It was a great pity, thought Caroline, that she had no son. Lily might have married him.

II

And what of Henry, what of the master of the house, the father of a boy who would soon be at Harrow and a daughter who in seven years' time might have been presented at Court? How was he enjoying life at Friar's End?

So Caroline often asked herself; and the answer was unexpectedly simple. To all practical purposes, he did not live there at all. He slept there, and had breakfast there, and on fine Sunday afternoons took tea under the cedar; but Caroline never really felt that he inhabited the same house with her. Their removal to Friar's End was the great achievement of Henry's life; yet, having once accomplished it, his heart seemed to turn more and more to Morton. When the car came round in the mornings he went out to it with alacrity: at night, descending, his habitual fatigue lent him an air almost of reluctance. He was tired out, of course: it would often be nine or ten at night, he would have dined on goodness knew what scraps of sandwiches; but there was never any sign of that relaxation, that thankful content, which a man should feel (thought Caroline) on getting back to his home. He came back to Friar's End for a night's lodging; and his nights were as short as possible.

It was not that he did not take an interest in the place. He liked, in the half hour before he was asleep, to hear Caroline talk about her neighbours and her subscriptions and the working parties at the Vicarage. He liked especially to hear about the Tregarthans. He took a silent but obvious pleasure in the fact that she had been accepted, and was even becoming in a mild way popular, as the chatelaine of Friar's End. As for Caroline, she clung to and fostered these brief, late-at-night conversations with all her might: they seemed the last link not only with the old life at Morton, but also with Henry himself. She had often read in books from the circulating library how sudden riches drove husband and wife apart: and though Henry had no devoted female secretary, and she herself knew no penniless viscounts, she felt she could quite see how it happened. Already two-thirds of Henry's life was unfamiliar to her. For though she told him in detail of all that happened at Friar's End, Henry did not speak in return of affairs at the factory. No doubt he wanted to rest his mind from it; but Caroline, who knew herself to be stupid on such topics, would have been quite content to hear, for instance, a word or two about the new canteen. . . . On one occasion she even questioned him.

"Is the canteen finished yet, Henry?"

"What canteen?"

"The new one. The one for the girls."

"That!" Henry turned back to the basin—he was just going to bed—and continued washing his hands. "It was finished three months ago."

"Is it—is it nice?"

"The girls seem to like it. It's all over yellow paint."

"Who chose it?"

"One of the welfare women. She saw to the whole thing. How are the Tregarthans?"

But for once Caroline persisted. She had in her mind a certain notion—a notion relating to those girls, and to that canteen, and to the welfare work in general, which she had long wished to lay before him, and though the opportunity was not good she might never have a better.

"Henry, you know all this welfare work—"

"And a proper nuisance it is," said Henry, reaching for the towel.

"I'm sure they mean well." Caroline frowned doubtfully; in whatever concerned the works Henry was, of course, right; but she could not help feeling that if Lily, for instance, ever had to work in a factory, it would be a great comfort to know that there was some nice motherly woman keeping an eye on her. For the moment, however, Caroline did not argue, but slightly shifted ground.

"I was thinking more of the canteen, Henry. I was wondering whether, as your wife, I oughtn't to have had something to do with it."

He looked at her in surprise.

"You didn't want to open it, Carrie? You could have, of course, only they were using one end before the other end was finished. If I'd thought—"

Caroline flushed.

"Of course I didn't! I'm not Cousin Maggie! But the china and pots and things, I *could* have helped with, and the welfare work I could still." She stopped: Henry's look, his next remark, was by no means promising.

"I should have thought you'd enough to do here. You always seem pretty busy."

"I am. It isn't that at all, Henry."

"If you must do something, why not send a—a dinner-set?"

"But they'll have a dinner-set already. They must have."

"Flower-pots, then. Though I don't know who'd look after them." He walked over to the windows, still with the towel in his hand, and twitched back a blind; he stood with his back to her staring over the garden. Automatically—mindful of air-raids—Caroline reached out to the switch: and for some moments they were both silent, as though the cutting off of the light had also cut off their conversation.

"Henry!" said Caroline softly.

He did not hear. It felt odd, sitting there in the darkness. She looked at her husband's back, dark against the square of the sky, and was vaguely troubled by a likeness she could not seize, by a flitting memory that hovered just out of reach. There had been another shadowy room, another man silhouetted at the window . . . and a garden outside that fell in three terraces. She was just beginning to remember when Henry turned.

"Aren't you happy here, Carrie?"

The words so shocked her that for a moment she could not speak. Not happy! Not happy with all that Henry had given her, with that house and the garden and Leonard and Lily! Why, it would be wicked not to be happy! 'I *am* wicked!' she accused herself. 'I'm wicked not to be more grateful, not to make him *see* how happy I am!' And then quickly—quickly!—the words tumbled out, any words that rose to her lips, so long as they expressed gratitude and tenderness and cheerful contented pride. . . . It never entered her head to examine the question calmly and give a truthful answer; it was not truth she was concerned with, but Henry's feelings. She had unwittingly wounded him; and there was nothing in her head or her heart but self-reproach and the desire to make whole again. She had left the bed and was standing beside him, her arm thrust through his, her shoulder pressing close. Foolishly enough, he still held the towel: he was a man ridiculous in shirt sleeves, with loosened collar and a dangling tie: but Caroline did not see him so. "Henry!" she repeated urgently—"Henry, dear!"—and then at last his head came round, and he was looking down at her with his usual veiled and unemotional glance.

"That's all right, Carrie." He put up his arm, held her a moment clumsily round the shoulders. He went back into the room and got on with his undressing.

III

The next morning Caroline went as far as Kingston and dispatched to Mathieson-Smith's one dozen green china flower vases and three dozen bunches of yellow immortelles. The conjunction was so pleasing that she bought two extra vases and six extra bunches for her own use. She put them on the morning-room mantelpiece, and there they remained until one day Lal came home from school, and threw them indignantly away.

IV

On the Thursday afternoon Caroline in her best frock, accompanied by Lily in starched muslin, set out to return the Tregarthan call. The car had taken Henry to Morton, and Caroline was not entirely regretful: had it been there at hand she would inevitably have been torn between respect for Lady Tregarthan (impelling her to use it) and dread of ostentation (since the distance was so short). As it was, they went on foot, dusted their shoes at the Court gates on a handful of dock leaves, and neither the butler or their hostess thought them a penny the worse.

"Don't go through the house!" called Lady Tregarthan, rising sudden as a partridge from the herbaceous border. "We're having tea on the lawn, and it's just round that hedge. This your daughter? Take off your hat, child, and let's have a look at you."

Obediently—'Thank goodness!' thought Caroline—Lily removed her wide-brimmed straw and held it between cotton-gloved fingers.

"Lanky, ain't she?" commented Lady Tregarthan. "Doesn't take after you, my dear. You can do without those gloves too, if you like. Now we'll go and find Marion."

The Smiths followed, they skirted the box hedge and found a wide lawn, bigger than the one at Friar's End, with two mulberry-trees and under them a tea-table. Beside it, in a green and white hammock, swung the most elegant creature Caroline had ever seen—tall, slim, short-haired, showing unbelievable lengths of unbelievably slender leg. This was Lady Westcott, Lady Tregarthan's married daughter; and Lily, it was plain, adored her at sight.

"My daughter Marion," said Lady Tregarthan; and the daughter raised herself delicately on her pillows and slid a foot to the ground.

"No, please!" begged Caroline, hurrying forward; for the lady, without doubt, was barely convalescent. If only they had thought, they might have brought her a bunch of grapes. . . .

"Get up at once, Marion, and stop shamming!" rapped Lady Tregarthan.

Caroline looked on in surprise, for as soon as Lady Westcott was on her feet she became lithe, alert, full of spring and vitality. She was another, though a slightly resentful person. And she was also immediately and completely aware of Lily's adoration.

"Do you play tennis?"

Lily shook her head. She was too fascinated to speak.

"I'll teach you. After tea. You'll have to play in your stockings."

"The grass—" began Caroline faintly.

"Dry as a bone," said Lady Tregarthan.

"Might as well be cement," added Lady Westcott.

All through tea—forgetful even of the fact that she was conversing with two ladies of title at once—Caroline listened fascinated to the contrast and similarity between those two voices. For the voices, at bottom, were precisely alike; both women had the same manner of speaking, in short dogmatic sentences that seemed to brook no denial; but whereas each word of the mother's came out curt and energetic, the daughter's dropped languidly, almost in a whisper, from that corner of her mouth unoccupied by a cigarette. One seemed to speak so from an abundance of vitality, the other from an almost complete lack of it; and yet the mother was sixty, and the daughter twenty-seven. 'I'm sure there is something amiss with her!' thought Caroline in bewilderment; and she made up her mind, with maternal irrelevance, that Lily should drink at least two glasses of milk a day.

"Did you enjoy the tennis?" she asked, as they were walking-home.

"Yes," said Lily. But she was not communicative. She was in fact so unusually silent that Caroline at last enquired whether she had a headache. Rather surprisingly—for Lily never as a rule admitted to indisposition—the child at once replied that she had.

"I think it's my hair," she added pathetically. "There's so *much* of it."

Caroline looked round in surprise. Lily's bobbed hair, though soft, was certainly very thick; but it couldn't well be shorter. Lily sighed.

"Couldn't I have it a fringe, Mother?"

Then Caroline remembered that Lady Westcott's hair, blonde, waved, flat as a pancake, was cut ruler-straight on a level with her eyebrows.

"Certainly not," said Caroline firmly.

CHAPTER III

I

HENRY now had a secretary.

His name was Eustace Jamieson, he had been to London University, and he treated Caroline, whenever he came down to Friar's End, with such extreme deference that he made her quite nervous. But she was glad, all the same, that Henry had not got one of the new, brightly efficient young women whose brightness and efficiency was one of the most familiar wartime phenomena. There seemed to be hundreds of them—hundreds, thousands, as many as were wanted—and yet until the war claimed them the vast majority had no doubt been living at home with their mothers, doing the flowers every Tuesday and Friday, and taking suburban dogs for walks on the Common. Now they drove cars, ran offices, secretaried the great, and in general kept the business system of the country swinging briskly along. Caroline admired them very much, but she was glad when Henry came home with Eustace. Before long she had determined to make use of him.

She had a secret project, a project hidden even from Henry, which for some months had been slowly forming in her mind. Eustace was to be her instrument. That he might refuse so to lend himself never even occurred to her; but she did feel, when the subject came to be broached, a certain embarrassment. For as Henry's wife, her position was delicate.

She got Mr. Jamieson to herself on a Sunday evening between tea and supper, and since he was not doing anything for Henry—he was engaged, in fact, with a book of poetry—she had no hesitation in interrupting him.

"Mr. Jamieson, I want you to do something for me."

He looked at once pleased, surprised, and slightly apprehensive.

"Of course, Mrs. Smith. Anything I can. . . ."

The silence prolonged itself uncomfortably. Eustace shut his book, using a tram ticket as marker, and waited for her instructions. 'He'll think I'm mad!' thought Caroline uneasily; but she was determined not to retreat.

"I want"—Caroline drew a deep breath—"I want you to get me a pair of boots."

"*Boots*, Mrs. Smith?"

He looked idiotically at her feet, and she felt an unreasonable desire to box his ears.

"Yes, boots, Mr. Jamieson. From the factory. Just an ordinary pair of boots, as they're ready to be sent out."

"But why—?"

He checked himself.

"You mean," said Caroline, flushing, "you mean 'Why don't I ask my husband?' I don't want to bother him. In fact I—I don't want him to know anything about it."

It was out. The worst was over. Even if the young man did think her mad he would hardly tell Henry; or would he? He was very conscientious. Caroline could just see him making a neat typewritten report headed 'State of Mrs. Smith's mind.' 'I'm being ridiculous!' she told herself; and indeed her involuntary smile, or else her habitual sanity, had evidently reassured him. He said quite cheerfully,

"As it happens there's a pair in the house now—new type of sole, new laces—ready to go up to the War Office. If you'll wait here, Mrs. Smith, I'll just slip out and fetch them."

Caroline hesitated: the suggestion was so eminently sensible that she could hardly refuse: and yet—and yet—it wouldn't suit her at all. For the mainspring of her action was nothing less than a dreadful suspicion of her own husband. Or rather she did not really *suspect*, she just wanted to have her mind at rest. For she had heard things . . . about boots with paper soles . . . and in that case what would be the use of samples? They would be sure to be all right. But she could not share these suspicions with Eustace Jamieson: they must remain locked and shameful in her bosom until finally thrown out by—by actual proof to the contrary. What could she do? Should she pretend she wanted to get a model of them cast in silver to commemorate Henry's war-work? Or that she wanted to sleep with them under her pillow, to bring good luck to the troops? 'If only women hadn't taken to being reasonable!' thought Caroline. 'If I were a kittenish little thing in a crinoline— or even in a bustle—he'd just put it down to playfulness—' She said desperately,

"No, don't do that. I don't want samples. I want just one pair as it comes straight off the bench. *Any* pair. You can get me one, can't you?"

"Should you be sending them back?" asked Mr. Jamieson.

"No, they wouldn't be any good," said Caroline incautiously. "I want them to keep. Now please, Mr. Jamieson, don't ask questions, but just do as I ask. I know you think I'm being silly—"

"Not at all," said Mr. Jamieson.

But he evidently did. He thought she wanted to preserve them as a souvenir, wrapped in tissue paper, in a bottom drawer with a lock of Lily's hair. He thought she was being very silly indeed: so that was all right.

II

Three days later, artfully disguised as a parcel of wool, the boots arrived. Caroline took them out to the tool-shed, and there waylaying the garden boy instructed him to wear them constantly until further notice. Luckily they were about the right size, and he was not particular. To make the test quite fair she also gave him two pairs of Army socks. After that she concealed his bicycle by locking it in an outhouse, and had nothing more to do but await results.

About once a week, as he was kneeling by a flower-bed, she came up behind and inspected the soles. They bore her scrutiny well. At the end of two months they showed hardly a sign of wear. At the end of three, with a light heart and quiet mind, she unlocked the outhouse and left the door ajar. This last act was a great relief to her, for she had been several times called upon for wonder and sympathy over the bicycle's disappearance; and was indeed even now forced to go and look at the outhouse with a display of astonishment.

"Well, I never!" said Caroline, shaking her head; and was surprised to feel, along with the proper guiltiness, a faint but undeniable stirring of something remarkably like conceit.

III

So now her spirit was at rest, her wicked suspicions were forever stilled. She could not believe she had ever harboured them. She was quite sure she had not; yet at the same time she felt a faint regret that the experiment had not been made sooner. For August and September had already gone by, October was a month of rejoicing; and on November the eleventh all troubles rolled away with the last sound of the firing. There was nothing left to worry about, scarcely anything to pray for, for the war to end wars was over, and no one would ever fight again.

In the Friar's Green church they rang the bells even while the Vicar was preaching. He preached on peace and goodwill, and the mighty works of the Lord, and said they mustn't hang the Kaiser. Caroline did not mind, she liked the sermon very much indeed; but there were some who considered that the Lord was being given too much credit. "Mighty works of the infantryman!" ejaculated the Doctor quite audibly; and the Vicar stopped and leaned over the pulpit. "But he *is* a work of the Lord," said the Vicar. "Probably the mightiest . . ."

As soon as she could Caroline walked back to Friar's End to ring up Henry. His voice sounded just as usual, but hers, as his first words showed, evidently did not.

"Been having a good cry, Carrie?"

"Yes, I have," said Caroline defiantly. "Are you shutting the works?"

"They've shut themselves. I'll be home for tea."

"Why can't you come now?"

"I'm trying to change a layout—advertisement—for the papers. Got to get 'Victory' in somewhere. What about 'Victory Brogues,' Carrie? and some flags?"

"Flags!" said Caroline. "That's just what we *do* want. Can you bring a Union Jack, Henry—a big one—and some of the Allies'?"

She heard him grunt, then the voice of Eustace, and Eustace taking over the receiver.

"Flags, Mrs. Smith? Certainly. Large Union Jacks, smaller flags of Allies. What about fireworks?"

The very thing! The very antithesis of restrictions and air-raids! They could be let off on the lawn, too, where all the children would see. . . .

"A whole lot," ordered Caroline.

She hung up the receiver and sat a moment with closed eyes. The first excitement had passed, leaving her even a little flat. It was all over.

"It's over!" said Caroline aloud.

Her head felt curiously light and clear, as though some background of accustomed sound—wearying, stupefying, but no longer consciously noticed—had suddenly come to an end. And there had been a picture as well, a picture of a white hill; but when Caroline tried to look at it, to take it out as it were, and triumph over the shape of darkness—when she sought for it in her memory, and under her closed lids—the hill had dwindled away and vanished, like a small heap of snow.

IV

The years of peace went faster than the years of war. The Smiths were established; they were the Smiths of Friar's End. Caroline was even that nice Mrs. Smith, the great friend of Lady Tregarthan, and patroness—in a mild, unobjectionable way—of Friar's Green. People liked her, and if they did not like Henry too it was because they scarcely ever saw him. He was certainly more at home, for though Mathieson-Smith's continued to prosper—or so Caroline, from lack of any information to the contrary, at any rate assumed that it did—there was no need for him to work on Saturdays; yet even during the week-end Henry managed to keep out of the public eye. He refused to learn golf and had no acquaintances outside his domestic circle. About once a month he accompanied Caroline to church, and spent the rest of the week-end either alone in his study or sitting in the garden with a pile of newspapers. He was becoming more and more silent, more and more reserved. Whenever he spoke to his wife, it was always with affection; but sometimes nearly a whole day would go by without his speaking at all. The old evening colloquies, so cherished by Caroline, were no longer the source of comfort they used to be; he listened with apparent interest, but took so little part himself that instead of conversations they were now monologues. Caroline at first worried, then—since the process was gradual—presently got used to it. "He has so much to think about!" she told Lady Tregarthan; and old Lady Tregarthan clucked like a hen and observed that it did sometimes take them that way. "They get tired of us, my dear," she said. "When a man's getting on he sometimes takes a notion that no woman's worth speaking to. But it passes off, and then there we are, poor fools, waiting to be noticed again." Caroline smiled, and said that Lady Tregarthan was doubtless right; but in her heart of hearts she did not believe it.

In far-away Morton Mrs. Platt died and Caroline sent a wreath. It was of chrysanthemums, large and showy, and just what Cousin Maggie would have liked. She had been one of the last links with Morton, sending a card every Christmas and receiving a calendar in return; the first year the card did not come—when she realized that such cards, frosted and lavish with robins, would never come again—Caroline felt a deeper pang than she could have believed possible. For Mrs. Platt had known Mrs. Chase, and her death somehow made that slight, ladylike figure more remote than ever. 'What would mother think of us here?' wondered Caroline; and decided that in a black dress, among her grandchildren at Friar's End, Mrs. Chase would have carried herself very well indeed. I don't suppose Leon and Lal would recognize her, thought Caroline; and then her thoughts turning easily to her children, she wondered whether old Mrs. Chase would have recognized *them*.

She hardly recognized them herself. As they left school—as Leon went to Cambridge and Lal to Somerville—she felt herself falling farther and farther behind in her efforts to keep up with them. Lal in particular displayed a quality of elegant brusqueness—there was no other word for it—that her awe-struck mother could only describe as aristocratic. She *was* aristocratic: by some inexplicable magic she had developed long narrow hands and feet, a long narrow silhouette, and a small but definite bridge to her small definite nose. And she wore her clothes, even the most expensive, as though she didn't know she had them on. . . .

'No one would ever think she was my daughter,' reflected Caroline.

Half grieved, half in pride, she had watched, marvelled, and now and then tried to check the astonishing transformation. But it was no use; she had no hold over them. They had forgotten Morton as completely as though they had never lived there; they accepted Friar's Green as their natural habitat. Towards their father they displayed a casual amiability: towards herself what Caroline believed to be a genuine if superior affection. They thought her an absolute duck, a perfect lamb; and Caroline, overwhelmed by such epithets, tried hard not to see that they also considered her to be almost completely lacking in intelligence.

Yet she on her side had a private standpoint, a patch of solid ground, from which she could still look benevolently down as a mother ought. She never ceased to be amazed, for example, at their extreme youthfulness. Lally at twenty-three, finally down from Somerville, was a mere child. She *looked* a child, with her short hair, long legs, and lounging contorted attitudes. She looked eighteen. Her occupations, since she had not yet made her choice of a career, consisted in riding, reading, visiting friends, and vaguely designing theatrical costumes. Caroline at that age had been a woman, married and expecting her first child. The idea of Lal running a house, or in any position of responsibility, was simply absurd. Nor was Leon much better. He had rejected the idea of going into the works, nor had Henry, rather surprisingly, shown any desire to have him. He wished to make films, and on payment of a large premium had become loosely attached to a studio on the outskirts of London. Caroline approved, because it made him happy, and disapproved, partly because she foresaw he would never earn a living at it, and partly because it took him away from home. She went up with him to Town, however, and saw him comfortably installed in a very nice Bayswater hotel. She wouldn't have trusted him to choose a lodging for the night.

'But he's like his father all the same,' thought Caroline. 'He never tells me anything—'

It was quite true. As Henry kept silence about the works so Leon kept silence about the studio. When his mother inquired whether he was liking it or whether he had made a film yet, he answered yes or no and changed the subject. If he were more communicative with Lally, no information was ever passed on. 'I used to tell *my* mother everything!' thought Caroline; and so as a rule she thoroughly believed. It was only on very rare occasions indeed that she remembered Vincent and the deserted garden, and her own shocking deceitfulness; and one of these occasions was the morning of her fifty-first birthday.

She had a picture of magnolias from Lal, a book on the cinema from Leon, and an opal pendant from her husband Henry.

CHAPTER IV

I

THE clock struck again. 'A quarter-past ten!' thought Caroline, 'and here I am day-dreaming!'

She put up her hands to open the window: they were good hands, if large; they were firm, still shapely, very creditable hands indeed for a woman of fifty-one. As a girl she had been quite vain of them. And—'I must speak to Lal about her nails!' thought Caroline; for the child had taken to a dreadful scarlet enamel, exactly the colour of blood, and whatever they did in society, Caroline could not consider it ladylike. With this thought uppermost in her mind she stepped out into the garden and stood looking and listening for signs of her daughter's whereabouts. It was a fine day, Lal had a friend staying with her, they would probably be on the tennis court; Caroline descended from the terrace and walked slowly towards it.

The garden was looking well. But it always did look well, and gave her no special pleasure; for as some pictures are artist's pictures, so this was a gardener's garden. It was perfectly designed, perfectly kept, and to Caroline completely uninteresting. She was allowed no share in it; she could not even get azaleas instead of geraniums in the tubs along the river. For though her original tyrant had departed, his successor, chosen specially by Caroline for his mild appearance, had proved a man of precisely the same caliber; with only this difference, that whereas the old man had feigned deafness, the new man simply agreed to everything Caroline said, and then went and did whatever he had in mind. He was certainly easier to get on with; but the result was the same.

'It's really no use,' reflected Caroline, thinking of next year's tulip bulbs. 'Whatever I tell him to put in, they'll come up red. . . .' She paused by a big flower-bed; it was filled, as by neatly-laid linoleum, with an intricate carpet-pattern in red, blue, and yellow; it was the one which on the previous Sunday had excited Henry's rare enthusiasm.

"There's been some work put in *there*," said Henry approvingly.

"*Hasn't* there?" agreed Caroline, following his glance with well-feigned admiration.

"It's one thing I always wanted you to have, Carrie—a good garden."

"I couldn't have a better than this," said Caroline; and then with genuine gratitude she had put her hands on his shoulders and given him a kiss. . . .

Caroline walked on. The way to the tennis court lay beside the rose-garden, which was a hollow square of beds and pergolas with a sundial in the middle. Here again she paused. She would have liked to pick some, only the gardener would be annoyed; he counted his roses, affirmed Lal and Leon, every morning and afternoon. Caroline scrutinized the bushes closely; if there were any drooping flowers or cankered buds, she would assert her rights and just nip them off. But no, Macadam had been before, the trees were spruce as guardsmen; even when she stepped into the bed, taking them as it were from the rear, not a single blemish met her eye. 'He is good,' admitted Caroline sadly; and she shut her eyes, as though to shut out the evidences of such goodness and sniffed the perfume. It came in sweet, warm gusts: it positively went to her head; for when she opened her eyes again she unhesitatingly reached out and picked a Lady Godiva.

The petals against her nose, she moved on, and observed, through the bushes, a tall lanky figure on the grass by the sundial. It was the young man Leon had brought down last night, the young man whose eyes, whenever they fell upon Lally, became at once dog-like with devotion. There was no one with him: extraordinary! reflected Caroline, how they let their guests roam unattended! But he seemed quite happy. He was strolling about, his hands in his pockets, smoking a cigarette; and suddenly, as Caroline watched, he took the cigarette from his mouth and began to declaim.

"'Twas brillig, and the slithy toves" said the young man,
"Did gyre and gimble in the wabe.
All mimsy were the borogroves,
And the mome raths outgrabe."

'Alice in Wonderland!' thought Caroline; and she took quite a liking to him. But Hilton was coming across the terrace, there was the gardener to be spoken to, and she had no time for conversation. She stepped back on to the gravel and waited for Hilton to come up.

"A message from Lady Tregarthan, Madam: if you like to go up, the mulberries are ripe."

"Good!" said Caroline. "If there's anybody waiting, say I don't know about Miss Lal and Mr. Leon, but I'll come this afternoon."

She felt quite pleased; she enjoyed tea with Lady Tregarthan, and she enjoyed eating mulberries. Hilton moved woodenly back to the house, his old man's gait stiffened by his butler's dignity. He was sixty-five, and Caroline sometimes wondered what they would do with him when he became seventy or even eighty. The children had once taken her to see a play called "The Cherry Orchard," in which an aged butler got shut up alone in an empty house; and the scene had left a deep impression on Caroline's mind. She did not really expect the same thing to happen to Hilton, but she was always relieved, after a holiday, to see him standing safe and sound at the hall door.

'He ought to have some one to look after him,' thought Caroline as she walked on. She was now near enough to the tennis court to hear Lal's voice and the friend's giggle; they were not yet playing, but lolling in negligent attitudes on the grass by the flower-beds. Leon was there, too, they made a charming modern group—Leon and Lal in white, the friend in pale yellow—against a background of summer green. As always the opportunity to take a good look at her children drove everything else out of Caroline's head; their slimness and straightness, the clear sunburn of their skins, filled her with what she herself would have been the last to recognize as a deep aesthetic pleasure. Consciously, she still thought Lally plain and Leon too thin; when Lady Tregarthan praised their looks, Caroline put it down to good nature, just as she put down her own partiality to maternal affection. She was so used, since the children grew up, to having her taste derided, that it never occurred to her that it might in this case be correct.

The other girl got up. *She* was attractive: she had pale gold hair, just darker than her frock, and she was putting on a green sweater. 'I'm sure they're much prettier than we used to be!' thought Caroline suddenly. She tried to think back, to remember herself as a young girl; and from a misty vision of corseted alpaca drew nothing to restore her conceit. A trim waist—that had been the great point; and if you weren't trim by nature you didn't exercise or eat fewer chocolates, you just held your breath and got some one to pull. And you were much more hide-bound about colours; if you were fair, you wore blue, if dark, maroon or pink . . . the one thing that seemed to have endured was the giggle; Lally's friend, looking at the intricate flower-bed, was giggling herself silly.

"What a hoot! What a scream! What a perfect gem!" Her piping voice shrilled higher and higher.

"I've never seen anything like it! I'm overcome! Are there any more?"

"There's one by the house," drawled Leon, "that looks as though its been laid with linoleum. *Very* natty."

"But what a hoot! What a scream! What a perfect—"

"Hush!" said Lally's voice urgently. "There's mother. She adores it. . . ."

Caroline gave them time to compose themselves, then emerged tranquilly on the lawn. At once Lal and her friend began to play, calling a fictitious score in high, clear voices. Leon scrambled to his feet—it was evidently one of the days when his manners were perfect—and opened a deck-chair.

"I'm not going to stay," said Caroline, sitting all the same. Leon dropped flat upon the turf again, arms and legs spreadeagled. He never stood if he could sit, and never sat if he could lie; and Caroline never ceased to hope that by occasional admonitions—not nagging the boy, but just a word now and then—she could break him of the habit.

"Sit up, dear," she said gently.

"Why?"

"Because I tell you to," said Caroline.

He did sit up, but she could see he was laughing at her. She said hastily,

"I've just seen that friend of yours, by himself in the rose-garden. Oughtn't you to fetch him?"

"No," said Leon. "He's all right."

"Is he one of the men in your film company?"

"No," said Leon.

Caroline was silent. It was perennially strange to her how the least question always put his back up. Yet Henry was just the same; alike in no other respect, they had both a positive mania for withholding information. 'Thank goodness Lal isn't like that!' thought Caroline. And Lal wasn't; Lal went to the other extreme. If she were about to read a book Caroline disapproved of, she announced her intention in advance; and if Caroline forbade her, she announced that she intended to disobey. "You needn't ever worry about me, darling," she had once said, "because if ever I'm going to do anything you don't like, I'll always tell you first . . ." Such candour was doubtless a virtue, but in her heart of hearts Caroline could not help feeling that it was also a little unfair. It simply shifted the responsibility, leaving Lal carefree and her mother doubly burdened. But there could be no question that Lal had very high principles. . . .

"Hilton's been looking for you," said Leon suddenly. Caroline nodded. That was something else she had to think of!

"I've seen him," she said. "It was a message from Lady Tregarthan."

"He's got a walk like a marionette. I'd like to use it some time."

'Use it?' thought Caroline. 'What does he mean, *use* it? Something to do with films?' But instead of asking, she said, aloud,

"I'm bothered about him. I believe he ought to have some one to look after him, and I know he won't like it. He didn't even like it when I told him to get a sleep in the afternoons."

"He mayn't have liked it, but he gets the sleep all right," said Leon. He looked at his mother and grinned. "In another year or so, darling, you'll be employing a male nurse disguised as a footman."

"I couldn't have a footman!" said Caroline in alarm. "I wouldn't know what to do with one. . . ."

"As a ball-boy, then," said Leon, reaching out to field one of Lal's wilder shots. He shied the ball back. Lal stopped it against her racket and flipped it gracefully up into her hand. That was Lal's game all over: a bad shot, an exquisite gesture. . . . The other girl played well—showing off, Caroline suspected, for the benefit of Leon: but she was getting very red in the face, whereas Lal remained cool and elegant and much more ladylike. Caroline watched her with complacency—a complacency quite undiminished by the fact that Lal was being soundly beaten; and then suddenly, unguardedly—prompted by the most curious mixture of pride, hope, and half-formed memories—spoke what was in her mind.

"I do hope she marries a gentleman!" said Caroline softly.

Leon started. Without seeing him, without looking round, she could feel the sudden movement of embarrassed surprise. The emotion communicated itself; for nothing, at that moment, could she have turned to meet his eye. With rising colour, resolutely in profile, she sat pretending not to have spoken; equally motionless, her son pretended not to have heard. The silence prolonged itself. Then with sudden energy Leon jumped to his feet, seized a tennis ball, and shied it on to the court.

II

Caroline was back in the rose-garden. Her cheeks were cool again, but she felt it desirable that some little time should elapse before she re-encountered Leon's eye. She couldn't expect him to forget, of course; but with time he might. . . get over it. 'What a thing to say,' thought Caroline unhappily. What a foolish, thoughtless, vulgar thing! For, of course, Lal would marry a gentleman. She was bound to. She could no more marry a man like—like Henry, than she, Caroline, could have married the boy in the old garden. Caroline turned that comparison in her mind, and for the name Henry hastily substituted the name Frederick Watts. Lal could no more marry a man like Frederick, than Ellen could have married the Macbeth boy. 'I'm a perfect fool,' thought Caroline crossly. 'I'd better forget all about it.'

With this end in view, she turned and walked quickly towards the house. She would have liked to make some beds, but they would all be done. 'Silver!' she thought. 'I'll just do the silver, and they can think what they like!' But before she reached the terrace she had to turn back across the grass; for there stood Leon's friend, still solitary, and beginning to look neglected.

"They're all on the tennis court," said Caroline. "Why don't you go and make up a four?"

The young man thanked her; but though he even took a few steps in the appropriate direction, Caroline received the definite impression that as soon as her back was turned he would just stay where he was. Well, she had done her best; and not to break off too abruptly, she added with a smile,

"Wasn't it you I heard by the sundial just now . . . reciting Jabberwocky?"

"No, it wasn't," said the young man offendedly. Caroline sighed. Another gaffe! But she still felt kindly towards him, both for his absurd recitation and equally absurd denial. She said placatingly, "I must have dreamed it. What inconsequent things dreams are!"

"They're not really," said the young man. "They're most important. They. . ." He relapsed into silence; he evidently gave her up. Caroline looked at a flowerbed and wondered what, if this young man were really going to be attracted to Lal, she would ever talk to him about. She also remembered that she had forgotten his name.

"You know, it's so absurd of me," she said, "but I didn't catch your name last night. Or else it's my memory—"

"William Galbraith," said the young man.

Caroline felt quite pleased with him. After so many Hugos, Drogos, and Sholtos, the primitive simplicity of William struck familiarly on her ear. And for short they would call him—not Willie, of course, that was quite gone out—but Bill. . . .

"I suppose your friends call you Bill?" she said confidently.

"No," said Mr. Galbraith. "Most people call me Togo."

"Well, I hope you enjoy your game," said Caroline, turning back towards the house. She felt slightly dispirited; it had not been, so far, a very successful morning.

CHAPTER V

I

ON HER way to Tregarthan Court that afternoon, Caroline, passing the Three Feathers, noticed a man outside drinking beer. There was nothing unusual in that, but the man himself, apart from being a stranger, was so altogether remarkable that Caroline could not help a second glance.

He was unusually tall, unusually broad, and wore some dark-coloured shirt open at the neck. The rest of his costume consisted of flannel trousers, an old tweed coat, and a pair of outlandish-looking white shoes with rope soles. These Caroline had a good opportunity of observing, since they were cocked up

on a table almost under her nose. They reminded her of a pair
Lal had brought home from France; they were laced in just the
same way, with white tape crossing over the bare foot; for the man
wore no socks. 'A foreigner?' wondered Caroline. But what was
a foreigner doing at Friar's Green? And in spite of his outland-
ishness, he did not look like a foreigner. A hiker, then? The rare
hikers encountered about Bushey Park did not look like that. They
were usually neat and genteel, the girls coquettish in coloured
headbands, the men spruce with brilliantine; this man was slov-
enly, almost dirty, and his hair needed cutting. . . .

The most curious thing of all was that Caroline, even after a
third and final glance, could not be sure whether he was a gentleman, or whether he wasn't.

'Well!' thought Caroline; and continued her way up to Tregarthan Court.

II

"I'm glad to see you," said Lady Tregarthan.

"I'm glad to be here," answered Caroline, sinking into a chair
under the mulberry trees.

The old woman—her hair was now quite white—looked at
her shrewdly.

"Finding them all a bit too much for you?"

"No," said Caroline. "It's just—it's just a hot day." Her fingers,
pulling at the grass, encountered a ripe mulberry; she picked it
up and ate it. At Friar's End she had left a cake from Fuller's, and
three sorts of sandwiches, in brown and white bread. They ought
to be all right. . . .

"Well, they're too much for me," said Lady Tregarthan. "I
don't mean your lot, my dear, I mean Marion. You know she was
down last week?"

Caroline sat up. She knew that much, but she was perfectly
willing to hear more; and it now transpired that Lady Westcott, to
mitigate the tedium of a two-day visit, brought with her a young
artist and a Saluki hound. Both of these she had left behind, the
second inadvertently, the first by design: she took him to lodgings
in the village and told him to get his meals at the Court. Subse-

quently, when telegraphing for the dog, she added three words to the effect that he was a vegetarian.

"Well!" said Caroline, when Lady Tregarthan had finished her recital. "Whoever is he?"

"*I* don't know, my dear. What I want to know is how I'm to get the dog up there. Can I give him to the guard?"

Caroline hesitated. Henry was going up in the morning, there would be nothing simpler than to put the dog in the car too and let the chauffeur take it on to its destination. But then Henry didn't like dogs—at least he had never said he *did* like them; and supposing at the last moment he refused to have it in?

"What's his name?" she asked.

"Akbar."

Akbar! Fancy asking Henry to take up a dog called Akbar! If only it had been called Jack or Pincher, Caroline felt, she wouldn't have minded so much. . . .

"Or did you mean the artist fellow?" asked Lady Tregarthan. "*His* name's Chalmers, and a proper ruffian he looks." She reached out for a scone and bit into it appreciatively. "Where Marion found him I dread to think. He's got no money, no manners, and no morals. He may have more than one shirt, but if so I haven't seen it. The one I have seen is dark purple."

Akbar forgotten, Caroline gaped over her cup.

"I believe I've seen him. Just now, outside the Three Feathers. He'd a dark shirt, and he looked like—like—"

"A prize-fighter run to seed," supplied Lady Tregarthan. "That's the fellow. He wore that shirt to dinner. When he came down I thought Phillips would have a fit. I nearly had one myself. And then he sat down and was rude to every one. He was even rude to Marion. He said her finger-nails made him feel sick."

"I didn't care for them myself," confessed Caroline. "Lal paints hers too, but I don't like it."

"Nor do I!" cried Lady Tregarthan energetically. "It makes me sick as a cat. But if Marion chooses to make a fool of herself it's either my place to tell her so, or her husband's if he's got enough guts, but it's certainly not the place of a distemper-daubing whippersnapper in a dirty purple shirt."

Caroline ate some more mulberries. This was what she enjoyed, to sit, slightly shocked, and listen to her friend's full-throated denunciations of whatever, at the moment, happened to be the special annoyance. The Vicar, the Misses Brodrick, the Government's foreign policy—all in turn had come under the flail of Lady Tregarthan's tongue; and though Caroline herself thought highly of all three, she had listened with great enjoyment. It was another of her unrecognized aesthetic pleasures. . . .

"The physique of a navvy with the brains of a guinea-pig," defined Lady Tregarthan. "That's what I told Marion; she said his brains didn't interest her."

"But I don't understand," said Caroline. "What is he staying here *for*?"

Lady Tregarthan paused. This was evidently the *bonne bouche*.

"He is staying, my dear, to cover the walls of the Sunday-school room with Anglo-Saxon saints."

"But—!"

"Exactly," said Lady Tregarthan. "I need hardly add that it was Marion's idea. She got at the Vicar, and she's actually put down money for it. I believe she's paid a month's rent in advance for his room at the Jackson. It looks to me like the masculine equivalent of being set up in a hat-shop."

Without quite comprehending, Caroline nevertheless received a definite impression that the man was not nice. And at once, as always in the face of any new or alarming circumstance, her thoughts flew to the children: how would they be affected, could they possibly take harm? Leon was going back to Town; but Lal—no, Lal would never be attracted by the physique of a navvy. She liked men—she had often said so, with what seemed to Caroline an almost presumptuous frankness—to be tall, very thin, and very intelligent. As for a dirty shirt, she would probably feel sick at the sight of one. She couldn't bear even a napkin that had been used more than once before. . . .

'That's all right!' thought Caroline comfortably; and she turned with renewed pleasure to a fresh handful of mulberries.

CHAPTER VI

I

IT WAS peculiarly unfortunate (thought Caroline afterwards) that the arrival of Lady Westcott's artist should have so exactly coincided with the departure from Friar's End of Leon, Togo Galbraith, and Lally's friend. For Lal was thus left at a loose end, and though normally aloof from all Friar's Green interests, she could not help noticing the stir caused therein by Mr. Chalmers' artistic and social activities.

He was at once popular and unpopular, both in a very high degree. By the rowdy set at the Three Feathers, by the silk-stockinged damsels who worked in Kingston, he was described as a caution, a cough-drop, and a proper oner. By the nice people like the Misses Brodrick, he was described as a scandal, a disgrace, and a menace to decent society. The tales of his doings were endless. He had been seen bathing stark in the river. He had been seen sun-bathing, practically stark, in the Jacksons' garden. He invited others to join him. He said that modesty was an invention of the devil, patented by the Anglican Church, and told the elder Miss Brodrick that he considered mixed nudist camps an excellent thing.

He told the Vicar that Buddhism was the only possible religion for a decent man.

He told Mr. Raymond, the R.A., that art began with Braque.

He told two Rover Scouts that the British Empire was the greatest force for hypocrisy the world had ever seen.

He told Lady Tregarthan that it was no use trying to converse with a woman unless you had slept with her first. Whereupon Lady Tregarthan had simply boxed his ears, and though she was now close on seventy a good box on the ear (as she told Caroline afterwards) is a matter less of strength than of knack. Mr. Chalmers went away smarting; and this was felt to be the only point scored on behalf of Church, Art, and established morality.

Lal alone, on hearing these rumours (which indeed Caroline tried to keep from her as much as possible), refused to be shocked. She observed, calmly, that it sounded just like the sort of talk Leon used to let off at Cambridge.

"Lal!" exclaimed Caroline. "I'm sure he didn't!"

"Nonsense, darling; they all did. It was the fashion, like flicks. It's only at places like Friar's Green that it sounds so daring."

Her mother was scandalized, but also relieved. Lal had a great contempt for undergraduates, and by tar from no other brush could the artist have been so effectually blackened. But Caroline had forgotten that beside this contempt flourished a great reverence for art, particularly in its more modern forms; and all her relief vanished when she found that Lal was walking at least once a day to the Sunday-school room to watch the progress of Anselm, Aidan, and the Venerable Bede.

"Wouldn't you like to have another girl down?" asked Caroline anxiously.

"No," said Lal. "I'm tired of girls. I think I'll do some work. . . ."

That night at dinner, without being spoken to, she appeared with nails a normal healthy pink. Caroline observed, but made no comment. She would have been just as pleased, for the moment, if Lal had dyed them black.

II

Two days later the worst happened. Lally, strolling into her mother's room, announced that she wished to learn to paint.

Caroline stopped brushing her hair (she was still absurdly vain of it) and looked at her daughter through the glass. Despite her customary air of nonchalant composure, Lal was evidently prepared to be stubborn. 'She wants to go away!' thought Caroline in a panic. 'Suppose she wants to go to Town?' And then came a third and more disquieting notion still—suppose Lally wanted to go to Paris?

"What did you say, dear?" asked Caroline mildly.

Lally looked at her with scorn. She knew—and Caroline knew that she knew—that her mother's question was just one more instance, such as she, Lally, spent her days critically noting, of the incurable weak-mindedness of age. She said severely,

"I want to learn to paint, Mother. I've just decided."

"You paint very nicely already, dear," said foolish Caroline.

Lal stamped her foot.

"I mean paint *properly*. Not water-colour landscapes with a tree in the middle."

"I suppose," said Caroline, with a desperate resolve to be weak-minded no longer, "you want to go to Town?"

"No, I don't," said Lal quickly. "I can take lessons here. I can take them off Mr. Chalmers."

The first part of her answer brought such a wave of relief that Caroline, for a moment, had no attention for anything else. Not want to go to Town! No idea, even, of going to Paris! It was too good to be true! And then, suddenly, she perceived that it *was* too good to be true. If Lal wanted to paint, and didn't want to go to Town to do it, then Friar's Green must have developed some new and overwhelming attraction. And what was there new at Friar's Green, save Gilbert Chalmers? Concealing her dismay, fearful of rousing Lal's stubbornness, she said mildly,

"Does he *give* lessons?"

"He would to me. And I could help him with his frescoes. There's a lot of donkey-work."

"I wish," said Caroline artfully, "that he'd sometimes change his shirt. It's really dirty."

"Is it?" said Lal, "I hadn't noticed. . . ."

That night Caroline lay awake an hour and at last woke Henry out of his sleep.

"Henry."

"What is it?"

"Lal wants to learn painting off that Mr. Chalmers."

"Well?"

"I—I don't think he's very nice."

"Then stop her," said Henry calmly.

III

Caroline's tactics, at this juncture, were extremely bad.

She was hardly to be blamed. She was on unfamiliar ground. But her first step could hardly have been worse.

"I've been talking to Mr. Raymond," she announced confidently, "and I really think, dear, if we asked him specially, he'd give you painting lessons himself."

Lal put down her cup—it was Sunday breakfast, but Henry had already retired with the papers—and looked her mother in the eye.

"Thank you, darling, but I'd rather not."

"But why, dear? He's an R.A.!"

"Because he can't paint," said Lal simply.

Half in awe, half in anger, Caroline looked at this astonishing young woman and wondered, not for the first time, however she had produced her. How *dared* Lal—how was it possible for Lal—to say Mr. Raymond couldn't paint? The Royal Academy, the final judge and exemplar of British Art, said that he could; but Lal disagreed. She disagreed calmly, confidently, as though she were a messenger from on high furnished with special information.

"Well!" said Caroline.

"He can't, you know, darling. I hate to destroy your illusions, but I'd sooner buy a painting-book and copy baskets of flowers."

Caroline got up from the table. She felt oddly offended. She had bought a picture from Mr. Raymond herself, a charming picture of autumn beech-woods and a man gathering sticks. Henry paid fifty pounds for it, and even he had not considered it dear. . . .

"How much does Mr. Chalmers get for his pictures?" she asked coldly.

"I've never asked. Anyway, price hasn't anything to do with their being good or not."

'Rubbish!' thought Caroline. Price had everything to do with it! How could you tell whether a picture was valuable, unless you knew the price?

But she did not voice these thoughts aloud. She wanted, above all else, to avoid giving an opening for one of Lal's celebrated displays of frankness and disobedience. She glanced at the clock: there was just time, before church, to slip up and see Lady Tregarthan.

IV

"You look worried, my dear," said Lady Tregarthan.

Caroline nodded. The walk, especially the last steep hundred yards, had left her slightly blown. As soon as she could speak, and with her usual instinct for plain dealing, she went straight to her trouble's heart.

"I'm very sorry to bother you, Lady Tregarthan; but could you send that Mr. Chalmers away?"

The old lady cackled.

"My dear! Don't tell me he's taken Hilton sun-bathing?"

"No," said Caroline soberly, "but he's going to give Lal painting lessons."

The statement, she was pleased to see, did not fail of effect. Lady Tregarthan was genuinely perturbed. "My dear! Do you think that's wise?"

"No, of course I don't," said Caroline impatiently. "But you know what Lal is. She gets an idea into her head and nothing will stop her. That's why I want you to send him away."

"If he were staying in the house, I would like a shot. But he isn't: he's staying with the Jacksons."

"Don't you own the cottage?"

"Not now. We used to: now we own nothing but this house and a couple of meadows. I could speak to the father, but it's Edie and Grace who bring in the money."

"Grace! the bar-maid at the Feathers! All bosom and red hair! And her sister—"

"Edie's my parlourmaid," said Lady Tregarthan. "They're baggages, both of 'em, who'd sooner disoblige me than not. I'll go down if you like, but I don't suppose it will be any good."

"I don't think anything's any good," said Caroline with unusual pessimism. "I can't lock Lal up."

"You can refuse to pay," pointed out Lady Tregarthan.

Caroline nodded; and the bells beginning to ring, she picked up her hymn-book and prepared to accompany her friend to church. She would try what prayer could do; and only a certain shyness prevented her asking Lady Tregarthan to pray as well.

V

Whether from lack of reinforcement, or because Caroline's own thoughts now and again wandered, her prayers produced no immediate result. On the contrary: for by Monday afternoon, the fat was definitely in the fire.

Lal came in about half-past four, went straight to her mother in the morning-room, and with one foot over the threshold launched her accusation.

"Mother! You've been to see Lady Tregarthan!"

"So I do practically every day, dear," said Caroline mildly.

"You went to see her to get Mr. Chalmers turned out of the Jacksons' cottage! It's a shame!"

"Lal!"

"It is! A disgusting shame! Just because you don't like him! You know how hard up he is and you try to stop me taking lessons. He's in the middle of an important piece of work, and you don't care. You dislike him because he hasn't any money, and yet you try to—to take away his livelihood. It's hateful!"

Caroline mastered her anger. The child was overwrought, she didn't know what she was saying. The thought rose to her lips, and she spoke it aloud.

"You don't know what you're saying, Lal. When you're quieter—"

"I do! Lady Tregarthan went there this morning, and when Gilbert went back for lunch old Jackson told him. And he said he'd like to oblige her. But it isn't his house, thank God, so he won't be able to. It's just what you'd expect of *her*, of course, she's always interfering with some one; but *you*, Mother! How *could* you?"

"Very well," said Caroline sharply, "if I thought it my duty. And I do. I don't think he's a—good influence in the village, and I don't want you to have lessons with him."

"Well, I shall," said Lally. "I'm sorry to disobey you, but I shall."

It was the *impasse*, the deadlock, that Caroline had so much dreaded. And she could do nothing. She had bungled the whole matter. Indeed, she was about to bungle it further, for in spite of her better judgment she could not refrain from making one of those sentimental appeals with her children so much disliked.

"Lal, how can you be so—so heartless to me?"

"I'm not!" said Lal. "I've said I'm sorry, and I am. And I'm not deceiving you: I could easily have sneaked off and had lessons and pretended I was somewhere else. You never think of *that*."

She was positively righteous! Her fury had died; her attitude was no longer one of anger at her mother's obstinacy, but of compassion for her lack of understanding.

"I'm sure you meant well," said Lal kindly.

Caroline played her last worthless card.

"I hope you don't expect me to pay for you."

"Of course not, darling. I wouldn't dream of letting you. I shall pay myself, out of my allowance."

For a moment the idea of stopping that allowance flashed through Caroline's mind. But it was no good. Lal would borrow from Leon, it would mean stopping Leon's allowance too. It would be endless! So Caroline kept silence; for it was one of her most remarkable qualities (according to Lady Tregarthan) that when she had nothing to say, she did not speak.

VI

With another portion of her allowance Lal bought two linen overalls, expensively smocked, in which she looked extremely attractive and about sixteen years old; and not out of her allowance, but out of Caroline's private pocket, was purchased a new evening dress to go and dance at the Grosvenor with Togo Galbraith.

"Did you have a nice time, dear?" asked Caroline.

"Not particularly," said Lal, who liked the Berkeley. She had had her twenty-first birthday party there, and Caroline, who was in charge of it, had been perfectly astounded at the amount of money Henry gave her to take with her. She had been even more astounded at coming back without it. Henry refused to go; he had no tail-coat, and didn't see why he should buy one.

"He seems a very nice young man, dear," said Caroline.

"Very," said Lal.

"I shall ask him for another week-end."

"Do," said Lal.

So Mr. Galbraith came down again, and since Lal was mostly absent, he and Caroline had a great deal of conversation. He seemed quite to have revised his original opinion of her. He told her all about himself. He was a doctor, three years qualified, in a quite decent practice on the other side of London. There were two other partners, who naturally landed him with all the panel work, but both were elderly and one at least might be expected to snuff out within a reasonable time. The only serious bar, in fact, to his, Togo's, progress, was his lack of a wife. For a doctor, explained the young man earnestly, ought to be married. A married doctor inspired confidence, a bachelor mistrust. He himself, of course, could not think of marriage for the moment; but as soon as a partner died—or supposing one of them retired—he didn't mind betting he'd have proposed before nightfall.

"Always supposing," added Dr. Galbraith mournfully, "that there's any one left that I want to propose to. . . ."

Caroline listened, and understood, and felt a great deal of sympathy. She liked the young man. It would not be a brilliant match; but she felt Lally would be safe with him. And since Lal would doubtless have some money, there was no reason why they should not marry quite soon. They could settle down where his practice was, not so near that Caroline—for she knew her own weakness—could keep popping in, but near enough for her to go over on Sundays and take her grandchildren out in the car. . . .

To the realization of this happy dream there were, however, two obstacles. In the first place, Lal apparently took no interest in the young man at all; and in the second Caroline very much doubted whether Henry would put down money for any one under an Honourable. Lal did know some Honourables; there had been two at the Berkeley dance, looking, to Caroline, much like any one else; and to these Henry's hopes might easily aspire. It was not long, indeed, since Caroline's hopes had so aspired also; but with Lal's head obviously full of—of nonsense, and confronted by the alarming example of Lady Westcott, she was beginning to think less of titles and more of respectability. She determined to be very cautious, very crafty; but the matter was so urgent in her mind that she invaded Henry's study and spoke to him that night.

"Henry, if Lal marries—"

He sat up.

"Lal? Who's she thinking of?"

"No one," said Caroline, remembering Mr. Chalmers and hoping it was true. "But I'm sure that young man—Dr. Galbraith—is thinking of Lal. He's practically told me so."

Henry reached for a slip of paper.

"What's his name?"

"Dr. William Galbraith. He's junior partner in a practice at Highbury." Caroline paused, half afraid that so modest a suitor would simply be turned down at once. But Henry, to her relieved surprise, showed no sign of annoyance or derision; he merely wrote down the name and address and looked at them thoughtfully. At last he said,

"What's he like, Carrie?"

"He's a gentleman," said Caroline at once. (She could say it to Henry, if not to Leon!) "He's only stayed here twice, but I like him. He's steady, and I think he'd make her a good husband. And there's no doubt he's very fond of her."

"What about Lal?"

For a moment Caroline was silent. She was weighing inescapable evidence against irrational hope. The best she could say, with honesty, was that Lal was indifferent, or rather that she was preoccupied. . . .

"She hasn't thought about him. But I think if he waits, and she gets to know him, it—it might come off."

Henry looked at the paper again. He had drawn a little border of crosses, and now, inside the crosses, was drawing a row of noughts. Caroline waited. He said suddenly,

"I'd like to see Lal married. If this is all right, Carrie, I'll give her five thousand pounds."

Caroline was extremely pleased. One of her obstacles had melted at a touch; and Henry, moreover, seemed pleased too. He looked positively cheerful. All that now remained was for Lal to fall properly in love, put this painting nonsense out of her head, and live happy ever after.

CHAPTER VII

I

SUMMER waned, a wet autumn played havoc with the garden;
Leon stayed in Town, Eustace Jamieson came every other week-
end, and Lal went almost daily to the Sunday-school room to take
her lessons of Mr. Chalmers.

Caroline asked him to dinner.

Her attitude towards him was unchanged, she still considered
him an undesirable acquaintance; but a sound instinct urged to
strip from him, as much as possible, the glamour of the forbidden
fruit. It was the same instinct that bade her feign, if not approval
of, at least indifference to the lessons themselves. Her wisdom
was belated, but it was none the less wisdom for that. She saw
Lal come and go without comment. She had the smocks washed,
one each week, and when the sleeve buttons came off sewed new
ones on. All these signs of grace Lal accepted, with some complacency, as the fruit of her own gentle firmness; but even Lal was
surprised at the invitation to dine.

"I don't for a moment suppose he'll come," she warned. "He
hates dinners. He thinks they're a waste of time."

'The jackanapes!' thought Caroline. It was the word she had
been used to apply—though, of course, only mentally—to some
of Leon's Cambridge acquaintances—and the fact that it was she
who now employed it of Gilbert Chalmers, while Lal was respectfully quoting his dictum about dinners, marked an interesting
change in their respective attitudes. With Caroline, familiarity
was breeding contempt: the man had been two months at Friar's
Green, and done no active harm that she knew of. A cold snap
had rendered his nudist doctrine unpopular; since none of the
nice people would speak to him, he could no longer be rude to
them. But Lal—Lal, who saw him every day—had ceased to mock.
She did not, like Lady Westcott, make appreciative comments
on his physique: she kept a complete silence. 'The child's getting
tired of him,' thought Caroline; and if she looked forward to the

dinner with a certain anxiety, it was more on Hilton's account than on her own.

But Hilton's sensibilities, as it happened, were spared, for Lal was right, and Mr. Chalmers did not come. He not only did not come, he also did not answer the invitation. When twelve days of the intervening fortnight had elapsed Caroline sent down the garden boy with a verbal message of enquiry; and the boy returned saying yes, Mr. Chalmers did remember the invitation, because he had made a sketch on the back: but he was very sorry he could not come.

'The jackanapes!' thought Caroline.

II

But she still, out of policy, kept up a mild interest in his saints. They were no longer, it seemed, exclusively Anglo-Saxon; they now included such well-known figures as the Virgin Mary, St. Catherine, and St. Joan. To Caroline's mind it all sounded dangerously Popish.

"I think I'll come and see how you're getting on," she told Lal; and Lal, after a good deal of obstructiveness, permitted her to walk across the green, while the artist was safely at lunch, and gaze for a quarter of an hour at the one completed wall. It showed a scene in Paradise, very flat and out of perspective, with St. Catherine and the Virgin engaged in picking flowers. The Virgin was in blue, St. Catherine in red: and each wore, in addition to her halo, a small wreath of daisies.

"What do you think of it, Mother?"

Caroline started. She had been quite lost for a moment in artistic contemplation, but her thoughts, now that she began consciously to unravel them, did not easily find words. It was all very pretty and—and innocent, but there was something lacking. She looked at the Virgin again, at the smooth golden hair and smiling countenance, and searched in vain for any sign of what she had undoubtedly gone through. This was Paradise, of course, where all tears were dried: but could any mother, wondered Caroline, ever so completely forget? To her mind, Mary in Heaven was a middle-aged woman, tranquil and happy to have her Son back again, but still a little worn. . . .

"Well?" said Lal impatiently.

"It's very pretty," said Caroline at last, "but—"

"But what, Mother?"

"It doesn't look to me like the work of a believer."

"It isn't meant to be," said Lal crossly. "It's a work of art."

III

About once a fortnight Dr. Galbraith, smelling faintly antiseptic, drove over in his car and stayed the night. Lal saw him at meals, and was perfectly amiable in an off-hand way. So, to Caroline's surprise, was Dr. Galbraith. She had hinted, with Henry's permission, that their daughter would not be undowered; but instead of immediately pressing his suit, the young man had seemed rather to draw back. Caroline, with conscious discretion, asked no questions; she simply watched and wondered, and presently began to acknowledge that his tactics had a certain merit. For if he proposed at once, Lal would certainly refuse him; and Lal had still a youthful dislike of changing her mind.

"But she likes to know he's there," reported Caroline to Henry. The words did not convey her exact meaning, which was indeed rather too subtle for either her own vocabulary or Henry's understanding. She had perceived, in fact, that while Lal liked to leave Dr. Galbraith and Eustace Jamieson playing tennis with each other, she would not have liked to leave them playing tennis with other young women. They were in a sense her property. It was an attitude which in any one else Caroline would have described as dog-in-the-manger.

"Then why doesn't she pay more attention to him?" asked Henry.

Caroline paused. How was it possible to explain—what she herself had only just begun to comprehend—that whereas to their generation the enjoyment of property consisted in taking care of it, Lal's enjoyment consisted in leaving it about? It was not possible; and partly to change the subject, partly from a genuine anxiety, she asked what was wrong with Eustace.

Henry looked at her.

"Eustace? Nothing that I know of. What should be wrong with him?"

"He's been looking poorly all summer. And"—Caroline paused, trying to define the exact impression made on her by the secretary's peaked and mournful countenance—"and as though he had something on his mind."

"You'd better ask him yourself," said Henry shortly. "There's nothing I know of."

But when Caroline did ask him, Mr. Jamieson earnestly denied both secret troubles and malnutrition. 'I believe it's his digestion all the same,' thought Caroline; and she was always careful, whenever he stayed the night, to leave a bottle of fruit salts handy by his bed.

IV

It was the purchase of those salts that led her, one late October morning, across the green to the chemist near the church. For Eustace was expected that night, and Caroline, casting an eye over his room, had seen that the bottle was empty. Thus confirmed in her suspicions, and finding no other supply in the house, she picked up her hat and bag and went down to the village. Coming back, the way led her past the Sunday-school room, which was built on behind the village hall; and without thinking, without any real motive, Caroline stepped impulsively across the grass, looked in at the window, and there saw Lal and Mr. Chalmers standing side by side.

They stood at a big table, evidently looking down at a sheet of drawings. Lal, as usual, held herself straight as an arrow, only her head bent a little to one side; but the artist, a good seven inches taller, was so slouched forward, one hand on the table, that their heads were level. The artist's other hand, the right one, was lying casually and heavily upon Lal's shoulder.

Caroline could hardly believe it, Lal—the detached and fastidious Lal—Lal who could scarcely submit to her mother's good-night kiss—thus passively accepting that off-hand masculine caress! And his hand (Caroline saw with horror) was not even clean. It was stained with paint. Lal had only to move her head—ever so little, just the fraction of an inch—and her pure and delicate cheek would positively touch it.

"Lal!" cried Caroline under her breath.

But the window was closed, they could not hear. Instead, at that moment, Lal did so turn, her cheek did so feel the rough contact; and she did not start away.

Caroline was so shocked that she went and did an extremely foolish thing. The disastrous results of her last visit notwithstanding, she went straight up to the Court and saw Lady Tregarthan.

CHAPTER VIII

I

"What's worrying you, my dear?" asked Lady Tregarthan.

It was almost exactly what she had said before; and as before Caroline nodded. If the actions of melodrama had not been so foreign to her, she would have torn her hair.

"That man."

"My dear!" Lady Tregarthan threw up her hands. "Don't tell me he's seduced your parlourmaid too!"

"No, he hasn't seduced my parlourmaid," said Caroline dryly (she had never pronounced that word 'seduce' before; to do so made her feel at once extraordinarily mature and experienced), "but I've just seen him and Lal." She looked at her friend's face, and saw half with gratitude, half with alarm, that the words, inadequate as they were to the circumstances, had driven all frivolity, all cynicism, from that wrinkled countenance. Lady Tregarthan sat grave as a judge. But instead of continuing Caroline harked back.

"Whose—whose parlourmaid is it?"

"Mine," answered Lady Tregarthan grimly. "Edie Jackson. If it had only been Grace, she'd have known how to take care of herself."

Caroline was silent. If Lal could know! But Lal did not know, and it was impossible to tell her. The weapon was good, but it was too dirty. . . .

"How far's it gone?" asked Lady Tregarthan suddenly.

Thus faced by a direct question, which so far she had not answered even to herself, Caroline took fright.

"It mayn't be anything," she said weakly. "It may be just my imagination. But Lal's always down at the school-room, and—"

"And I suppose you've seen him kissing her?"

"Certainly not!" cried Caroline. "I'm sure Lal would never dream of letting him!"

"You may be perfectly sure she would," said Lady Tregarthan brutally. "That child's just about due for a love-affair. And there seems no doubt the ruffian's got a way with him."

"I can't understand it!" cried Caroline, throwing all pretence aside. For she knew the other woman was right. There had been, in that one observed caress, something that thoroughly alarmed her. It was so—so casual! No first caress could be as casual as that! It was not indifferent, it was . . . intimate. "I can't understand it," said Caroline again. "I should have thought he'd be the last man on earth to attract her! He's—"

"He's a hulking great brute," said Lady Tregarthan. "But there's no accounting for tastes. One of my cousins, I remember, fell in love with the bailiff: he looked just like a gorilla, but *she* didn't care."

"What did they do with her?" asked Caroline anxiously.

"Sent her to Egypt, where she fell in love with a policeman. Not the native sort, of course, but a young man from Clapham. So then my poor aunt sent for her home again, and she finally married a High Church curate. My poor aunt was Low."

Caroline sighed; the example was not encouraging. But a curate, after all, was better than a gorilla, and if it would do Lal good she was perfectly willing to take her at least to Torquay. Only would Lal go?

She voiced her ultimate fear.

"Suppose—suppose Lal takes it into her head to marry him?"

"She can't do that," said Lady Tregarthan promptly. "He's got a wife already."

A great load lifted from Caroline's heart. A wife already! Here indeed was a weapon to her hand! She felt like hurrying home and telling Lal at once. And if the child liked, they would go to

Torquay as well. If Lal had been a little in love, she would need something to cheer her up. They would go to Torquay, and have a nice holiday, and Lal would forget her foolishness. At Christmas—Caroline's thoughts leapt joyfully ahead—she would invite Dr. Galbraith to stay as long as he could. . . .

"Where is she?" asked Caroline suddenly.

"His wife? I don't know. All I know about her is that Marion told me she existed. I imagine they have nine children, and haven't met for years."

The picture aroused no sympathy; already Caroline felt a positive dislike for the woman. For if Mrs. Chalmers had kept by her husband, as a wife should, all this—argued Caroline, perhaps unjustly—could never have happened. But her relief outweighed even righteous indignation. She walked home quite lightly: she felt ten years younger.

II

Lal did not come in to lunch. She did not come in till nearly five o'clock, and Caroline, primed as she was with sympathy, revelations, and plans for the future, found the delay so trying that she had to go up to the linen closet to steady her mind with sheets. On further consideration she had decided to begin with Torquay, and if Lal should prove amenable, not to mention Mrs. Chalmers at all; for Caroline had also made up her mind that that misguided lady was one of the facts of life of which Lal ought, if possible, to remain in ignorance. It might not be possible; Lally might be obstinate: but were she obstinate as a mule, Caroline swore to herself that no word of that other fact of life—the scandalous, disgraceful fact that was Edie Jackson—should be allowed to sully Lal's ear. So prepared—tactful as a courtier, loving as a pelican—Caroline stood among the shelves, counting the same pile of pillow-slips over and over again, till she heard a step outside and the opening of Lal's door.

"Lal!" she called.

Lal came down the passage. She was wearing a white frock, she looked extraordinarily young. 'There can't be anything!' thought Caroline. . . .

"What a domestic sight!" said Lal benevolently, leaning against the door.

"Lal, would you like to go to Torquay?"

"No," said Lal.

It was not an auspicious beginning. To gain time Caroline unfolded a towel, looked at the laundry-mark, and folded it up again.

"Why?" asked Lal.

She suspected something already! Her attitude was still negligent, but her eyes, fixed on her mother's face, had become suddenly watchful.

"I just feel I need a change," said Caroline, with attempted airiness. "If you don't like Torquay, dear, we might go somewhere else. Somewhere warm. We might even try one of those cruises. Miss Brodrick—"

"If you want to get me away from Friar's Green," said Lal distinctly, "why can't you say so straight out?"

Caroline's heart sank. This was the one mood of Lal's that she feared, the one mood she could not deal with. And knowing that for every moment of hesitation her daughter despised her still more, she yet could not help hesitating longer. She even reached for another towel. . . .

"That's the one you've just looked at," said Lal.

Caroline dropped it like a hot potato. She said nervously,

"Very well, then, I do. And that's no way to speak to your mother. I'm going to Torquay next week, and you're coming with me."

"No, dear," said Lal.

She said it gently, firmly, in what Caroline immediately recognized as just the tone she herself ought to have used. And gently, firmly, Lal continued,

"I know what's on your mind, darling, and if you'd only be frank with me, I'd be frank with you. I was going to be, anyway. Gilbert and I—"

"Stop!" said Caroline.

Lal stopped obligingly.

"That man," began Caroline; and then she stopped too. She had realized how inferior was her own style to her daughter's. She tried again.

"Mr. Chalmers may be a very clever artist, dear, but I don't think you quite understand what—what kind of a person he is. He's not like Leon's friends, who just talk about things: he really . . . does them. You don't know—"

"I do!" flashed Lal. "And I'm sorry, Mother, but I don't think it's much good your trying to talk about Gilbert. You've never liked him—"

"I should think not!" cried Caroline incautiously.

"There you are." Lal shrugged her shoulders. "It's pure prejudice."

"It is not," said Caroline. She heard her voice quiver, partly with anger, partly with nervousness. For they were approaching perilous ground, which she saw but could not avoid; she trembled, but went on. "Lal, you don't know anything about this man—"

"I do!" flashed Lal again.

Caroline paused. She was faced by a dilemma. She felt certain that on Lal in her present mood, the name of Mrs. Chalmers would make no impression. The weapon was useless in her hand. The other weapon she had sworn not to use. Yet how could she refrain from fighting? How could she leave Lal unwarned? And how, save by chapter and verse, could she drive the warning home? Quite unconsciously, Caroline sighed.

"I suppose you're working up to tell me," said Lal brutally, "that he's had an affair with Edie Jackson."

"Lily!"

"Well, he had, but it's over. In any case it was mostly her fault: she flung herself at his head. But people always blame the man."

Caroline sat down on a laundry basket. She was more shocked than she had ever been before. And Lal stood looking down at her, Lal slim, straight, immaculate in virgin white, and talked about affairs with Edie Jackson—

"How did you know?"

"From Gilbert, of course."

Caroline gasped. The man was even worse than she had believed! To seduce Edie Jackson was bad enough, but to tell Lal about it afterwards—! And what else had he told her? What other appalling conversations had accompanied the delineation of those mild and celibate saints? Caroline simply dared not think. And as though reading her mother's mind, Lal added calmly,

"He's told me everything. . ."

"Did he tell you he had a wife?"

Lal nodded.

"In Hampstead. She likes Hampstead. She's the sort that does."

The words were evidently an echo: Lal had never been to Hampstead in her life. And why shouldn't a woman like Hampstead? It was a very nice place. Aware that her mind was wandering from the point, aware that now was the vital moment for a show of firmness, Caroline gathered her forces.

"Then as you know so much, Lal, I shan't have to explain why I forbid you to see Mr. Chalmers any more. You understand?"

"It's you who don't understand," said Lal. "I don't blame you in a way, I suppose your generation can't—"

"What don't I understand, pray?" said Caroline, nettled. Lal paused. Her defiance cooled and hardened. She looked her mother straight in the face.

"That I love him," said Lal.

She turned quickly, and went.

CHAPTER IX

I

FOR a quarter of an hour, unconscious of her surroundings, Caroline continued to sit on the laundry basket. She was not thinking; she was simply stunned, physically as well as mentally, as though by a material blow. But at the end of that time, her brain beginning to work again, she perceived two things. The first was her own culpability in not looking after Lal better, the second that their conversation had been left unfinished. Beyond that one bare statement Lal had said nothing: how much more had she to tell?

What disastrous theories, what appalling projects, were still to be unfolded? For projects and theories Lal inevitably had: she was no Viola, to love hopelessly and with resignation. The headlines of a recent divorce case, blatant and horrible, flashed dreadfully through Caroline's mind. 'Nothing like that,' she thought. 'It couldn't be anything like that!' she got up; she felt stiff and tired, but her brain was now clear. Before anything else she must talk to Lal again, discover the worst; if necessary, put the worst clearly before her, shock her as she herself had been shocked. 'She hasn't realized,' thought Caroline. 'She doesn't know what it means. . . .'

Very slowly—slowly as an old woman—Caroline walked down the corridor to her daughter's room.

II

Lal was lying on the bed. Her face was pressed into the pillow, but she was not crying. Caroline advanced to the bed-side and stood looking down at her.

"Darling, I want to talk to you."

At once Lal stiffened. Every inch of her long fluent body was suddenly quite still. But her voice, when at last it came, was now light and nonchalant.

"Is it time to dress?"

Caroline came a step nearer.

"Sit up, Lal."

"Why?"

"Because I want to see your face."

Deliberately, half defiantly, as one meeting a challenge, Lal swung her feet to the floor and so looked straight up into her mother's eyes.

"Well?"

"Dear, you know I only want you to be happy?"

"I suppose so."

"Don't you believe me, Lal?"

The child actually appeared to consider.

"I think you want me to be happy all right, but in your own way. I don't think you've ever considered whether your way's the same as mine. Personally I don't think it is."

Caroline looked behind her and saw the dressing-stool. She felt she must sit down.

"What is your way, Lal?"

"Not being interfered with, and having enough money to live on, and being always with Gilbert." Involuntarily, at that ready and explicit answer, Caroline frowned. The child had been right: except for the money, their ways did not coincide at all. "You see!" said Lal.

"But your way isn't possible!" cried Caroline, in genuine distress. "My darling, if you loved this man and could marry him it would be different, but you can't! You can't do anything about it, and neither can he! I understand how you may have got . . . fond of each other, but nothing can come of it!"

"It can," said Lal.

"But what? Do you mean"—Caroline's lips felt suddenly stiff, as though with extreme cold—"do you mean his wife is going to divorce him?"

"No," said Lal evenly. "She won't. She's too mean."

Relief flooded Caroline's soul. The worst could not happen! Lal was safe, Lal would get over it. It must seem dreadful now to her, poor child, but she was so young! In another year—in another six months—all would be forgotten; it was just a matter for time and patience, and loving-kindness. . . .

"Not that that makes any difference," added Lal.

"My dear," said Caroline, with what she considered to be great understanding, "it mayn't make any difference to your being fond of him, but it must to everything else. I'm sure if I speak to Mr. Chalmers—"

"Mother!"

Lal's eyes blazed.

"If you say a word, I'll go to him tomorrow!"

Caroline did not understand. Of course Lal would run to him, and probably upset herself, and make all sorts of wild promises. What promises had she not made already?

"I won't if I can help it," promised Caroline soothingly. "I don't want to see him any more than I expect he wants to see me." She paused: it was no good abusing the man. "But, my darling, you don't see what it means. You think you can wait: but it may be for years and years, without even being sure that there's anything to wait for. You're just at the beginning of it, Lal. And it isn't very . . . nice, is it, waiting for—for something to happen?"

"For another women to die," said Lal brutally. "That's what I think. It's disgusting. So we're not going to."

She swung her feet on to the bed again and sat up cross-legged. She looked about fourteen. Caroline stared at her in horror.

"Do you mean—do you mean you're going to run off with him, Lal?"

"Probably. Not just yet, of course, because he hasn't finished the frescoes."

To Caroline's Philistine soul the words brought a ray of hope. If he thought more of his paintings than of Lal, surely, surely there was still some way out! Paintings weren't like a business. You could leave them whenever you wanted to; and for a moment—so touchy a thing is maternal pride—Caroline felt almost offended. The emotion braced her; she said quite calmly,

"And when does he expect to be ready, dear?"

"Perhaps in another three weeks. But, of course, I shall tell you first."

For one unnatural moment Caroline wished she wouldn't. To have a daughter elope—that might happen to any one: but to *let* one's daughter elope, after due warning—that was disgraceful. And yet what could she do? She couldn't—how that old thought returned!—she couldn't lock Lal up. . . .

"I hope you realize," said Caroline, suddenly inspired, "that you won't get a penny from your father?"

"We wouldn't take one," said Lal. "Money doesn't mean anything to Gilbert at all."

Surmising from this that Mr. Chalmers had a private income, Caroline fell silent. Her daughter looked at her benevolently.

"But we shall never, darling—whatever happens—do anything underhand."

She was positively priggish. For the first time in years, dismay and apprehension notwithstanding, Caroline felt her palm tingle with an almost overwhelming impulse to slap.

III

"Henry!" said Caroline that night.

He turned over. He was not asleep, but Caroline knew that in a moment he would pretend to be. Without waiting for further preparation, she said urgently,

"Henry, Lal's in love with that artist!"

"Oh!" said Henry. "I thought it was the doctor."

"Well, it isn't. I never said it was. And he's married already!"

"Then why do you keep having him here?"

"Not Dr. Galbraith, Henry: Mr. Chalmers," said Caroline impatiently. "And, Henry, she says she's going to run off with him!"

"Then stop her," said Henry.

CHAPTER X

I

A FORTNIGHT—the worst fortnight of Caroline's life—slowly passed. Lal continued to go daily to the school-room; at home she behaved with extreme docility and unusual consideration. She was never late for meals. She darned her stockings. When Dr. Galbraith came down she stayed and entertained him. She behaved towards Caroline as though Caroline were a little ill. She seemed really anxious to make the home cheerful.

And Caroline did nothing. She had spoken to Henry, but to no avail. She had written to Leon, urgently desiring him to come down, and received no answer. She did not dare speak to Gilbert Chalmers lest Lal should carry out her threat and openly depart to the Jacksons' cottage.

She could do nothing but worry. A first shading of grey appeared in the hair over her temples: it was the only tangible result, from which Caroline derived a morbid pleasure. She felt that if only she could come down one morning with her hair completely white, then—then Lal would see! But her hair, it seemed, partook of her own unspectacular character: it would whiten in a reasonable way. Once, in an effort to attract sympathetic attention, she had breakfast in bed: Lal followed the tray, put lavender water on her mother's handkerchief, and then went off to the Sunday-school room.

Caroline would very much have liked to follow. It was one of her worst troubles that while the progress of the murals was of supreme importance to her, she had no means of keeping an eye on it. She could not question Lal; she still, almost unconsciously, clung to the old belief that if she took no notice Lal would give over. It was so she got her out of the habit of whistling, which Caroline considered unladylike: Lal at eleven had whistled defiantly for days on end; but her mother pretended not to hear, and Lal had stopped. If only the same thing could happen again! Caroline hardly expected it would; but she was careful not to mention the paintings.

They were none the less constantly in her mind, and she concocted several hopeless plans to retard their progress. There had been a story she knew as a child about some one called Penelope, who, to deceive her suitors, unpicked by night the embroidery she did by day; but though Caroline thought of it often, she could not seriously visualize herself stealing-out of Friar's End, between two and three in the morning, with a torch and a pail of whitewash. Even when quite small, she had been surprised that the suitors did not notice. She also considered faked cablegrams, summoning Mr. Chalmers to Australia, or a more practicable telegram to his wife summoning her from Hampstead. But Caroline had never faked even a postcard, and she was not altogether sure what the effect of Mrs. Chalmers's arrival would be. It might simply shorten the time of waiting, and though waiting was bad enough Caroline had no illusions as to the respective heats of a frying-pan and a fire.

So she did nothing, until on the last day of the fortnight Lal announced her intention of going up to Town to see about clothes. She did not wish for company, she said she had plenty of money; and this, to Caroline, sounded so suggestive of preparations for departure, that after a morning of anxious deliberation she flung caution to the winds and walked across the Green to interview Mr. Chalmers.

II

She found him leaning against a portion of dry wall contemplating a portion of wet. He had a pipe in his mouth, his hands in his pockets, and apparently saw no reason, in Caroline's appearance, to alter his position. He continued to lean, to smoke, and, after one brief glance, to contemplate the wall.

"Good afternoon," said Caroline from the doorway.

Mr. Chalmers frowned.

"I want to speak to you," said Caroline.

He dragged out a hand and removed the pipe. His voice, when it came, was extraordinarily deep and extremely irritable.

"Sorry, I'm working."

"So I see," said Caroline, in what she hoped was a tone of irony. "I want you to stop."

For a moment they stood looking at each other. Then Caroline walked into the room, removed his coat from a chair, and sat down.

"Very well," said Mr. Chalmers reluctantly.

His whole air was that of a man foolishly pestered in the middle of serious work. He shrugged his shoulders, looked at the clock. He might have been Michelangelo interrupted by a cook.

"First of all," began Caroline methodically, "I want to say that in all this I don't care in the least about you. I only care about Lal. I don't like you—"

"Why?" asked Mr. Chalmers unexpectedly.

Caroline paused. It was an *embarras de richesse*. Then instinctively, from a positive welter of vices, she picked what was only his most immediate characteristic.

"Because you're so rude. You're very rude to me, and I don't like it. But I didn't come here to complain of your manners; I came to ask you some questions."

Mr. Chalmers grinned.

"You think I'm rude enough to be truthful?"

"I think I can tell if you're lying," said Caroline calmly. "In the first place, do you want to marry Lal?"

Mr. Chalmers frowned.

"The question of marriage simply hasn't arisen. Lal knew I had a wife as soon as she knew me."

"There are such things," said Caroline slowly, "though I very much dislike them, as divorces."

"You can put that out of your head," said Mr. Chalmers at once. "My wife wouldn't think of it. She's a woman of high principles."

Caroline had a sudden flash of insight.

"And I suppose you're just as pleased that she is?" she said tartly.

Without answering, the artist heaved himself away from the wall and on to the edge of the table. All his movements were heavy, loose, and somehow extremely masculine. He was now so close that Caroline's nose could distinguish a faint odour of tobacco, turpentine, and ancient tweed. An extremely masculine odour. . . .

"How old are you?" she asked suddenly.

"Thirty-five."

"Then you're old enough to see how—how disastrous this must be for Lal. For you don't expect it to last?"

"It doesn't generally," admitted Mr. Chalmers.

The answer, so shocking in its implications, affected Caroline less than she would have believed possible. For her mind was already busied with a new and unexpected impression, which, as their interview progressed, had been growing stronger and stronger: that the passive spirit, in all this terrible business, was the man's, the active Lal's. She looked at him again: he sat frowning, sulky, as though the whole affair were simply a nuisance to him. And so, Caroline suddenly perceived, it was. He was that most destructive of all male types: the drifter. He had doubtless drifted into marriage as he had once drifted into love affairs; any woman who came his way would simply sweep him along. His wife had swept him to Hampstead, Lady Westcott to Friar's Green; now Lal was proposing to sweep him somewhere else, and as long as it gave him no trouble, he would doubtless let her. But Lal. What would happen to Lal when another, stronger current swept him away from her? The blow to her pride would be heavier than the blow to her heart.

"If you like," said Mr. Chalmers suddenly, "I'll write to my wife. She may have changed her mind."

'There you are!' thought Caroline. 'He doesn't mean it, but he says it to keep me quiet! To save trouble!'

"So until I've heard from her," added Mr. Chalmers, "I don't think it's much good our talking."

He got up from the table with an air of relief. He was evidently congratulating himself on his brilliant idea. Caroline rose to go. She quite agreed with him: it was no use their talking, because he would say whatever, at the time, made things easiest for him. But she did not immediately go: for a moment, as they stood face to face, she looked at him searchingly, trying to see what it was Lal found so irresistibly attractive. She saw a heavy countenance, not good-looking, with a deep furrow between the eyes: a skin now rather colourless without its tan, a mouth curving higher on one side than the other. . . .

"Wondering what they see in me?" asked Mr. Chalmers.

"Yes," said Caroline; and at that moment—just for one instant— she did see it. She saw him as something huge, untamed, like those creatures half-horse, half-man, that Ancient Greeks used to carve in stone. The image was gone almost before she could seize it; but she had, for that instant, felt the desire to know, challenge, and master something strange, powerful, and ruthless.

'Nonsense!' Caroline told herself sharply. 'He's weak as water!'

"I'll write tonight," Mr. Chalmers was promising, "and as soon as I hear, I'll let you know."

Caroline nodded. She was thinking of something more important.

"Mr. Chalmers!" she said from the doorway. "I don't want Lal to know I've been here. You're not to tell her. If you do"— Caroline's voice was suddenly humorous—"she'll make you go off tomorrow!"

III

A little wearily, but on the whole in better spirits than she set out, Caroline walked back to Friar's End. Her problem was to some extent simplified: for she now saw that if she could deal with Lal she would have dealt with Gilbert Chalmers too. There was no fear of an abduction—unless, indeed, Lal abducted Mr.

Chalmers; and the state of the school-room walls, which she had not failed to examine, gave her additional comfort.

'They won't be done for weeks!' thought Caroline.

She turned in at Friar's End gate, walked up the drive, and saw, standing before the house, a strange car.

CHAPTER XI

I

IT WAS strange, not only to Caroline's eye, but also to that immaculate gravel: it was at least fifteen years old, it was extremely dirty, and it bore in addition the unmistakable stamp of the car which is never garaged but simply left outside. A little in front of it stood the girl-driver; she had not yet, apparently, rung the bell, but stood doubtfully gazing first at the house, then at the gardens, then at a small piece of paper she had taken from her pocket. 'She's come to the wrong place,' thought Caroline; and stepped helpfully forward.

The girl swung round. She was tall, slim, to Caroline's eye rather plain, and wore a heavy tweed coat and a red cotton handkerchief knotted loosely round her neck.

"Does Mrs. Smith live here?"

In some surprise Caroline disclosed her identity. The girl gave her a swift considering look, nodded, and without any further preparation said baldly,

"I've come about Leon. He's rather ill."

There is this to be said for understatement, that if it does not necessarily check alarm, and very rarely deceives, it at least helps to steady the emotional temperature. Like a cue in the theatre, it can be answered only in its own key, or in one so very little higher that the progress towards panic is considerably retarded. Caroline was very much alarmed indeed, but she was not panic-struck. If the girl showed no emotion, neither would she. Automatically leading the way in, passing through the hall to the morning-room, she said calmly,

"I'm so sorry, I don't remember your name." The girl smiled.

"You couldn't. You've never seen me before. My name's Margaret—Meg—Halliday, and I'm a friend of Leon's. He got a fearful cold, and didn't look after it, and it turned into influenza, so I took him into my studio. I've nursed him all right, and he's had a doctor, but he's still pretty queer. In fact, if you can come up to Town, I think you'd better."

For a minute, before this flood of information so nonchalantly loosed, Caroline stood dumb. Lal and Mr. Chalmers were both wiped from her mind: she had thoughts for no-one but Leon. Leon ill, Leon—from the way this young woman spoke of him—apparently destitute, Leon no longer in that nice boarding house, but dependent on this young woman for roof and succour! What could have been happening? What violent and secret calamity could have so suddenly overtaken him? 'I—I'll have to tell his father!' thought Caroline vaguely. . . . Then fear caught her again, and she put out a hand and steadied herself against the girl's shoulder.

"He isn't going to die," said Miss Halliday, with her usual distinctness.

"You should have fetched me before," muttered Caroline. "You should have fetched me at once!"

"I couldn't. Leon was too ill to be bothered, and I didn't know where you lived."

For an instant Caroline was startled from her distress. She knew Leon well enough, this young woman, to take him into her home, and yet she did not know where his family lived! Like everything else it was inexplicable! And even so—

"They'd have known at the hotel!" said Caroline.

"What hotel?"

"The Kensington Gardens, where Leon lives."

"But he doesn't. He lives in Coram Street!"

It was like a conversation in a nightmare, a conversation in which nothing makes sense. Miss Halliday went on.

"That was where I did get your address in the end. I dashed round to see if any letters had come for him, and there was one forwarded from here. I believe there was another address on it as well."

Caroline stood in bewilderment. She felt as though a door in her own house, that she passed every day, had suddenly been thrown open: as though behind it lay a whole range of rooms and closets, staircases and corridors, of which she had never before suspected the existence. 'I don't know anything about him!' she thought. 'I don't know anything at all!'

"Would you like me to drive you up now?" asked Miss Halliday. "Because if not, I ought to be getting back."

"Of course," said Caroline quickly. The moment of bewilderment had passed: she was her proper self again, calm, methodical, perfectly able—whatever Leon had done—to deal with both it and him. Her mind, back on its natural plane, began to work quickly and easily, even reminding her, as she mentally counted up her ready cash, that Miss Halliday might be glad of some tea—or possibly sherry, which would be a good deal quicker. . . . She rang; gave instructions, and added that she herself would be away for the night. She would pack her own bag, and be off in about ten minutes. Then, instinctively waiting until the butler had gone, she turned back to Miss Halliday.

"Does Leon want any clothes?"

"Only pyjamas," said Meg easily. "He's got six pairs already, but he likes to change them twice a day."

Caroline went upstairs and put together one of her own cambric nightgowns and four more pairs of Leon's silk pyjamas. While she was packing them she heard a step outside; the door opened and there was Lal.

"*Lal!*" said Caroline. She stood and stared at her; for the first time in her life she had forgotten that she had a daughter.

"*Lal!*" said Caroline again.

"What's happened?" asked Lal, advancing into the room. "Has father had a fit?"

"Leon's ill, and I'm going up to see him. I shall be away for the night, perhaps longer." Caroline hesitated; appalling thoughts were suddenly awake in her mind. "Lal," she said a third time, "you won't—while I'm gone—do anything silly?"

"You mean I won't do a bunk with Gilbert?" said Lal more precisely. "Well, I shan't, darling; but I don't think you need have bothered. Haven't I always promised I'd tell you first?"

She waited, righteous and aloof, as one expecting an apology; but no apology came. For once, in her anxiety for one child, Caroline seemed to have forgotten what was due to the other.

II

Miss Halliday's studio, which they reached about five o'clock, was large, well lit, but to Caroline's eye (now used to the luxury of Friar's End) almost poverty-stricken in its bareness. It occupied nearly the whole first floor of an ancient Bloomsbury mansion, and might have been the very drawing-room in which Miss Swartz played her three pieces while Amelia waited for George Osborne. But the house, since then, had come badly down in the world: there were five extra door-bells, each with its visiting-card, and not one of the six inhabitants seemed ever to have heard of brass polish. Steps, hall, and staircase were all equally dirty, nor was Miss Halliday's studio particularly clean. It was cleaner than the rest, however, and Caroline's eye, instinctively recoiling from a half-finished nude, lit with positive pleasure on a large laundry basket.

"Jane's been," whispered Miss Halliday, with an air of relief.

"Jane?"

"She lives upstairs. I asked her to give an eye to Leon. She's taken in the laundry. I expect Leon's asleep, but of course you'd like to see him?"

Caroline nodded, and moved to the door. But Miss Halliday, instead of leading the way to another apartment, made for a great seven-fold Chinese screen that jutted from the outer wall (concealing the last of the three long windows) half-way into the room. Caroline followed: and behind it found her son Leon asleep in Miss Halliday's bed.

III

Only the fear of waking him kept her from exclaiming aloud. He was thin, white, unbelievably aged by a week's growth of beard: he looked as though he had been ill for months, and as though he would take months to recover. The tears started to her eyes. "Leonard," whispered Caroline. "My dearest boy!" He did not stir, he had not heard; she might be as foolish as she wished. She stood half smiling, half weeping, murmuring the childish endearments to which both he and Lal so strongly objected: she indulged herself to the full.

A sound from the outer room, as of some one entering, brought her back to her senses; and shifting her eyes from Leon's face she began to examine his surroundings. The bed he lay in was of the truckle or camp variety, covered with two blankets, a motor rug, and a woman's tweed coat. More female garments, among them a spotted dressing-gown, hung in close proximity to Leon's trousers. His underwear occupied one chair, his tray and water-jug another: there was also a flat-topped trunk on which his shaving tackle and soap lay cheek by jowl with Miss Halliday's brushes.

It was practically—thought Caroline with a shock—a double bedroom.

She was still trying to assimilate the fact, and in particular to discover her own mental attitude to it, when a light tapping on the screen heralded Miss Halliday's reappearance. Her aplomb was staggering: she carried the new pile of pyjamas in one hand, her own coat and muffler in the other, and it seemed as though neither hand knew what the other did.

"Do you want to see the doctor?" she asked softly; and taking the answer for granted, stood back to let Caroline pass. Either from motives of delicacy, however, or quite possibly because she simply wanted to use a comb, she herself remained behind the screen; but she waited just long enough to effect an introduction.

"Dr. Baker, Mrs. Smith," said Miss Halliday correctly.

Caroline looked at him with something like horror. He was extremely young, scarcely older than Leon himself, and his small fair mustache was not yet properly grown. She wouldn't have trusted him with a cut finger. . . .

"Mrs. Smith?" he repeated.

"Yes," said Caroline almost accusingly. "Will you please tell me exactly what has happened?"

"There's nothing to worry about," said the young man quickly. "It's just a bad go of influenza. Meg—Miss Halliday—found him ill, and called me in as soon as she got him here. I can assure you, Mrs. Smith, she's done everything possible—"

"She has indeed," interrupted Caroline severely, "and I'm very grateful to her. But what I do not understand is *why* she had to. Why didn't you send him straight to a nursing home?"

Dr. Baker hesitated. ('As well he may!' thought Caroline.) But his answer, when it came, was not at all what she expected.

"You see, Mrs. Smith—nursing homes are rather expensive things."

It was now Caroline's turn to pause. Nursing homes *were* expensive, of course: but couldn't Leon afford them? Or if he hadn't the money in hand, could he possibly have doubted that his family would foot the bill? There was something here, she felt, that she did not understand; and with her usual directness she went straight to the point.

"Didn't you think Leon could pay?"

"No," said Dr. Baker, with equal simplicity. "He always seemed as hard up as the rest of us."

It was at this point in their conversation—the second fantastic, dream-conversation of the day—that Miss Halliday's voice broke cheerfully in.

"He's awake," she said, "and I've told him you're here."

Caroline turned and left them.

IV

Her first thought, even at that slightly melodramatic moment, was that whereas she had left Leon in yellow pyjamas, he was now wearing green. They made him look even more pallid than before, but his eyes were lively.

"Well, my dear?" said Caroline, as detached a parent as could be imagined.

Leon grinned feebly.

"Aren't you going to shed a single tear over me?"

"Certainly not," said Caroline. "I'm going to give you a good talking to. As soon as you're better, Leon, you'll have a lot to explain."

At once his expression changed. He seemed to close up, to retire behind invisible defences.

"I gather Meg's been making a fool of herself," he said wearily.

"If you mean by coming down to Friar's End," said Caroline, "she's done nothing of the kind. She ought to have come long ago, and I've no doubt she would have, if only you hadn't been so—so silly. Leon, *why*—?" She broke off: it was obviously impossible, at that moment, to start cross-examining him. 'I must wait till he's better,' she thought, 'then it will all have to be gone into.' Without a word, therefore, she opened her bag, took out five one-pound notes, and slipped them under his pillow. Leon moved his head impatiently.

"What's that for?"

"You seem," said Caroline, not without irony, "to be penniless." She paused, half expecting an explanation—some tale of wild extravagance, or of a bogus film company, or even—Caroline winced—of a rapacious chorus girl. She winced, but she would have understood. Faced by the most brassy-haired charmer in London, she would have fought Leon's battles, borne him scatheless away, and then forgiven him. But no such comfort was now offered her: and when Leon at last spoke it was simply to evade the issue.

"If you don't mind," he said politely, "I think I'll go to sleep."

An old, long-forgotten formula rose in Caroline's mind.

"And perhaps you'll wake up in a better temper," she said severely.

His lips moved; she bent over him, inquiring. "What is it, my dear?"

"I'm asking God," said Leon clearly, "to make me a better boy."

CHAPTER XII

I

IN THREE days, said Dr. Baker, Leon could go down to Friar's End: and since for that short time, it was not worth moving him to a nursing home, he remained where he was. Miss Halliday too stayed where she was, only sleeping with Jane upstairs instead of on the couch in the studio. As for Caroline, she took a small room in a Bloomsbury hotel which she found for herself and enjoyed the experience very much indeed.

"What's it called?" asked Meg.

"The Glen Lomond," said Caroline complacently. "It's just round the corner, so whenever you want me, I can be here in a minute. I'd stay all day, my dear, willingly, but it might interfere with your work." Meg looked up over her drawing-board with a wary eye. Caroline was to come every morning to perform Leon's toilet, every noon to get his lunch, and every night to put him to bed. She said quickly,

"It would rather, Mrs. Smith, because I'm having a model."

"A model?" repeated Caroline.

"That sort of thing," Meg nodded her head towards a couple of realistic male nudes. "As a matter of fact it's the same man."

Caroline started.

"Here?"

"At half-past two. If you drew yourself," said Meg amicably, "of course I'd ask you to stay; but we can't have spectators."

Caroline glanced from Miss Halliday to the nudes, and from the nudes back to Miss Halliday.

"You mean you have him *alone*?"

"No such luck," said Miss Halliday simply. "I can't afford it. Jane comes down from upstairs, and a couple of men. It's half-a-crown an hour."

The medley of art, morality, and economics was more than Caroline could cope with. She half rose: a step sounded outside: might it not be the model himself, about to burst in, fling off his clothes, and spring into the forceful attitude of the Discobolus? The precision of the image—the astounding flight of her own imagination—sent the blood to her face; and blushing furiously Caroline hurried downstairs, hurried along the street, back to the soothing and respectable atmosphere of the Glen Lomond Private Hotel.

II

The Glen Lomond was small, shabby, but to Caroline, from the circumstances of her staying there alone, a place of novel and adventurous charm. There was a large dining-room, hung with engravings after Landseer, where she took her meals at a table all to herself. The waiter, small and shabby like the hotel, looked after her beautifully, and the excitement of not knowing what was coming lent an added interest to every meal. The food at Friar's End was perhaps better cooked, but then she had ordered it herself, not only with care, but also with foresight. Here, if there was mutton for lunch, one never knew whether it would reappear as mince or rissoles—or even as *vol-au-vent*—for the evening's entrée. After dinner she took coffee in the lounge, a room even larger than the dining-room where Indian students—for the place was absolutely cosmopolitan—sat perpetually sipping and smoking cigarettes. A good many of them were residents, and curry occurred frequently on the menu; but Caroline, unprejudiced by Anglo-Indian contacts, was not disturbed. She liked the whole place very much indeed, and on the third evening, wishing to give Miss Halliday a treat, confidently and benevolently invited her to dinner.

"What about Leon?" asked Meg.

"He can go to sleep," Caroline looked at her son—he was sleeping then—with sensible calm. Her panic had been brief: as soon as she knew that Leon was not in danger she had at once reverted to the fundamental maxim—doubly proved on his youthful measles and chicken-pox—of never thinking him, or letting him think himself, worse than he was. "We'll have dinner at seven, dear," she said, "and then if you like to go to the pictures, I'll come back here."

Meg smiled. She had a vision of herself being left at the cinema door with a three-and-sixpenny ticket thrust firmly into her hand: and such indeed was Caroline's design. But she had another object as well. She had been thinking about Miss Halliday a great deal. She thought about Leon too, of course; but the subjects were to a certain extent one, and the other half of the Leon problem—the question of his extraordinary indigence—would obviously have to wait till he was well enough to be scolded. But Meg she could and did think about: and as a result of her thoughts had come to a very important conclusion.

She was resolved, when Meg and Leon should acknowledge their engagement, to put no obstacles in their way.

He could certainly have done better: but he might also do a great deal worse. Whatever her antecedents (and Caroline determined to look them up as soon as possible), Miss Halliday was undoubtedly a lady. In an extremely difficult situation she had carried herself with great dignity. And what a situation it was! Everything to be explained, and no one to explain it! For Leon, the only person competent, was evidently too ill even to recognize this obvious duty. Perhaps he thought Meg had explained already: that by simple announcement of their betrothal she had already regularized her position; not realizing (in his masculine obtuseness) that it was something no nice girl could possibly do. Miss Halliday had not done so: and Caroline greatly admired both her delicacy and self-restraint.

So she asked Meg to dinner, and after they had finished their fruit salad led her to the ladies' drawing-room. It was rather cold, because no one ever went there, but as a price of privacy Caroline was perfectly content to wear a woolly jacket. She offered one to Meg, but Meg refused.

"The child's nervous!" thought Caroline; and without further delay said kindly,

"My dear, you needn't be afraid to tell me. . . . I suppose you and Leon are engaged?"

"Oh, *no*," said Miss Halliday.

They looked at each other in mutual surprise. Miss Halliday put down her coffee-cup and turned squarely to face her hostess. "We're not, really, Mrs. Smith. I'd have told you."

Seeing, as she thought, her mistake, Caroline tried again.

"But you're going to be, my dear? When Leon's better and everything's cleared up?"

"Oh, no!" said Margaret again. She looked at Caroline consideringly: she seemed (thought Caroline without rancour) to be wondering how much the old lady could understand. "You've got it all wrong, Mrs. Smith. I'm awfully fond of Leon, but I'm not in love with him, nor is he with me. We've no more idea of marrying each other than of jumping over the moon. When he was so awfully ill, I had to bring him here because there was nothing else to do; I didn't know then, of course, that he was so disgustingly rich. But I'd have done the same for any one—any one that I liked; and I hope Leon would have done it for me. If he wouldn't," finished Miss Halliday crisply, "he damn well ought."

The extraordinary young woman was then silent, and Caroline, as usual after any speech of Miss Halliday's, felt her brain stagger beneath a flood of astonishing information. What sort of world was this, she asked herself, in which the young of different sexes took each other literally into their beds, nursed each other through sickness, and then refused to get married? In what odd pocket of society had Leon so effectually taken root? And there was another phrase, a phrase that stuck and rankled: *'so disgustingly rich'* said Miss Halliday: and she had uttered it casually, *en passant*, obviously with no intent to wound. Why 'disgustingly'? There was nothing disgusting about riches—so long, of course, as they were honestly earned. If Miss Halliday was as unworldly as all that, reflected Caroline ironically, it was perhaps just as well she did *not* want to marry Leon; and here her thoughts coming full circle, Leon's mother found herself suddenly back in her original position. She said firmly, "Whatever you may feel about Leon, I'm sure he's fond of *you*, my dear."

"Oh, he's quite *fond* of me," agreed Miss Halliday.

"And if he does ask you to marry him, I hope you'll at least think carefully about it."

Miss Halliday smiled. She looked at Caroline with genuine affection.

"I suppose that means you're going to make him, Mrs. Smith, so that I shan't lose my reputation?" Now this was exactly what Caroline did mean, though she would not have put it so crudely. Without giving a direct answer, she said gently,

"My dear, *we* know—I know, that you did it from the best possible motives; and I'm more grateful than I can say. But if any one else were to hear of it—"

"But they have," said Miss Halliday. "Every one."

"Every one?"

"Well, Jerry—that's Dr. Baker—and the charwoman, and the girl upstairs who came down while I had to go out, and of course all my friends and all Leon's friends, and I expect one or two people at *his* place—and—oh, everybody, Mrs. Smith! And really it hasn't damaged my reputation in the least. Perhaps"— she smiled—"you'd think I hadn't much of a one to start with—"

"Oh, no!" said Caroline quickly. "I'm sure—I could tell at once— that you were nice. No one could ever think anything else. If you weren't, how could I want Leon to marry you? And as it is I do want him to—not just because of your reputation, my dear, but because I should like you for a daughter-in-law." Miss Halliday did a most unexpected thing. She flew across the room, caught Caroline round the shoulders and gave her a violent school-boy hug.

"I'd have you for a mother-in-law any day!" she cried regretfully. "It's such a pity it won't happen!"

III

The next day, in the car sent on from the works, swathed with rugs and shawls against the cold, Leon was taken to Friar's End. He showed no signs of pleasure (such as Caroline expected) at getting back to his comfortable home. He was docile, but not enthusiastic. On the back seat, less swathed but warmly wrapped up, sat Meg Halliday.

"I'm not match-making," Caroline told her son firmly, "but I like her, and I'm indebted to her, and I think she needs a holiday. I've asked her for a week."

"You'd better ask that doctor-fellow too," said Leon.

Caroline was at once interested.

"Are they engaged?"

"Not *engaged*," Leon said patiently, "but he's very keen on her. Besides, you like him, and you're indebted to him, and he needs a holiday."

"Nonsense!" said Caroline.

Now looking back over her shoulder, she was very pleased to see Meg there. For the explanation given to Leon had not been altogether candid. She had invited Meg partly indeed from pure benevolence—the girl obviously wanted feeding up—but partly, also, on less altruistic grounds because she felt that in the coming negotiations between herself and her children Miss Halliday might be useful in the role of interpreter. She was of their generation, talked and behaved in the same sort of way, and yet was oddly sympathetic to Caroline as well. Her father (now dead) had been an admiral.

The car slid over Ham Common, paused at the Kingston traffic, and ten minutes later was in sight of Friar's Green. Leon looked at his mother in surprise. She was sitting bolt upright, her face suddenly anxious; and as he thus examined her he noticed for the first time that there was grey in her hair.

Remorsefully, pricked by compunction, he slid a hand under her arm.

"Sorry I gave you a fright, darling!"

To his great astonishment, there was no response. Caroline did not even look round. The car had stopped; assisted from the rear by Hilton, she was already getting out. Regardless of her son, regardless of her guest, she walked straight into the hall and from the very threshold sent a sharp call echoing through the house.

"Lal!" called Caroline.

On the landing above a door opened. Caroline looked up and with a great show of nonchalance began to remove her gloves. It was all right. Lal was still there.

CHAPTER XIII

I

IF LEON were well enough to go out, he was well enough to be scolded, and when, observing a brilliantly fine morning, he announced his intention of walking down to the village, Caroline decided that she would talk to him that afternoon.

In the meantime she made him put on two mufflers, one round his neck, the other under his overcoat and pinned behind the back. She also went with him herself, so that with Lal and Meg Halliday they made a party of four. "Quite a family outing!"

said Leon; but to Caroline, who considered family outings very nice things, the remark was not annoying. Lal, on the other hand, frowned. She had no mind to be escorted to the school-room by her mother, her brother, and her brother's possible fiancée. She walked a little apart, her overall in her hand, and would not join in the conversation.

"I like this!" cried Meg Halliday, as they approached the wintry Green. "It's absolutely Dutch!"

"You ought to see it in summer," said Caroline, gratified but a little puzzled. "When the may trees are out, it's a real picture."

"Miss Halliday," said Leon, "prefers trees without leaves and the Living Skeleton to the Venus de Milo. Don't you, darling?"

Caroline glanced from one to the other. The first part of his speech was of course nonsense; but had that last word been 'darling,' or hadn't it? It had been said so quickly, so lightly, that she was not sure; and since their countenances gave her no indication—since Meg's continued unblushing, and Leon's unabashed—she was still in a puzzle over it when her thoughts, like every one else's, were suddenly diverted by the appearance on the path outside the Three Feathers, of a tall masculine figure moving uncertainly towards them.

"Good God!" cried Miss Halliday. "There's Gilbert Chalmers!"

II

For a moment no one answered her. But they continued to walk on, and Mr. Chalmers standing his ground, another few steps brought them all within ear-shot. It was then that Caroline asked, a trifle belatedly, whether Meg had met him before.

"Rather," said Meg. "We used to live in the same studios."

"She's probably nursed him through diphtheria," added Leon with a grin.

"On the contrary, *he* nursed me—which is more than you ever did." Meg raised her voice to a cheerful shout. "What the hell are you doing here, Gilbert?" she called. "Corrupting the local morals?"

"They don't need it," called back Mr. Chalmers, now advancing in turn. "And what the hell are *you*?"

He seemed unaffectedly glad to see her. They did not shake hands, but stood exchanging a species of insulting pleasantries while the Smiths waited beside in what was practically a family group. Caroline glanced quickly at her two children: Leon was grinning with amusement, evidently looking for the first opportunity to join in; but Lal stood aloof—not gauchely sulking, but as though she had temporarily retired into a private world of her own. She looked as though she might be thinking about Primitives.

"But what *are* you doing here?" asked Meg suddenly.

"I'm frescoing a Sunday-school room. I'm the industrious apprentice. I've done two walls in three months. I'd like you to have a look at them."

"Who's been helping you?" asked Meg promptly.

The artist looked across at Lal. She was gazing at the landscape with an air of concentration.

"Lal has. She's got a remarkable talent for it." He walked across and took her familiarly by the elbow. "Come and show off, Lal, before I take all the credit."

"Certainly," said Lal. "If Miss Halliday would be interested."

"Interested! It's her job," said Mr. Chalmers. He swung round and with the other hand seized hold of Meg. "We'll have some instructive criticism, and probably a stand-up fight. She's the rudest woman in England, when she gives her mind to it."

"May I come and hold the sponge?" asked Leon politely.

"No, you mayn't!" cried Caroline, suddenly alert. "You'll catch your death of cold! You're coming home now, with me!" And she in turn grasped hold of Leon, swinging him to her side of the road. Meg laughed. Lal said coldly,

"Well, if we're not going to waste the morning, let's go."

She moved, the others followed; and Caroline, as she and Leon turned the corner, caught a last glimpse of Mr. Chalmers, striding cheerfully and easily between the two women.

III

Lal reappeared for lunch, and immediately afterward went back to the school-room. She did not invite Meg to accompany her, and Meg, when asked what she would like to do, said she thought she would read *Treasure Island*. Caroline smiled approvingly, foreseeing an undisturbed hour with Leon; but as though Leon foresaw it too, he perversely asked Meg to read *Treasure Island* aloud.

"Nonsense!" exclaimed Caroline, "Miss Halliday's here for a rest!"

"Then you read it to both of us," suggested Leon.

Meg picked up the book and tucked it under her arm.

"I won't read aloud, and I won't be read to. And I hope"—she smiled amiably—"you have a very pleasant afternoon. *Au revoir!*"

The door shut behind her. Caroline looked at her son, and Leon looked at his mother.

"If you *do* marry her," said Caroline suddenly, "I shall be very pleased."

"Thank you," said Leon, "I'd as soon marry a lady M.P. I like them clinging."

Caroline looked at him in alarm. What did Leon know of women who—who clung?

"Clinging?" she repeated aloud.

"With large blue eyes," elaborated Leon, "and fluffy fair hair. And possibly the least little hint of a babyish lisp."

The description, to Caroline's ear so precise, renewed one of her early fears. She said, quickly,

"Leon, you're not—you're not married, are you?"

"No, darling, I'm not."

"Then what," demanded Caroline, with the air of one following up a cunning attack, "have you done with all your money?"

Leon lay back on the sofa and looked at the ceiling.

"Nothing, darling."

"But what's become of it? Where *is* it?"

He closed his eyes.

"In the bank, darling."

Completely bewildered, more than a little incredulous, Caroline got up and came to the sofa.

"Then if you haven't spent it, why did you leave that nice hotel where I left you?"

188 | MARGERY SHARP

"If you really want to know—because it was just my idea of hell, dar—"

"Stop calling me darling!" cried Caroline sharply. "You call me darling, darling, darling, and you show no more consideration for my feelings—you don't care how much I worry—you lie there and think you're being amusing, and whether you're telling me the truth or not I don't know!"

She broke off, incoherent. Leon sat up in genuine solicitude.

"Every word I've told you is the exact truth. The money's in the bank. I left that hotel because I couldn't stand it any longer. I'm sorry if I've hurt you, but I do hate these—these investigations."

"But I must know what you're doing!" cried Caroline.

He did not answer; if he had, she suspected, it would have been to say he didn't see why. 'Investigations!' thought Caroline with bitterness: she asked him three questions a year, he didn't answer them, and then said he disliked investigations!

"Well, I'm going to investigate now," she said firmly. "I can understand your leaving, if you didn't like the place, but why didn't you let me know? And why did you go somewhere where they didn't even take care of you?"

"Because it was cheap," said Leon.

Caroline paused. He might be telling the truth, but to her it didn't make sense. He had plenty of money, but he wanted somewhere cheap. He didn't like the Kensington Gardens Hotel, presumably because it wasn't comfortable, and yet he went somewhere ten times more uncomfortable still. In any one except Leon, she would have called it the act of a miser. . . . A thought, suddenly comforting, flashed through her head.

"Were you saving up for anything?"

"No, darling," said Leon. He looked at her anxious face and frowned. It was exactly how Henry frowned, when he saw that a verbal explanation could no longer be put off. "On the contrary," said Leon gloomily. "I was trying to get rid of things. If it had been mine to give away—"

"What, Leon?"

"The money."

It was at that moment, as she stood bewildered, that a phrase of Meg Halliday's returned to Caroline's ear. *"So disgustingly rich"* Miss Halliday had said; and, *"as hard up as the rest of us ..."*

Slowly, dimly, Caroline began to understand. Once given the clew, she could even parallel, from her own experience, the workings of Leon's mind. Had she not suffered herself, in those last days at Morton, from the sense of being undeservedly better off than her neighbours? That Leon, who had been brought up to wealth, should feel so too was strange to her, but not incomprehensible. She remembered the bareness of Meg's studio, the shabbiness of Dr. Baker's clothes; they were not like the people in Morton, who disliked wealth because they envied it; on the contrary, they rather despised money, and enjoyed being poor. They considered it a virtue. Caroline did not agree with them because (she reflected) she was old enough to have sense; but she saw the attitude's charm as one particularly becoming to the young. Leon was in good company; if he could survive the week's disgrace, she would do her best to leave him there.

"Leon," she said at last, "would you like me to stop your allowance?"

He stared at her speechless. For once in their joint lives (observed Caroline with complacency) she had thoroughly astounded him. She went on,

"What do they give you now at that film place?"

"Three pounds a week."

"Plenty!" said Caroline.

Leon jumped up and caught her by the shoulders.

"You're the most extraordinary woman I've ever come across!"

"You're not to leave here till you're better, mind!"

"Right."

"And now," added Caroline, fearful of marring her triumph, "I think you'd better go to sleep."

Outside the door she paused. She was feeling extremely pleased with herself. Leon—the unimpressionable!—had called her an extraordinary woman! And even so he had not seen all that was in her mind; for with maternal treachery Caroline was already reflecting that three pounds a week, with a good home behind

you, was a very different thing from just three pounds a week—

IV

Henry seemed pleased to see his wife again, but showed little curiosity about her three days' absence; and this was fortunate, since Caroline, with so much of interest to communicate, had decided, for reasons not clear even to herself, to tell him practically nothing at all. She told him merely that Leon had had influenza, that she had brought him home, and that a very nice Miss Halliday was staying for the week. But she did, just as she was dropping off to sleep—and with the male model, Miss Halliday's reputation, and several other odd facts still stirring in her mind—add one last unguarded remark.

"Things *are* different, Henry!" said Caroline.

But Henry had stopped listening.

CHAPTER XIV

I

THE following morning Caroline, passing the morning-room where she had left Meg Halliday alone, was surprised to hear voices through the open door. Lal had evidently returned.

"Gilbert wants to know," Lal was saying coldly, "whether you'd care to come down and lend a hand?"

"What, with the masterpiece? Not on your life," replied Miss Halliday.

There was a rustle of paper as she returned to *The Times*, then, after a moment's pause, Lal's quick light steps receding through the terrace door. As soon as they were quite gone Caroline entered the room and found Meg sprawling in a chair with the paper scattered round her feet.

"Was that Lal?" asked Caroline disingenuously. Meg swung down her feet.

"Yes. She's just gone back to work. I'm idle."

"And so you should be," said Caroline warmly. "A rest is just what you need." She paused, straightening a cushion, while Meg watched and smiled. For Meg (as Caroline was aware) could not begin, though they both knew exactly what was coming. They were going to have a long, intimate talk on the subject of Lal and Mr. Chalmers.

"Have you known Mr. Chalmers long?" asked Caroline at last.

"About six years, off and on." Meg paused, then made a deliberate addition. "Ever since he married, in fact. His wife used to be at the Slade with me."

"Is she—is she nice?"

"Depends how you like them. Personally," said Miss Halliday, "I always found her a bit elfin."

There was a short pause. 'Elfin?' Caroline was thinking. 'Why *elfin*?' But she brushed the question aside: and when she spoke again it was with accents of such shrewd simplicity that Meg sat up in her chair.

"*Why* did he marry her?" asked Caroline.

"Because her father turned up and made him."

Caroline nodded thoughtfully, as though it were the answer she had expected. It did flash across her mind that this was a very odd way to be talking to a young girl; but Meg seemed quite calm and self-possessed, and she *did* have men models in her studio, and in any case Caroline found it a great relief. She said boldly,

"Lal wants to marry him."

Meg nodded.

"But she can't, of course, unless his wife divorces him. And if his wife doesn't divorce him—"

"She won't," said Meg.

"How do you know?"

"From experience." Meg grinned. "Not that I ever wanted to marry him myself, but I've known a good many women who did."

"And as they couldn't marry him," asked Caroline carefully, "did—did anything happen?"

Meg picked up the scattered paper and began putting it together again. There happened to be an illustrated supplement, which took a good deal of time.

"Gilbert's very . . . dilatory," she said at last.

"You mean," said Caroline sharply, "he doesn't like doing anything that will give him trouble?"

"I mean he doesn't like doing *anything*. He's got no initiative. How did he get here in the first place? Because Lady Westcott brought him. And now he *is* here, he'd stay for months and months, quite happily, until some one moved him on again."

It was a view that exactly coincided with Caroline's own. It embraced the same reading of Mr. Chalmers' character, and the same admission that—some one *might* move him. But it was a different view from Lal's, and Caroline said anxiously,

"But when his painting's finished? Won't he go then?"

"It never will be finished," said Meg calmly. "He never finishes anything. It's a pity, too, because he could do some good stuff. He ought to have been a medieval craftsman working under a foreman with a cudgel."

Caroline sighed. It began to look as though the elopement might be indefinitely postponed, but then so too would be Mr. Chalmers' departure, and until the man were finally removed from Lal's neighbourhood, she felt she would not know a quiet hour. If only—the thought rose unbidden in her mind—if only Miss Halliday would remove him! But Meg was obviously outside the sphere of his attraction. She had too much sense.

"I wish you knew Lal better," said Caroline suddenly.

"She's awfully attractive."

Caroline sighed again. It was no use discussing the child, Miss Halliday was quite right; and besides, she must have seen at once, from that very first encounter, exactly how matters stood.

"What do you think I had better do?" asked Caroline frankly.

"Nothing," said Miss Halliday.

Since that was exactly what she had been doing all along, Caroline ought to have been better pleased; but in spite of Miss Halliday's evident though tacit sympathy, in spite of the relief of having spoken to some one, the conversation was not nearly so satisfactory as yesterday's talk with Leon. Caroline no longer felt extraordinary. She felt just as usual—puzzled and rather stupid. And she felt that if something did not happen soon—if the strain were not rapidly eased—she would decline even from being stupid, and become bad-tempered as well.

II

Miss Halliday's visit, however, progressed comfortably enough. The girl was easy to entertain; in the mornings she amused herself, either reading, or going for walks, or conversing with Leon, and in the afternoon, since the weather was fine though cold, Caroline took them both for motor-drives and tea at some café. Caroline quite enjoyed herself, and Leon, though he pretended to be bored, always ate plenty of cakes and came back hungry. Lal stood aloof; except to deliver a message from Mr. Chalmers, she hardly spoke to Meg at all. The messages were all the same, for it seemed as though he could not bring himself to believe that Meg really intended to remain idle at the house when she might be helping him in the schoolroom. Lal herself added no persuasions: it was bad enough—as Caroline quite sympathetically realized—to have to carry such messages at all; but Gilbert Chalmers was evidently not the man to put any one else's feelings above his own comfort. A note involved finding paper, and an envelope, and some one to carry it; not to employ Lal (who was going back to Friar's End in any case) would have struck him as simply foolish. But on the third morning the waste of Meg's labour proved finally unbearable, and he walked up himself to argue with her in person. It was the first visit he had ever paid to Lal's home.

"There's Chalmers," said Leon, looking out of the window.

Both Lal and Miss Halliday followed his glance, but Caroline, after the first start of surprise, looked at her daughter. Lal was standing very straight, a faint frown between her eyes; and then suddenly, urgently, as though she had just taken a decision, she turned to her neighbour.

"Meg—do come this morning!" said Lal cheerfully.

Miss Halliday raised her eyebrows.

"Are *you* determined to make me work too?"

"Yes," said Lal. "I'm sure you'll be frightfully brilliant. I'll lend you an overall." And without waiting for an answer she jumped up, opened the door, and met Gilbert Chalmers on the threshold.

"Isn't it nice, Gilbert," said Lal gayly, "Meg's coming down too!"

III

So after that Miss Halliday went each morning to the Sunday-school room and assisted with the designs for a St. Crispin and a St. Mark. It was understood by every one that she did so purely to oblige Lal.

Lal was evidently resolved on bold measures, for when Dr. Galbraith came down for the Saturday she left Meg and Gilbert working-together and came back to go for a walk with him. Even after lunch the knowledge that Gilbert was waiting alone did not hurry her away; for Meg and Leon, Eustace and Dr. Galbraith, had settled down to bridge, and Lal showed a marked reluctance to leave them. It was the situation Caroline had once visualized, and drawing further on her imagination she gave the four their tea early and sent them off to Kingston to see a film. Dr. Galbraith indeed would have lingered, but Caroline packed him into the car with strict injunctions to keep an eye on Leon. "The minute you think he's tired," she ordered, "you're to come home; and if the others want to stay, they must take a 'bus."

Dr. Galbraith looked at her affectionately.

"Aren't you going to give me the money for the seats?"

"I'll give Meg the money for some chocolates!" cried Caroline. And she did: she opened her bag, and gave Meg half-a-crown.

IV

Returning through the hall she saw Henry come out of his study and stand looking towards the stairs. It was an odd look, as though the stairs were—were something difficult. Caroline went up behind him and slipped her arm through his.

"Tired, dear?"

His shoulders at once straightened.

"Where are all the others?"

"I've sent them to the pictures. Come and have your tea, Henry."

She led him into the morning-room, poured him fresh tea and another cup for herself. It was so long since they had sat thus together, one on each side of the fire, with no Lal and no Eustace, that Caroline felt quite sentimental.

"It's like Morton!" she said cheerfully. "Do you remember, Henry?"

She would have liked to reminisce a little, to talk about her mother and Cousin Maggie and the house in Cleveland Road; but he would not follow.

"That's a long time ago," said Henry.

There was a short silence: and looking at him again, remembering the extraordinary weariness of his attitude in the hall, Caroline felt a vague uneasiness. She said cautiously,

"Is anything bothering you, dear?"

Henry looked at her sharply.

"What should be bothering me?"

"You mayn't be bothered," said Caroline boldly, "but I do think you're overworked. I'm sure you could get home earlier if you tried."

"You don't know anything about it," said Henry.

"I asked Eustace—"

"Then I wish you wouldn't. If there's anything I dislike it's to know you and Jamieson are discussing me behind my back."

It was the first time he had ever spoken to her with anger, and Caroline was so shocked and distressed that for a moment she could not speak. She sat very still, staring into the fire in the hope that its heat would dry the tears before they fell from her eyes. 'It's because he's always been so good to me,' she told herself, 'I'm not used to it!' And she stared into the coals till a red cavern suddenly crashed and fell in.

"You and Jamieson—" began Henry again.

"We don't!" cried Caroline. "I've never discussed you with him, I wouldn't dream of it! I simply asked him if he didn't think you looked tired, and he said yes. He didn't say another word, he just walked away."

Henry sank back in his chair. His anger seemed to have vanished as suddenly as it had arisen. He looked very tired.

"That's all right, Carrie. Give me another cup of tea."

She poured it out and took it over to him. She wondered whether other wives felt this same impassable barrier between all they felt and all they could say. Would Lal, should she ever marry Dr. Galbraith, be similarly tongue-tied? Caroline could not imagine it; but then she could not imagine Lal anything but young and pretty. When you were young and pretty you could sit on a man's knee and put your cheek against his, and then the barriers disappeared. But a heavy middle-aged woman—! 'I'd seem a perfect fool!' thought Caroline. But she did put her hand, gently and tentatively, upon his shoulder, and Henry smiled.

"What are you doing about Christmas, Carrie?"

"Nothing," said Caroline in surprise. "I hope Leon will be home, and—" she broke off; 'and Lal,' she had been going to say: but whether Lal would be home or not was still a matter for conjecture. Henry, however, did not notice.

"Ask Dr. Galbraith," he said, "and that young woman who's here now. Let's have some people, Carrie, and make a do of it."

"Well!" said Caroline. She felt pleased and astonished; Henry usually hated people, and whenever they had guests kept resolutely out of the way. Caroline liked them: there was nothing she more enjoyed than seeing a tableful of people sit down to a really good tea. But her pleasure in this case was only half in anticipation of the party; she was pleased and touched, and very grateful, because Henry was trying to make up to her.

"We'll have a good time!" promised Caroline.

And impulsively—middle-aged and heavy though she was—she slipped on to the arm of his chair and laid her cheek lightly to his.

CHAPTER XV

I

LATE that night, as Caroline was going to bed, she noticed Lal's door ajar. Automatically her step slackened; she would have liked to go in, to exchange a few comfortable mother-and-daughter commonplaces while Lal was undressing; but such visits were not encouraged. She sighed, she was about to pass on; when at that moment Lal appeared in the doorway.

"Hello, darling," said Lal, in tones of surprise.

She was in her dressing-gown, very slim and youthful, and had a hair-brush in her hand. Instead of shutting the door, however, she even opened it a little wider.

Caroline paused. Lal had been silent all evening, refusing to play cards after dinner, and sitting alone with a book which Caroline suspected her of having already read. But now, as she stood swinging her hair-brush, looking not at her mother but at the corridor beyond, she seemed trying to overcome her own reticence. Caroline felt sure that she was about to say something, that there was something the child wished to communicate, but disliked putting into words; and so indeed it was, for after a moment's silence Lal swung her hair-brush again, looked over Caroline's shoulder, and so, nonchalantly—half in the corridor, half in her room—broke the dreadful news.

"He wants me to go to South America."

II

Caroline's heart seemed to stop. South America! The other side of the world! How could she—how *could* she let Lal go to South America! But if Lal were determined, how could she stop her? Lal was over age. She couldn't be locked up. 'But I will stop her!' thought Caroline desperately. 'I must!' At that moment, had Gilbert Chalmers been at hand, and a precipice adjacent, she would have committed murder without a qualm. Without a qualm, and without a scruple; she felt she could kill Gilbert Chalmers and yet remain a perfectly good wife, mother, and Wesleyan Methodist. Aloud she said idiotically,

"Do you mean Mr. Chalmers?"

Lal nodded.

"And he wants—wants you to go with him?"

"Or Meg," said Lal coldly.

Caroline did not understand. She was not sure even that she had heard. What had Meg Halliday to do with it? Why should Lal mention *her*. It wasn't sense—

"He wants," elaborated Lally, still in that cold, detached voice, "either Meg or me to go with him. I don't think he minds much which. But he doesn't like travelling alone."

With a great effort Caroline imitated, if not her daughter's directness, at least her daughter's nonchalance.

"And is—is Meg going?"

"No," said Lal. "She's not such a fool."

Caroline moistened her lips.

"And you, Lal?"

"I'm not such a fool either," said Lally.

Late into that night Caroline lay awake. She was too thankful to sleep, just as Lal, she suspected, was too unhappy: but while it seemed heartless thus to rejoice, while she did not minimize Lal's hurt, she knew that her own emotion was lasting and Lal's evanescent. The child would cry into her pillow, perhaps grieve a month or two, and then get over it. Her pride, as she had already shown, might be safely depended upon. And though Torquay was now out of the question, Caroline was already determined that after Christmas—not too soon, not too obviously—she would suggest a visit to Switzerland for the winter sports.

'I'd like to go myself!' thought Caroline, almost in surprise.

The plenitude of her relief, the sudden lightness of her heart, were evidently having an odd effect on her. For her fancy quickened; she visualized not only Switzerland, but Paris and Italy, Spain, and the Riviera. Having once crossed the Channel, what was there to stop them? 'I've never been out of England!' thought Caroline. She felt quite indignant; she felt positively reckless. For two pins she'd have gone round the world.

IV

The next day Dr. Baker came down to drive Meg back to Town, and Caroline, to whom all the world was just then her friend, promptly kept him to lunch. She did not, however, find him particularly interesting. He was a nice young man, but not so nice as Dr. Galbraith; he was clever, but not so clever as Leon. Caroline saw that he made a good meal, and took little further notice of him. About an hour after lunch, however, passing through the drawing-room, she found him and Lally still sitting over their coffee-cups, and apparently deep in conversation. Not for the first time that day, Caroline looked at her daughter anxiously;

Lal was less white than she had been at breakfast, less white than when, after a morning spent at the school room, she had returned silently to lunch; but for all that there were rings under her eyes, and Caroline wanted her to lie down. She glanced at the young man, therefore, without concealing her surprise, and asked where Meg was.

"With Gilbert," said Lal, pronouncing the name very distinctly. "She'll be back by tea."

Caroline looked at Dr. Baker again, and said that as the day was fine and there were some very pretty walks, he might like to take one. But the stratagem failed, for the young man in turned looked at Lal, who very unnecessarily offered to accompany him. However, they were back in good time, bringing Meg with them, and at eight o'clock that night Caroline and Henry, Lally and Leon were able to take their dinner together, without any stranger present, in the dining-room at Friar's End.

That night, for the first time in many months, Caroline looked upon her assembled family with a quiet heart. She understood Leon, no longer feared for Lal, discovered, in her happiness, fewer signs of fatigue in Henry's face. She was even talking more, asking Leon questions about the film trade, to which Leon replied with unusual goodwill. Though Lal said little, she ate her dinner; it was as much as could be expected of the child, and Caroline was content. Her contentment indeed overflowed, for as Hilton came in with the soup, and contrary to all tradition at Friar's End:

"For what we are about to receive," said Caroline, "the Lord make us truly thankful."

CHAPTER XVI

I

NEVER before had Caroline prepared for Christmas in such a genuine spirit of peace and goodwill. There was peace at Friar's End, goodwill in her heart, and after inviting Meg and Dr. Galbraith each for three days she nearly wrote to Morton and invited Ellen Watts. But to Henry's goodwill, if not to her own, there was a definite limit; and Caroline contented herself with sending a hamper for Ellen and silk stockings for the girls. She nearly sent them dolls: she still visualized them, despite every effort, as the three Whiners, just as she still visualized Ellen as a woman of forty in the fashions of 1918.

"I wonder if she still gives music lessons?" said Caroline aloud.

"Who does?" asked Lally, looking up from a pile of Christmas cards. She was writing on one side of the table, her mother at the other; but whereas Caroline's cards were all gayly coloured, Lal's were mostly severe black-and-white woodcuts, varied by an occasional reproduction of a Van Gogh. "Who does?" said Lally.

"Ellen Watts, dear." Caroline sighed. "You wouldn't remember."

"Yes, I do," said Lal. "She wanted to teach me music, and she had the Whiners, and she was beastly to kiss. I simply loathed her."

"Lal!" cried Caroline automatically.

"So did you, darling; only your conscience wouldn't let you admit it. The more you hated her, the more you asked her to tea." Lal stared at her mother with sudden suspicion. "You're not thinking of having her for Christmas, are you?"

Caroline shook her head.

"Your father wouldn't like it. Which do you think for Miss Brodrick, dear—the church or the mail-coach?"

Lal did not answer. Instead, very casually, she made a most unexpected suggestion.

"What about Dr. Baker?"

"For a Christmas card?" Caroline looked at the mail-coach doubtfully. It *was* rather masculine, perhaps, with all those horses.

. . .

"I mean to stay," said Lal, more unexpectedly still.

"To stay!" repeated Caroline in surprise. "But we hardly know him!"

"He looked after Leon. And he's got nowhere to go. I'm sure he'd come if you asked him."

Suddenly intelligent, Caroline nodded.

"Because of Meg. Leon told me there was something."

"Something? Does he mean they're engaged?"

"Not *engaged*," quoted Caroline, "but he's very fond of her. I'll ask him with pleasure, if you think Meg would like it."

"Then do," said Lal; and returned to addressing envelopes.

Meg came, Dr. Galbraith came, Dr. Baker followed, Henry brought Eustace Jamieson, and Caroline was in her element. She put holly over all the pictures and a great bunch of mistletoe in the hall; she had coloured candles for the dinner-table, and enough boxes of crackers to fill a cupboard. She refused to be kept out of the kitchen, and with her own hands made eight dozen mince pies. This was in the house alone: outside she helped decorate the church, dressed a Christmas-tree for the Sunday school, and provided an after-the-performance supper for the Boy Scouts' entertainment. The children watched with amusement; but the pleasure was infectious, and when a holly-garland fell it was Lal and Dr. Baker who ran to put it up again, and when the mince pies appeared it was Leon who ate them between meals. "The house feels like Christmas!" said Caroline, surveying her work.

On the twenty-fourth Lady Tregarthan came to dinner and added considerably to the gayety of the meal. Her quick old eyes, glancing shrewdly over the table, were bright with amusement; she mocked the young men, jeered benevolently at Lal and Meg, and made even Henry laugh with a lively social history of the old Friar's Green. The R.A., it seemed, had once had an affair with Miss Ada Brodrick: they were passionately in love, they were on the point of elopement, only the sudden distemper of a puppy—Pekingese, in those days—had saved the name of the one, the virtue of the other. "And that's why she now breeds Labradors," added Lady Tregarthan. "I believe they're considerably hardier. . . ."

Looking down the table, Caroline saw Hilton move forward to fill his master's glass. Henry was drinking a little more than usual, and it was evidently good for him; he suddenly began to talk, telling a long story about an intricate correspondence with the War Office, and though no one quite followed, it transpired that the official concerned was a distant connection of Lady Tregarthan's. Distant indeed, but not too distant for her to know all his social history, too, and Henry listened with enjoyment to a couple of scandalous anecdotes. The enjoyment was general; and when Caroline left the table it was with the pleasing conviction that her dinner had gone well.

By the drawing-room fire, a little apart from the two girls, Lady Tregarthan suddenly turned and smiled at her.

"Where's that Chalmers fellow, my dear? I suppose you didn't invite him as well?"

Caroline stared. She had forgotten all about him! For months her constant preoccupation, the artist, during the last week, had vanished completely from her mind.

"I'd forgotten all about him!" she cried.

"Shows your good sense," said Lady Tregarthan. "As a matter of fact, he's gone off to Marion's. She sent a wire for him, and I strongly suspect his train-fare as well. All I hope is she doesn't give him his train-fare back again."

"Oh, well," said Caroline tolerantly, "I suppose he's got to finish his pictures."

"He'll never finish anything, my dear. He's just like an uncle of mine who was constantly making rockeries. The garden looked like a brick-yard, but it never got any forarder. If he isn't back in a month, we'll have the place decently white-washed and that will be that." Lady Tregarthan looked at her hostess with appreciation. "You're a very wise woman, my dear. The way you handled this Lal business—"

"But I haven't!" protested Caroline. "I didn't handle it at all. I should have, and I tried to; but I only made things worse."

Lady Tregarthan sniffed.

"Nonsense, my dear. Didn't you bring that young Halliday woman down?"

"I asked her to stay, because she had been kind to Leon. I never expected her to—to—"

"To come in so useful," supplied Lady Tregarthan. "I grant that may have been luck, but you also kept your head. You didn't fuss, and you didn't nag. And that waiting game's the hardest of all."

"It is!" said Caroline fervently. She almost shuddered. Looking back on those months of suspense was like looking back on a nightmare. But when a nightmare was once over, a sensible person did not look back; and though Caroline disclaimed wisdom, she had quite a high opinion of her sense. There was one dreadful moment, however, that still lingered in her mind; and with a sudden impulse to confession, she said hurriedly,

"Do you know, I once—when I thought he was going to take Lal to South America—I once imagined myself killing him?"

"And quite right too!" said Lady Tregarthan heartily.

III

That night Caroline received her first Christmas present; for as the party broke up Lady Tregarthan suddenly produced, from the pocket of her woollen under-jacket, a roll of ancient creamy lace.

"It's rose-point, my dear," she said curtly. "I don't know what you'll do with it. I'm just giving it you to remember an old woman by."

Deeply touched, Caroline took the package in her hand.

"It's the loveliest thing I've ever had," she said sincerely, "but as for remembering you—it'll be a long time yet—"

"I'm not so sure," snapped Lady Tregarthan. "I'm a tough old crow, but I'm getting on. I had a look at our brasses the other day, and we none of us seem to have seen eighty."

Caroline started. She also knew the Tregarthan tablets: they were just across the aisle from the Friar's End pew. It would be strange if one Sunday she saw her friend's name there as well!

"I had a look at the vault, too," added Lady Tregarthan. "It's getting extremely damp, but I don't suppose that will worry me. It's a comforting thought that one's bones won't feel rheumatism."

"If you've any doubts," suggested Leon politely, "what about cremation?"

Lady Tregarthan sniffed.

"I'm not going to be put into an oven at my age, young man. I shall be buried with decency. And if you come to the funeral in flannel trousers, you'll find orders to turn you out."

Caroline listened in silence. She wouldn't much mind being buried, she thought, if only she could be put straight into the earth without all the paraphernalia of coffins and things—Just straight into the earth, among the roots and pebbles and—yes—and the worms if you liked, with the good soil settling comfortably round her as it settled round a bulb or a young tree. . . . A shroud? Well, she wouldn't mind a shroud, that would soon be rid of; but as for great lumps of tree-trunk—still worse, great lumps of lead—thrust indigestibly into the kind bosom of the earth—it was positively barbarous!

"Of course, mother ought to have a mausoleum," said Lal affectionately, "something with harps and cherubs and a nice front door!"

IV

Christmas Day, Boxing Day, passed, and Caroline continued to enjoy herself. So did every one else, and even the bridge Leon insisted on in the afternoons sounded and looked like a round game. Neither Henry nor Caroline played, but the other five cut in and out, and dummy and the odd man quite often did something else. The dummy was frequently Lal, especially when the odd man was Togo Galbraith, and they constantly distracted the others by the vivacity of their conversation. "Lal, dear!" said Caroline reprovingly, as Dr. Baker revoked for the third time; but there was no reproof in her heart; she was only too pleased at the spectacle of Lal's flirtatiousness. There was no other word for it: Lal was flirting outrageously with Togo Galbraith. But she did not forget her duty to the guests; as soon as the last rubber was over she spent a full hour listening to Dr. Baker play tunes on the piano. In Caroline's opinion they were very dull tunes indeed; but Lal listened politely and even kept asking for more. Eustace disappeared with Henry, Meg and Leon very sensibly went out to get up an appetite for dinner, and Caroline indulged herself with a nice lie down; she felt that as soon as Dr. Baker stopped, Togo Galbraith would be able to cut in and take Lal for a walk too. If the tunes went on much longer, indeed, Caroline was determined to go downstairs and say that Henry was working. She rehearsed the phrase drowsily; but before the plan could be realized, the tunes had sent her to sleep.

CHAPTER XVII

I

ON THE morning after Boxing Day the visitors departed; but there was still one Christmas engagement for Caroline to look forward to. This was a dinner at Tregarthan Court, on the following Saturday, and in anticipation of it Caroline added to her brown silk dress a fichu of Lady Tregarthan's lace. Since the lace was long, and far too precious to cut, the adornment was voluminous; but Caroline tucked an end in here, pinned fold back there, and regarded the result with a good deal of satisfaction. Lal, however, did not.

"There's no *need*, really, Mother," she said. "Lady Tregarthan knows you like it. Besides—"

"Besides what?" asked Caroline pugnaciously.

Lal hesitated.

"Darling, if you gave *her* a piece of lace, you wouldn't expect her to wear it the very next time she came here?"

"Yes, I should," said Caroline. "Or at any rate I'd be very pleased if she did. And she'll be pleased to see *me*. She'll be pleased to see how nice it looks, and that I'm making use of it." Caroline looked again into the glass and settled the lace complacently about her shoulders. The boldness of her defence, so surprising to her daughter, was almost equally surprising to herself: but for once she meant to have her own way. And the lace—she picked up the hand-mirror—was really handsome! It was good enough for a duchess! She said firmly,

"I'm sure it looks very nice, Lal. And when I'm gone, mind you're to have it."

Lal looked at her with eyes grown suddenly wide and startled.

"I can't imagine you gone," she said quickly. "You're like the Rock of Ages."

"Well!" exclaimed Caroline, quite huffed, "I'm not so old as that yet!"

II

Looking forward to the new year, indeed, Caroline felt herself suddenly much younger, for the future smiled to her: she visualized Leon industrious and communicative, Lal married and settling down, Henry spending less time at the works and more at Friar's End. She had an idea that once Lal and Leon were out of the way he would feel more at home there; and though the notion should undoubtedly have reflected on both parent and children, Caroline somehow managed in her mind that it did not. The children were not ordinary children, nor was Henry an ordinary father; he had important things to think about, his mind was naturally preoccupied. And the children, separated, from him by the enormous gulf of their different education and outlook, could hardly make the first advances. They spoke another language: Caroline, bi-lingual, had for years been their interpreter. She had explained the stoppage of Leon's allowance by saying, not that the boy was ashamed of having money, but that he desired to make his own way in the world. Henry had seemed quite satisfied, and even pleased; but when he attempted, a day or two later, to give Leon a word of encouragement, both praise and advice fell sadly flat. Henry had been awkward, Leon embarrassed, until Caroline, in mortal dread of being found out, quickly guided the conversation into a more impersonal channel. Caroline had sometimes a difficult time of it; only with her husband alone, or with her children alone, was she completely at ease. 'And Henry is at ease with me,' she thought. 'He'll talk when we're by ourselves . . .'

That was another thing she had to make right in her mind. She knew, though she would not admit it, that Henry was shy of talking before his children. They seemed to know so much more than he did. They were so extraordinarily well-informed. And they had a quick, glancing mode of speech—like the dialogue in the new films—with which he could not keep pace. Caroline was often left behind herself, but for her it did not matter; they knew she was slow, and made rather a joke of it. But Henry did not care to be made a joke of, so he held his tongue and let them chatter. 'It's simply that he hasn't time,' thought Caroline loyally. 'If he took films seriously, he'd know more about them than Leon. If he'd had Leon's opportunities, he—he'd have been Prime Minister!'

She thoroughly believed it. Her faith, like her love, knew no limits. And in these days, as though at the prospect of living once more with her husband, that love gathered new force. She felt more closely attached to him, more nearly one with him, than ever before. He was always in her mind. For the past year or more she had been forced to think constantly of either Lal or Leon; now, that double anxiety relieved, she could think solely of her husband.

It was perhaps for these reasons that when a telephone rang, and was not answered, her heart knew better than her happy and confident mind.

III

The call was made on the afternoon of the Saturday on which they were to dine at Tregarthan Court. Caroline had come in to lunch and found a message from Eustace Jamieson saying that Mr. Smith was working late, and would not be home for tea; she lunched in her usual tranquillity, but afterwards reflected that Henry might possibly have forgotten the evening's engagement. Eustace Jamieson might have gone home, the works were certainly shut, but she could still get through to Henry's private number. 'I'd better ring him up!' thought Caroline; and she went into the morning-room to use the telephone.

IV

There was no answer.

Caroline looked at the time. It was a quarter to three, and Henry had said definitely that he would be home late. He might, of course, be in some other part of the building; and as the thought came into her head Caroline suddenly saw quite distinctly the image of a minute solitary figure moving at random through the vast deserted works. Only Henry never did move at random, and there was no reason at all why that odd picture should have brought with it a sudden pang of pity. "Try again, please," said Caroline; and she sat down in a chair with the receiver at her ear.

There was no answer. She rang again at three o'clock, again at a quarter past. No one answered. It was odd, but there was of course no cause for alarm.

In ten minutes she rang again. There was no answer.

'I'm being absurd!' thought Caroline uneasily.

But uneasy she was. She went to an upstairs window and looked along the main road. No car, bringing Henry home early, was to be seen approaching. Caroline waited some minutes, then went back to the telephone and rang again. There was no answer.

And now alarm, unreasonable though she knew it to be, nebulous though it remained, definitely seized her. She had only one idea, to get to Morton as quickly as possible. Most possibly (she told herself) she would cross Henry on the way, or miss him, find his office empty, and come foolishly home again. But she was still determined to go. She rang for Hilton, told him to order the car from the Three Feathers, and so, scolding herself the while, went upstairs again to seize a hat and coat.

V

"Is Mr. Smith still here?" asked Caroline.

The door-keeper at Mathieson-Smith's looked at her curiously. She wondered whether her voice sounded to his ears as strangely as it did to her own.

"Yes, he's here," admitted the doorman.

"Then will you please take me to him? I'm Mrs. Smith."

The man looked at her again, so that for a moment Caroline felt as though she were expected to produce her credentials. He had never seen her before, no wonder he was surprised! But the extreme respectability of her looks seemed to reassure him; he let her through, led her down a passage, and so to the foot of a narrow stair that wound up and up about a locked lift shaft.

"You'll have to walk," he warned her.

"Doesn't the lift work?"

"Not this afternoon. The man's gone."

Caroline nodded and began the ascent. She was only too thankful—remembering Henry's look of fatigue before the staircase at Friar's End—that there was a lift at all. Up two flights she toiled, pausing once or twice for breath, till on the second landing the man thrust open a door and disclosed a large unoccupied room furnished as an office. Opposite, indicated by a jerk of his head, was another door, closed, and marked 'Private.'

"Thank you," said Caroline. She heard his footsteps descending; then crossed the empty room, knocked, and receiving no answer, walked diffidently into Henry's office.

VI

Henry was there.

He was sitting at his desk, but in so collapsed and drooping an attitude that his left hand brushed against the floor. He did not appear to have heard her.

Caroline ran forward, and kneeling beside him, so that she could look into his face, gently raised him up. He was not, as she had first imagined, dead. But he was very ill. His face was the colour of chalk, his eyes, though open, did not focus on her. For a moment Caroline knelt distracted, foolishly chafing his hand, foolishly murmuring his name. Then she remembered the doorman, still perhaps on the stairs, and forced herself to her feet. What words she called, as she ran back through the outer room, she could not afterwards remember: they echoed in her ears only as a loud inarticulate cry. But they reached the man below; and Caroline, clinging to the banister, saw him stop and look up.

"Telephone for a doctor, quickly!" she called.

To her horror the man turned as though to re-ascend. Caroline took a quick step downwards.

"Don't come up!" she ordered furiously. "Mr. Smith is ill, get a doctor at once! If you can't, ring up the police and ask them to send one. Say there's not a moment to lose."

She saw him go, then ran back to the office. Henry was still as she had placed him, leaning back in the chair; she fancied, but could not be sure, that his breathing was a little stronger. On a second table stood a half-empty carafe: Caroline filled her palm with water and sprinkled it over Henry's face. She saw that his eyes were now shut, and willfully believed that this was a good sign. But the water was all gone, and still he had not stirred; and overcome by a sudden dreadful weakness she sank again on her knees beside him.

The minutes passed. His hand, limp between hers, was still faintly alive. She pressed it gently, held it to her cheek; but no conscious vibration answered. Every few moments she looked up into his face; there was no consciousness there either. "Henry!" she said softly. "Henry!" she repeated; for a hundred urgent questions—questions that she had never asked, that he would now never answer—were thronging into her mind. 'Henry,' she wanted to say, 'have you been happy? Have I been a good wife to you? Were you ever disappointed that there wasn't another son, to come into the business instead of Leonard? Were you, Henry? Have you ever been a little lonely, my dear? I have—I do—love you, Henry. Sometimes I think I haven't shown it enough, but you never seemed to want me to. And you've been so good to me, Henry. No woman could have had a better husband. And I have loved the garden. Henry, I do love you so. . .

Her lips were moving, she was murmuring the words aloud.

"Henry, my dear, you know I've been happy, don't you? You made me happy. Henry, my dear, I love you. . . . "

Suddenly his eyes were open. His lips moved. His voice was quite normal.

"I'm glad you came, Carrie," he said calmly; and so died.

CHAPTER XVIII

I

ACCORDING to a will made five years earlier, Henry left everything to his wife. It amounted to some three hundred and fifty pounds.

For Mathieson-Smith's belonged to the creditors. There was a mortgage on Friar's End, a mortgage on Henry's insurance policy. So far as Caroline understood, she, Lal, and Leon possessed nothing but their clothes. She did not, indeed, understand much; when Eustace Jamieson talked to her of slumps, of over-expansion, of dwindling foreign markets, she listened and tried to take it in, but without much success. The works had been always mysterious to her; the fact that they had disappeared was no more surprising than the fact that they had ever been. Henry's death, as she saw it, had simply wiped them out. She bore no resentment to him for having kept her in ignorance; she had always been kept in ignorance. She was only sorry that her husband must have had, for some years, a trouble she could not share.

Caroline mourned very quietly. She wore black, and wept a great deal, but she did not noisily lament. She did not greedily claim sympathy. Her children, for once silent under the greatness of the disaster, were silenced also by the dignity of their mother's sorrow. There was not, indeed, very much that they could say. Essentially, they had never known their father at all: to pretend to an equal grief would have been presumption, and so they felt it. But they were quiet, obedient, and very affectionate, and thus they comforted their mother.

For Henry himself Caroline had no fears. Her strong faith assured her that he was in heaven, her equally strong sense that he was not playing a harp. In the Father's house were many mansions: the Lord, out of His infinite resources, would provide some more suitable form of bliss; and Caroline pictured her husband as constantly busied and absorbed in some new, unimaginable occupation. When she herself died, or at the Resurrection if that happened first, he would tell her all about it.

In heaven he would tell her everything.

It was her one great regret that she had not known how bad his heart was, or indeed that it was bad at all. Yet perhaps even this was just as well: she could not have helped questioning him, and Henry did so hate to be questioned. Moreover, according to Eustace Jamieson, he had seen the right doctors and done everything possible. The only thing he had not done was to work less hard. 'And I couldn't have made him do that!' thought Caroline.

Eustace was very good to her. As sole executor he arranged everything, even the funeral, which took place very quietly in the church at Friar's Green. It seemed strange to Caroline, since they were all going away, that Henry should be left behind.

II

For the Smiths were leaving Friar's End. They had no option; if they did not go of their own accord the village would have the interesting experience of seeing them turned out. "We must leave at once," said Caroline; and Lal and Leon, sitting soberly with her in the morning-room, nodded agreement.

It was two days after the funeral. Lal, against her principles, but to please her mother, was wearing a black frock. She was pale, but very composed. Leon, also to please his mother, was not lounging but sitting up at the table, a writing-pad and ink before him: and at the top of the sheet he had written 'Three hundred and fifty pounds.'

It was Leon who spoke first. Pushing back the pad, he said, suddenly,

"I'm getting four pounds a week, and a bit more from articles, Mother, and I can manage on that. If Lal gets some sort of a job—"

He broke off and looked inquiringly at his sister; but before Lal could speak the door opened and Hilton came in. His demeanour was that of an archbishop visiting bereaved royalty, for though—unlike the family butler of fiction—he had omitted to offer Caroline his savings, his manner to her since the disaster had become even more reverential than before. In low and apologetic tones he announced that Dr. Baker had called, and was in the drawing-room.

"Oh, dear!" said Caroline.

It was nice of the young man to call, especially as he must have come all the way from Town, but she did not particularly like him—or rather she had no feelings towards him whatsoever—and she was moreover physically tired. For once in her life she was faced by an obvious duty—trivial indeed, but a duty nevertheless—and felt herself unequal to it.

"Where's Mr. Jamieson?" she asked weakly; and at once remembered that he was going through Henry's bureau. As Hilton reproduced this information, however, Lal said abruptly,

"You go and talk to him a minute, Leon. Tell him I'm just coming."

Leon hesitated, then, as though reading something more in Lal's glance, preceded Hilton from the room. There was a moment's silence. Caroline sank back in her chair, too tired to wonder at or be annoyed by her daughter's interference. The respite was grateful to her. She wanted neither to speak nor to listen, but jut to sit, until Leon came back.

"Mother," said Lal.

Caroline sighed. Lally no doubt had a plan too, a plan noble and generous and touching as Leon's, to show a proper interest in which it would be necessary to sit up. Grateful indeed, but physically reluctant, Caroline did so; and at once, as though she had been waiting for just that movement, Lal went on.

"I'm not going to get a job, darling, because it isn't necessary. I'm going to be married to Jeremy Baker."

"You're *what*?" said Caroline.

She could not if she wished have concealed her astonishment. For the name, at that moment, conveyed nothing at all. So far as she knew there was not a single Jeremy of their acquaintance. She looked at her daughter so blankly that Lal smiled.

"Dr. Baker, darling. I'm going to marry him. He came down yesterday, and it's all settled."

Caroline sat speechless. For enlightenment, instead of diminishing her surprise, had increased it. Dr. Baker! That peculiarly uninteresting, peculiarly colourless, most ordinary young man! What was Lal thinking of? If she had to get married—a step sensible enough, particularly in the present circumstances—why didn't she marry Dr. Galbraith?

"Dr. *Baker*?" said Caroline aloud.

"Yes, darling. He's got a panel job in Hammersmith, and we're frightfully in love with each other, so there's no point in waiting."

"Well!" said Caroline. Words failed her: she simply could not take in the astonishing and so suddenly presented fact. Lal and Dr. Baker! Lal the brilliant, Lal the fastidious, and a young man so ordinary that Caroline could not even recollect his personal appearance! She tried, and she could not do it. She remembered faintly an unimposing mustache, and that was the end. As for his mental qualities, she had never noticed that he had any. She had just never noticed him at all. . . .

"You do like him, don't you?" said Lal.

Caroline evaded the question. She neither liked nor disliked, but it was no use telling that to Lal. Instead, she said gently,

"My darling, if he makes you happy, that's all I care about. But will he, Lal? You've got to be quite sure. I should have thought—"

"That I'm not exactly cut out for a panel doctor's wife," supplied Lal. "That's what Jeremy thought too: we've been arguing about it for weeks. But I am, darling, if the doctor's Jeremy. I'd marry him if he were the hangman."

The extravagance of this sentiment, no less than the energy of Lal's manner, surprised Caroline afresh. Lal always knew her own mind, but not even at the height of her infatuation for Gilbert Chalmers had she displayed cheeks so flushed or eyes so bright. And it was all—marvelled Caroline—for Dr. Baker!

"He seems," she said doubtfully, "a very nice young man—"

"He's splendid," said Lal.

Caroline gave it up. If Lal could see splendour in Dr. Baker, she must love him indeed. Only love could be so irrational. And Caroline also determined, with her usual fairness, that she would consider the young man again and if possible revise her judgment of him. For it was plain that Lal saw something in him which she did not, and Lal, being so much cleverer, was sure to be right.

"I must talk to him!" exclaimed Caroline.

"He wants you to," said Lal. "That's what he's come for. He likes you awfully, darling."

Pleasantly flattered (since her opinion of the young man was already rising), Caroline forgot her weariness and stood up.

"I'll go now," she said. "I can talk to Leon afterwards. And I'm very glad, my darling, that you're going to be happy. I don't think it matters much being poor: when your father and I married I dare say we had less than you'll have now; and—and we were very happy indeed, Lal, because we loved each other, and had you and Leonard, and—"

A growing restlessness in her daughter's attitude warned her that it was time to stop. She broke off; she moved hastily across the room; but a further delay was inevitable, for at that moment the door was opened from without by Eustace Jamieson. He carried an envelope in his hand, and seemed greatly excited.

"Mrs. Smith, do you remember any one called Partridge?" asked Mr. Jamieson.

III

Suddenly as everything else happened at this time, Caroline found herself a woman of means. They were not very large; but Mr. Partridge's original two thousand pounds were now increased, in obedience to the comfortable laws of compound interest, to something like four thousand pounds, and she would have a certain income of nearly £120 a year. £120 a year, just over two pounds ten a week; but she had also her £350, and after setting a hundred aside for immediate expenses, Caroline mentally divided the remainder into five hundred ten-shillings, and thus brought her weekly income—for the next ten years—up to a round three pounds. Further than ten years she did not look; in the meantime she would be able to manage nicely.

For she was determined to live alone. Leon, with every appearance of sincerity, had pressed her to share a flat with him; Lal—possibly more sincere still—had suggested her taking the top floor in the same house with herself and Jeremy; for both of these offers Caroline was properly grateful, but both she refused. She had a fixed idea that all youthful couples should be left alone for at least five years; she had also an idea that for all his cordiality Leon would prefer to be by himself. And besides—

"Besides," she said to Lady Tregarthan, "I'm too old for living in other people's houses. I need a place of my own."

Lady Tregarthan nodded.

"You're quite right, my dear. But while you're looking round, and if you want to do me a kindness, why don't you come to the Court?"

Gratefully, reluctantly, Caroline shook her head. She could not speak, for the tears, which just then came so easily, were ready to overwhelm her. So she just shook her head, and the old woman looked at her with understanding.

"You're quite right," she said again. "You'll be better away. But I'm sorry, for you're a very nice woman."

Caroline was so much moved that she leant forward and kissed Lady Tregarthan on her old withered cheek. And Lady Tregarthan kissed Caroline. They were two old creatures kissing each other good-by. It was a clumsy business, even slightly absurd, for both remained seated and Lady Tregarthan at least was very stiff. Caroline felt glad afterwards that neither Lal nor Leon chose that moment to come in; but she was glad also that the incident had taken place.

IV

The month preceding her daughter's marriage was spent by Caroline at the Glen Lomond Hotel. Lal, despising it, stayed in far less comfort with Meg Halliday, but spent most of her time enameling, distempering, and laying linoleum in an extremely shabby old house behind Hammersmith Broadway. She appeared to have no more thoughts of a trousseau than she had of a honeymoon; she said she had plenty of clothes already, and when Caroline wanted to give her fifty pounds refused it with indignation.

Caroline did not insist; she saw that Lal, like Leon, was temporarily in love with poverty; but she laid out some of the money herself, and instead of looking for a flat spent her days guiltily stitching at hand-made underwear. Lal caught her halfway through, scolded her thoroughly, and then suggested that the rest of the material might as well be made into a layette. "Lal!" cried Caroline, quite alarmed.

"It's all right, darling," Lal reassured her. "I'm only looking ahead. As a matter of fact, it won't be needed for another five years at least."

Caroline was shocked, but said nothing. She merely resolved that if her daughter were mistaken, the layette should not be wanting. . . .

One concession only did Lal make either to convention or to Caroline. She was married in a church. As she explained to Leon, it pleased her mother and did herself and Jeremy no harm. Jeremy's own parents were both dead, but he too was perfectly willing to give pleasure to Caroline. He liked his future mother-in-law extremely, and Caroline in time grew very fond of him. He would never set the Thames on fire, but he was good and hard-working, and devoted to Lal, and these were qualities far more important than mere brilliance. 'You can't have everything,' thought Caroline sensibly; and she gave him a very nice clock for a wedding-present.

The ceremony was naturally as quiet as possible; but Caroline wore a grey dress instead of a black—she knew Henry would not mind—and made Lal carry a great bunch of violets. The bunch was so large, and the violets so fine, that the air was quite sweet with them; and Caroline, as she cried a little into her handkerchief, determined to slip out to Boots, as soon as the service was over, and send Lal a bottle of the same perfume. It was just the sentimental thought—so natural to herself, so foreign to her children—which she had never been able to resist. . . .

PART IV

CHAPTER I

I

"THIS is where I shall stay," thought Caroline.

She was alone on the second floor of a large and old-fashioned house whose situation, on the dubious borderline between Holland Park and Shepherd's Bush, combined the so often irreconcilable advantages of dignity and cheapness. The address was good, the rent low; but what had really taken Caroline's fancy was the generous scale of the front room. It was really large, well-proportioned, lit by two long windows; and she had come upon it fresh from the inspection of half-a-dozen minute American flatlets selected for her by Lal. The other accommodation consisted of a small bed-chamber, a kitchen containing a bath (or a bathroom containing a cooker) and a large cupboard. A lathe-and-paper partition, run diagonally across the common landing, provided privacy and a front door. The bedroom window, at the back, looked over the roof of a built-out bathroom below into a small mews; but Caroline had not yet admitted to Lal that that bathroom roof was also one of the attractions. 'She'll never believe I can do it!' thought Caroline. . . .

The landlord did not seem to believe it either. He looked at his new tenant, looked at the window, and doubtfully inquired how Mrs. Smith would get out.

"With orange-boxes," said Caroline. "One outside, and one in. It will be most convenient." She smiled reassuringly, and the landlord returned to his notebook.

"You want rails and a trellis all round, and three boxes of earth—"

"With holes in the bottom and standing on pieces of brick," added Caroline.

He made a note of it.

"What colour?"

"Green." The tubs at Friar's End had been green, but Caroline had no intention of growing scarlet geraniums. She was going to cultivate nasturtiums, mignonette, and Aesopus tulips. She was also going to buy packets of seeds and mix them together. She would plant nothing in rows. . . .

As the landlord went downstairs he crossed Lal coming up, and for a moment Caroline held her breath to hear what he would say. But he said nothing, Lal was running up too fast; and Caroline moved quickly away from the window before her daughter came and looked out. The suitability of those seven square yards of leads as the site of a roof-garden was so obvious to her that she could not imagine its failing to strike any one else; or that Lal, glancing out, should not immediately conjure up the trellis, the flower-boxes, and a middle-aged lady climbing in and out of the window. So Caroline moved away, and found her daughter critically at gaze before the sitting-room door.

"Well, darling?"

"I've taken it," said Caroline.

"Mother! Didn't you go to any of the places I gave you?"

"I went to them all," said Caroline apologetically.

"And they were very nice, dear, and most convenient, but—"

"But what, Mother?"

"So extremely small. I should have felt as though I were sitting in a cupboard."

Lal looked at the wallpaper distrustfully.

"Are they going to do it up for you?"

"Well, not just yet, dear." Caroline suppressed a slight feeling of guilt; she had compounded fresh papers for the arrangements on the bathroom roof. "I shall ask them next year. And it's very cheap for furnished."

"So it ought to be," said Lal. "Look at the furniture!"

Caroline looked, and saw nothing to displease her. The room contained a round mahogany table, an oak buffet, a walnut writing-desk, and five odd mahogany chairs. All were shabby, but all had originally been good. They would polish up very nicely. On the floor was a very old Turkey carpet, which Caroline was already planning to treat with tea-leaves. The curtains were much faded, but properly made, with a good lining. They must have been up years and years, ever since the house was first occupied. Caroline took a fold in her hand, and saw a faint pattern, shiny on a dull ground, of roses and fleurs-de-lys.

"Silk damask!" she said proudly.

"They don't look much like it now," said Lal.

Her quick disparaging glance had already passed on. She moved impatiently towards the door, and Caroline followed. They went first into the bathroom, where Lal pointed out the poor condition of the linoleum, then to the bedroom, where she found a badly discoloured ceiling. Caroline looked at it without disgust; at Morton, in the old days of gas, every ceiling had been a little discoloured. She looked at the useless bracket, still carrying its shade of frilly pink glass, and felt her heart quite go out to it. It was a pretty shade, it must have been bought for the drawing-room; and then—thought Caroline rapidly—the other got broken, and this one was sent upstairs. . . .

"Fancy putting electric light in, and not having the ceilings done!" cried Lal indignantly.

Caroline moved away from the bracket, and to divert her daughter's attention altered the level of a window-blind. Unfortunately it stuck, and Lal was on her in a flash.

"There you are! The whole place is coming to pieces!"

"It's only caught," said Caroline mildly. She jerked once or twice at the cord, but nothing happened, and she was forced to turn back and meet her daughter's eye. Lal was standing in the middle of the room, her feet close together, her whole attitude that of a person trying to occupy the minimum of space in a crowded railway carriage: and suddenly, at the sight of her, Caroline forgot all about the window-blind, and the garden on the roof, and remembered only the astounding fact that Lal was married.

She didn't look married. She wore a dark blue skirt, a loose white coat, and a blue straw hat like a plate with a ribbon on it. She looked twenty at most. She also looked remarkably carefree. There was a casualness about her, as though she didn't know where her next meal was coming from, but was merely sure that it would be there. To Caroline's eye she didn't look married at all.

"How is Jeremy?" asked Caroline almost sternly.

"Grand. Half the children in Hammersmith have measles, all their mothers are having babies, and he was called out twice last night. I've got to dash back now to give him a meal." She caught her mother's eye and grinned. "It's Irish stew, dear. Very nourishing."

"What time did you put it on?" asked Caroline.

"Half-past four. It's full of onions. There's also a bread-and-butter pudding for the char to put on at six." Lal paused; she looked extremely pleased with herself; and with sudden insight Caroline realized that if Lal married had still the air of a child, it was because, like a happy child, she lived surrounded by love and praise. There would be praise awaiting her now: Jeremy no doubt considered it extremely clever of her, at the age of twenty-five, to be able to cook a stew. And so, for that matter, did Caroline herself. She looked at Lal and marvelled.

"Who told you how, dear?"

"No one," said Lal conceitedly. "I did it by the light of nature and a cookery book. I try the things first when Jeremy's not going to be in, and if they're all right he gets them later on. He's never had pastry yet."

"It's a knack," said Caroline. She had that knack herself, and there was nothing she would have liked better than to give Lal a lesson; but Lal, as Caroline well knew, preferred to make her own experiments. She was as stubborn over her cooking as she had been over Gilbert Chalmers—

"I'll find it in time," said Lal confidently. "I rather like pastry, it's so nice to push about. And I like making pancakes, and shelling peas, and scraping new potatoes. In fact, the only thing I really hated was washing-up; so now I don't do it."

"You don't *do* it?" repeated Caroline, startled.

"Never, dear. You'll be shocked to hear that I leave it all to the char in the morning. It's about her only useful activity."

"But suppose," persisted Caroline, "you were to run out of things?"

"We do," said Lal calmly. "Then I buy more at Woolworth's. We're getting cupboardsful. If it were all clean at once, we could do a Lord Mayor's banquet."

"Well!" said Caroline. She was shocked indeed, shocked to the marrow. She said severely,

"You ought to be ashamed of yourself!"

"Why?"

It was Lal's old question: Caroline opened her lips to reply, and as of old found that she did not know the answer. Why *should* Lal be ashamed of not washing-up, when she disliked it and could get it done by some one else? Because of her extravagance in buying more crockery? But Woolworth's was cheap, and Caroline moreover had a strong suspicion that the cupboardsful were exaggerated. *Why* ought Lal to be ashamed of herself?

"Jeremy," added Lal, "thinks it's a very good idea."

At once, in an instant, all Caroline's perplexities vanished. Of Dr. Baker as a young man she thought very little: for his opinions as Lal's husband she had a great respect. For a husband always knew best: and if Jeremy approved, Lal might be perfectly sure she was right.

II

Two days later Caroline's own belongings arrived. They were not many: she had two trunks of clothes, a rose-wood work-box, a picture of lilies given her by Lal, and a number of *objets d'art* presented year by year by both Lal and Leon. Only on her birthday, it seemed, did Caroline ever acquire any personal posses-sions: she had never, like the children, bought books or pictures or bric-a-brac for herself. But there also arrived at Prince's Crescent two wooden cases, one large and shallow, one a square sugar-box, which the children would not have recognized; for they were cases which had been packed over twelve years earlier, which had come with the Smiths from Morton and lain ever since unopened in the attic at Friar's End. Caroline approached them first of all: extracting—with eagerness, with anxiety, with final triumph—from the one a large glazed text, from the other a fine collection of Goss armorial china.

CHAPTER II

I

ON A fine May afternoon Caroline sat out in her garden admir-ing the Aesopus tulips. She sat in a deck-chair, kept permanently on the roof under a piece of mackintosh; and this chair, and the tulips, and Caroline's substantial slow-moving figure, were already well-known features of Prince's Mews.

"Well!" said Caroline complacently.

The six tulips stood straight as soldiers, proud as dukes, and gay as cockatoos. Their streaked petals, pink and creamy-white, had edges delicately fluted like the lip of a seashell. They were at once shells, birds, and elegant warriors; but even while her imagination thus rioted, Caroline's habitual sense kept it well in hand. She knew, all the time, that they were really just tulips. . . .

On the other side of the mews a window opened and a cat was thrust out. Caroline looked at it with interest: it was Tiger, it belonged to two old ladies, and when inflamed by passion it kept the whole mews awake. But the ladies, approached by a deputation, had stated quite positively that Tiger spent every night at the foot of one or other of their beds; they had heard the bad cat, indeed, but it was not Tiger. So now the deputation, which consisted of two gentlemen from the same house, was lying in wait to catch Tiger in the act; and when it did one gentleman was to watch the beast outside while the other, at whatever hour of the night, was going straight up to the Misses Buxton's flat to demand either Tiger or an apology. To Caroline, who had heard the story from the First Floor, the sight of the animal was thus extremely interesting: she watched it walk purposefully along a wall, drop on to a shed below, and there, like a man who suddenly decides to throw up an appointment, abruptly turn, sit, and begin to wash itself. It looked, thought Caroline, a very nice cat indeed, and though all the evidence was against them she hoped the Misses Buxton might be right. "Tiger!" called Caroline softly; but the beast took no notice, and the opening of another window, quite near at hand, distracted her attention.

It was a window with flower-pots, and as such had long been an object of interest; for this, her first glimpse of the owner, Caroline frankly strained her eyes. She saw two small quick hands, a flash of glass bangles, and then all at once the whole head and shoulders of a girl with brilliantly red hair and a face, even at that distance, gayly coloured as a doll's.

The girl was leaning right out, and she was addressing Caroline.

"I say! Would you mind telling me the name of those tulips?"

Caroline was so surprised that for a moment, instead of answering, she continued to stare at the bright apparition. The girl pointed.

"Those pink-and-white ones. What's their name?"

"Aesopus," replied Caroline.

"How much?"

"Aesopus. A-e-s-o-p-u-s."

"Thanks awf'ly," said the girl. "It's for my husband. He's taken such a fancy to them he wants to know their name. He's like that." She nodded amiably, and as suddenly as she had appeared, without a single glance for the three pots of wallflowers, retreated inside. Caroline stared after her: her curiosity, far from being appeased, was merely whetted. For the girl looked—well, not the sort of girl who *has* a husband; yet she had, and one who liked flowers, and one for whom Caroline was already conscious of a fellow-feeling. It was most odd. 'The people who get married!' reflected Caroline vaguely; and at once her thoughts flew to Lal and Jeremy Baker. How *could* the child have fallen in love with him? And yet she had, and was happy, and settling down as easily and naturally as any other girl. Perhaps—astonishing thought!—she *was* like any other girl. . . . Caroline considered the notion with surprise: was it possible that her children, after all, were not so extraordinary as she had always thought them?

'But they are!' Caroline assured herself: and then smiled indulgently. For what did it matter whether they were extraordinary or not? They were Lal and Leon, and she was their mother, and she knew that whatever they did would continue to be remarkable to her. If Lal had a baby, for instance, it would be the most remarkable baby in the world. . . .

A cloud edged towards the sun, and still Caroline sat, not consciously musing, but letting long inconsequent thoughts of Morton, and Henry, and Friar's Green, and the children, drift slowly through her mind. She remembered walking to church with her mother, and stopping to look through the gates of the houses on the Common. She remembered how they had once met Miss Dupré, and how Miss Dupré had passed without seeing them. She remembered a house behind the Dairy Farm, with a garden that fell in terraces and vast shadowy rooms. She remembered Vincent. He was the only person, so far as she knew, who had ever thought her beautiful; and she now saw that for whatever she had suffered, during their brief acquaintance, she had by this been amply repaid. He had given her that personal, physical pride, which in excess may become devastating, but without which no woman can come to her full stature. In Caroline it had not so exceeded, and it had been, throughout her life, a hidden source of strength and dignity. She remembered and was grateful.

She remembered the fête, and Ellen Watts and Cousin Maggie in her brick-red gown; and then suddenly her thoughts leapt forward, and she was at Bournemouth with her husband, walking along the cliffs in the wake of a galloping donkey-chair. The donkey was being beaten, Caroline was passionately arguing, and then suddenly Henry had laughed and hurried her towards the sands. But they were too late, Mr. Partridge had turned, and as the donkey-chair rattled towards them the Caroline of the present, on her sunny roof, felt the tears start to her eyes. To whom did she owe gratitude, if not Mr. Partridge? He had made possible her six Aesopus tulips. It was as though, foreshadowing all, he had put out a hand and kept Caroline safe.

'But it was Henry!' thought Caroline. Mr. Partridge had made no conditions: if Henry had taken the money when she offered it, it too would have gone with the rest. She had pressed it upon him, been bitterly disappointed when he refused: but Henry as usual knew best, and so it was he, and not Mr. Partridge, who had finally safeguarded her.

"Henry!" said Caroline aloud.

She did not expect him to hear. His new occupations would be too engrossing; for Caroline knew that while she herself, even in heaven, would still have one thought out of two for Leon and Lal, Henry was different. He was always utterly absorbed in whatever he was doing. And she would not have distracted him if she could; she spoke his name not to call his attention but because its shape was pleasant and familiar to her lips. "Henry!" she said; and the sound brought back Morton and Bournemouth and the house at Friar's End. It resumed the last thirty years of her life. For the future, she had Lal and Leon, and perhaps grandchildren to look forward to, and such immediate trivial interests as the fate of Miss Buxton's Tiger. She had also her garden, where next year she would plant twelve tulips instead of six. It was plenty.

'I've had a good life,' thought Caroline.

For so indeed it seemed to her. She had neither explored deserts, nor flown oceans, nor received the tumultuous applause of crowded theatres. She had never even been to Switzerland. Indeed, when she came to think of it, she herself, in her own person, had done nothing at all. She owed everything to her husband and her children; and to Mr. Partridge and the boy Vincent; and farther back still to her mother and Grandpa Pole in the flat over the grocer's shop.

'But most to Henry,' thought Caroline.

The sun dropped: it was too cold to stay out longer. Stiffly, carefully, Caroline mounted the sugar-box and insinuated herself backwards through the window. It reminded her of getting out of the car: only now there was no Lily or Leonard to upset her with ribald comment. 'I had enough of that, anyway!' thought Caroline, coming down heavily on the other side.

She went along to the kitchenette, put a kettle on the ring and cut some nice thin bread and butter. There was also a cake, so that if Lal did by any chance come in, the child could have something to eat, and would also—Caroline hoped—be impressed by the comfort, and even luxury, of her mother's domestic arrangements. With this end in view Caroline further drew out an elaborately crocheted tea-cloth and a cosy in a crochet cover. She had brought them from Friar's End, not without misgiving; but they had been made after all by her own hands, and Eustace Jamieson, when consulted, gave an unqualified assent. 'He'd have let me take the silver teapot!' thought Caroline; and she smiled affectionately, for Eustace was coming, the next Saturday night, to take her to the cinema. He had a new post, something quite important, and he would tell her all about it; and then the talk would turn to Henry, and she would hear for the hundredth time how brave and clever he had been, and how ill-luck had dogged him, and how no other man could have held on half so long. . . .

"Henry!" said Caroline again.

Still smiling, her lips still shaped by that name, she picked up the tray and carried it into the sitting-room. The distance was no more than a step: her new and last domain was the smallest of which she had ever been mistress. But it was hers, it was an abiding place, and it contented her. It was where she would stay.

As she passed the front door she had noticed, on the mat, the faint white oblong of a newly arrived letter. Letters were rare to her, this was one of the first that had come to Prince's Crescent; and the knowledge that it must be for herself—and not, as at

Friar's End, probably for Lal or Leon—gave her a pleasing and absurd satisfaction. She was the householder!

Setting down her tray, Caroline eagerly returned. She stooped, took the envelope in her hand, and saw that it had been re-addressed from Friar's Green. The post-mistress's scrawl, obliterating everything else, had left a pale 'Please forward' in the top corner; and that writing too was familiar, for the letter was from Ellen Watts.

THE END

FURROWED MIDDLEBROW

15210 Rosenkrans Ave
La Mirada Hpm

Made in the USA
Monee, IL
03 November 2021